FINE LINE

A. D. JUSTICE

FINE LINE.

A CROSSING LINES NOVEL.

Copyright © 2019 A.D. Justice.

Cover photo by Wander Aguiar.

Cover model is Jonny James.

Cover design by Sommer Stein, Perfect Pear Creative Covers

PROLOGUE

A Terrible Idea
Nick

"For the record, this is a terrible idea."

My director, Calvin Montgomery, locks his angry eyes on me while speaking to the handler who will be assigned to me—if Calvin approves the operation, that is.

"Sir, Special Agent Nick Tucker has repeatedly proved what a valuable asset he is in the field. He's one of our best. He has outscored most of his peers in both field and psychological profile tests—even those who have previous undercover experience. We can't deny the man has the skills we need on this assignment. He deserves this chance."

"Yes, I can read the reports as well as you can, Jack. But Nick doesn't have any true undercover experience—not even on short-term cases, and the others do. Maybe they didn't score as well on the psych tests because they're already accustomed to living among the criminal element and acting as one of them. Did that ever occur to you? We both know how hard this life is even for a few months, but the case you're asking me to put Nick on is potentially a multiyear mission."

Calvin turns his penetrating gaze to me, constantly assessing my every reaction, looking for a weakness and a reason to deny my involvement. I've been in hectic firefights before and kept my cool, though. My time in the military, working for Steele Security, and providing private security for billionaire Dominic Powers before joining the DEA prepared me for most every perilous situation they can throw at me. Drawing on my inner strength, I keep my expression passive, my breathing regular, and my instinct to remind him he's driven a desk for too many years to remember what working in the field is actually like under wraps.

"You'll be cut off from everyone you know, Nick. You'll essentially divorce your entire life—for years. Your friends, your family, wife, girlfriend, boyfriend. *Everyone.* You hear me? And that's the easy part of the job. Even contact with Jack will be sparse, especially due to the group you'll infiltrate, so you'll be making decisions on the fly. Any outside affiliation will be scrutinized—and these guys won't ask questions first.

They'll shoot you in the head and replace you with the next guy in line. I'm not convinced you truly understand what you'll have to do to be one of them."

"I can assure you, I do understand."

"Is that right? This UC op has been issued special permission to break the very laws you've sworn to uphold. Your psych profile shows a strong sense of duty and a penchant for following the rules to the letter. So, you'd be fine if they order you to force some young kid to sell drugs on the street corner and bring you every penny of the money he made? Then rough him up if he doesn't bring you enough?"

The visual that pops into my brain before I can stop it makes my heart rate increase instantly, the artery in my neck jerking and giving away my reaction.

"Or maybe it's not a him. Maybe it's a her. You'd willingly force a young woman into prostitution, selling her to any Joe Blow off the street, who'll do whatever the fuck he wants to do to her? You can make them believe you don't care about her at all, just how much money she brings in for getting her John's rocks off? What if that means her customer gets to beat the shit out of her just because he has mommy issues? I mean, as long as he doesn't kill her and she can perform for her next trick, what the fuck does it matter, right?"

My stomach churns with disgust, and the room

around me turns red with my rage. But I tamp down those feelings inside my chest until they form a mangled ball full of drive and determination to see this through to the end.

"I'll do whatever the fuck I have to do to stop these bastards. The longer we sit here repeatedly arguing the same points and imagining hypothetical situations, the more time they have to commit those very crimes. Sir."

"I'm sure I don't have to remind you we're after the major charges to shut them down for good. Small-time hoods are a dime a dozen. We want the source—their suppliers. Local reports say this group is using a prescription drug that hasn't even cleared the FDA yet. It's highly effective and lethal in the wrong hands. That's in addition to the influx of opioids and other controlled substances from their Mexican drug cartel affiliation. We can't blow the entire operation because you feel the need to feed your savior complex over every sob story you hear. Most of those women asked for it anyway—they probably even enjoy it."

"I'm well aware of what we're after and how to do my job." Inside, I'm seething; outside, I display a calm demeanor.

He's testing me, that much I know. His last comment was to gauge my knee-jerk reaction because that's exactly how this gang thinks. If Calvin approves my request for undercover work, the group I'll join will say and do a lot worse to me than my director has ever even thought about. If I can't handle my boss yanking my chain inside the comfort of his office in our secure, air-conditioned building, I have no business being an undercover agent where anything and everything can go wrong.

Will go wrong.

Something always does.

To stay alive, I have to think fast on my feet, improvise, and give an award-winning performance.

No time like the present to start earning a few of those golden statuettes.

"Sir, I can handle anything they throw at me. I've been in intense situations in my career, starting in the Army, through private details, and in my time with the DEA. I'm ready to take my career to the next level, and I need undercover experience to do that. This wasn't Jack's idea—I requested to be assigned to this case."

The muscles around Calvin's eyes contract, crinkling the skin until only small slits remain. He draws a slow circle around his mouth with his thumb and forefinger before resting his chin on his hand. With my gaze locked on to his, I wait for him to make his decision. The first one to blink will be Calvin, because I am all in.

"All right, Special Agent Tucker, you've convinced me to give you a chance. On one condition."

"What condition is that?"

"If at any time you suspect your cover is blown, or your gut warns you that something is off and they've turned on you, get out of there. To hell with the case and the charges. Call Jack, get to the safe house, do whatever it takes to extract yourself from the situation."

"I appreciate your concern, sir, but it won't come to that. I'll see this through till the end."

"All right. We'll get your name, background, and criminal history established. Congratulations, Nick. You have the distinct honor of pledging to one of the most notorious motorcycle gangs in the world. The Devil's Dominion rules their LA territory with an iron fist. I only hope they don't turn that fist on you."

"Thank you, sir. I won't let you down."

◆

Six Months Later

"ARE YOU SURE YOU'RE READY TO APPROACH THEM, Nick? No need to rush things." Jack paces in his kitchen while I sit at the table and finish my coffee.

Jack Collins fits the bill for a retired biker. He is a handler, but he's curated his entire life around the motorcycle club lifestyle to avoid arousing any suspicions. He hasn't pledged to any outfit, but he is known by enough bikers that no one questions his presence, and no one crosses him. He has the don't-fuck-with-me air down pat.

His long black and gray hair is pulled back in a low ponytail. His sun-weathered skin bears the ravages of years on the open road—the deep-set wrinkles, the sunspots, the year-round dark tan. His brown eyes are keen, assessing a man and his intentions with a quick glance. The skin on his hands matches his face, but his grip is as strong as a man half his age. The long span of his career gives him advantages others could only hope to attain one day.

"It's time, Jack. You're my handler, you know I'm ready, and you know that shit is escalating out there. My hair has grown out, along with my beard. All my ink is finished—nothing overly distinguishable but still believable. My criminal background is airtight, and my stints in San Quentin and Pelican Bay legitimize my badass felon status."

"You can't use words like *legitimize* around these guys, Nick." Jack scrubs his hand down his face.

"I can talk real dumb too, Jack. Like I ain't got no schooling or nothing."

"Make fun of this all you want, Nick. But I'm telling you, these guys have a grittiness about them, a certain way they talk, a language all their own. It's a combination of the motorcycle gang lingo and prison slang."

"Trust me, I got this. I've mastered how they speak, the motorcycle gang terms, and the prison slang. I've memorized my background and rehearsed how I became a badass ex-convict, looking to join the baddest MC club around. One point that is pure genius on your part is showing I was part of a Tijuana-based gang before I was sent to prison. Thanks for that."

"Anything I can do to keep you from having to murder someone as part of your initiation. Because that's what they usually require—and could still order you to do it. But we'll cross that bridge when we have to. If you can patch in, you won't have to do the lowly probie bullshit. That'll at least give you a leg up in earning their trust and working your way up the chain faster than most.

"If you have to improvise and add anything to your history, don't forget to tell me immediately. We can build your experience around whatever you need, but it could take a little time to get it on paper. And don't say gang. You know how one-percenters feel about that word."

"Striking the word gang from my vocabulary now. And I'll try to keep the improvisation to a minimum, but I'm sure it'll come up. My documented history is solid, but that doesn't account for the things I never got caught doing. If you happen to have any former gang members in your back pocket, that would be useful too."

"I'll see what I can do. You never know, this old dog may still have a few tricks you don't know about."

One thing about Jack Collins, he always has another trick up his sleeve no one else knows about. How he stayed one step ahead of the agents under his charge when he went weeks without hearing from them is a mystery in our world. He takes his job home with him every night, and the safety of his agents is his first priority. I know I am in good hands.

"Thanks for the coffee. I'm heading back to my dinky little apartment to get into character. They're having a party at their clubhouse tomorrow night, so I'll use that opportunity to make my presence known."

"Good luck, kid. Don't die."

"That's the nicest thing you've ever said to me, Jack." I smile over my shoulder as I leave his bachelor pad and climb onto my bike.

My new life waits for me, in the gritty, dirty underbelly of the criminal world. Getting the approval for this level of undercover work is a boost to my ego and a rush to my senses. The heightened danger, constantly surveilling my surroundings, and testing my ability to decipher friend from foe within a matter of seconds will take my career to the next level.

I feel as if I've found my purpose in life. Finally.

~

Major Mistakes

Savannah

THE WOMAN STARING AT ME LOOKS FAMILIAR, BUT I don't know her. Not anymore anyway. Her red hair is longer than when she was younger. Her deep green eyes hold so many secrets, ones she'll never tell. She's also much thinner than she used to be—a telltale sign of stress and depression settling in over the long haul. The sad fact is, I used to know her very well. But now she's only the outer shell of the vibrant, bubbly personality I remember from just a couple of years ago. The light in her eyes is dim now, barely perceptible even when I'm searching for it.

"When did this happen, exactly? How did I become *this* woman?" I stare into the hollow green eyes reflected in the mirror, talking to myself. Again.

A loud bang on my apartment door abruptly ends my one-sided conversation. My heart drops, and a groan escapes from my throat. Dread covers me like a lead blanket. There's only one person that can be... the one person I really don't want to see, much less spend the evening around. But I don't have a choice. I'm trapped, like a frightened, timid animal in a cage.

After removing the door chain and unlocking the multiple bolts I had installed, the door swings open before I can even grab the knob.

"Why the fuck do you have the door locked like that? Who are you hiding in here?" Butch pushes past me, moving from one room to the next through my apartment as he searches for the invisible man.

"There's no one here except me. Just like last time. And the time before that. You know I always keep all the door locks in place when I'm here alone."

It's a phobia I have—an intense fear that drives me to check the locks several times before going to bed every night. He knows this about me, because he's complained about it every time he's stayed at my apartment. Thankfully, that hasn't happened in a very long time.

He stomps toward me in his heavy leather boots, the ones he wears every day because they best protect his feet and ankles while he's riding his motorcycle. It's strange how what I initially thought was intriguing, dangerous, and sexy about him when we met are the very traits that make me want to run away and start a new life somewhere else today.

I just haven't figured out how to get away from him yet.

"Pack all your shit. We're leaving."

"What?" I whirl around on my heel and stare at him, completely dumbfounded.

"We're moving. Prez is sending me and a couple of other guys to DC to induct a smaller club into ours. We have to try them out, see if they're worthy enough to wear the Devil's Dominion colors. This is my chance to show him I'm officer material and get on the voting ballot to move up in the club. I've been waiting years for this day."

The only thought in my mind is that my opportunity to get away from him is finally here. The day I've been waiting to come for far too long. There's no way I can move from LA to DC—they're at completely opposite ends of the country. Literally from one coast to the other. My entire life is here in LA, including my job and the few friends I had before I started seeing Butch.

Maybe my friends will take me back when I get rid of him.

"That's great news for you, Butch. I'm glad the president finally sees your potential in the club, and I hope they make you an officer soon. But I can't just up and move across country with you. My job is here —my entire career I've worked years to establish. I also have a lease on this apartment I can't just break."

I'm listing every logical reason I can think of, no matter how lame it will inevitably sound to him. He doesn't care about excuses—he only cares about results. More specifically, he only cares about the results he wants to see.

"Wouldn't that just fucking thrill you? Wouldn't you just love for me to go across the fucking country for the next six months and leave you here alone so you can fuck every swinging dick that crosses your path? Of course you're going with me, you stupid bitch. Who the fuck do you think is gonna drive the truck behind us and haul our shit across the country? All our stuff won't fit on our fucking bikes, you moron. Now, pack your shit like I said."

With his final command, he shoves me and slams my head into the wall, catching the edge of the doorframe with the full blunt force of the impact. Even with my eyes closed, I can feel the room spinning. Nausea settles into my gut and the bile churns, threatening to work its way up my throat. The pain in my skull makes me whimper. His only reply is a disgusted huff.

"Now, rent the fucking moving truck, pack your shit, and let's go to DC before I'm too old to ride my damn bike anymore."

After I hear the door open, he hurls one last threat at me. "If you even think of trying to get out of this, I'll kill every single person you love. All your fucking friends from the hospital. Your mom. Your sister. Try me, bitch. I dare you."

He stomps out, the chains on his boots and belt clinking with every step, growing fainter until I hear the engine of his bike roar to life. Funny, or not funny, how it reminds me so much of his own terrible roar. After he rides away, I open my eyes and gingerly move off the wall where he left me.

The door to my apartment is standing wide open.

He knows my paralyzing fear of leaving the door unlocked. Irrational or not, it's still there.

I want to rush to lock every bolt, but the first step

in that direction reminds me of my head injury. The disorientation, nausea, and I are not new friends. With slow movements, I lift my hand to feel the goose egg forming behind my ear. I'm not even surprised to find blood on my fingers when I lower my arm again.

My walk to the door is slow as I calculate each step and how much farther I have to go. My chest is heaving from the building anxiety. When the door is finally locked—every bolt is secured and every chain is in place, my pounding heart slows enough so I can breathe normally again.

After I put a cold compress on the back of my head, I slide onto the couch and carefully lie back on the throw pillows. I waste a few minutes daydreaming about never leaving my apartment again, never unlocking the door again, while waiting for the throbbing in my head to subside. As often as I dream about this, I should've already found the master plan for leaving Butch in my dust.

Since nothing else I've tried so far has worked, I pick up my laptop and rent the moving van as the asshole commanded. A one-way trip to Washington, DC coming up, sans the excitement a cross-country trip should elicit. The only way I can describe how I feel about what I just did is I'm positive I've just signed my own death certificate.

In fact, the longer I'm around Butch, the more I realize that outcome is inevitable—it's only a matter of time. The odds there will come a day when it's him or me increase with our every encounter. I let my eyes drift up to the ceiling, staring at nothing in particular while thinking about my situation. My job as an emergency room nurse is stressful and adrenaline-filled, but it pales in comparison to a single interaction with Butch. In an ironic twist, I would be required by law to report potential domestic abuse if one of my patients presented with the same signs I bear.

He wasn't always like this. When I first met him, the tall, muscular, brooding man was much sexier. His brown hair was longer than other men I'd dated before, but it gave him an edgier appearance. Eyes so brown they're almost black sparkled with playfulness and teasing. But it was all a charade—he was pretending to be someone he wasn't. And he was so good at it for so long—long enough to ensure I fell for him. Long enough to ensure I was caught in his trap. When I look at him now, all I see is the ugliness inside. Any desire that once burned for him has long been doused.

Thankfully, those nights with him have dwindled to an occasional visit—and only when he needs me to do something for him. He disappeared for a couple of weeks one time, and I thought he'd found someone else to prey upon. Selfishly, I hoped he had—but then I immediately felt bad for wishing him on anyone else. Unfortunately, one day, he simply walked back into my apartment as if he'd been here all along. No explanation. No questions.

His visits have been sporadic since that day. Usually when he's drunk and looking for somewhere to crash after a night out with his friends. He passes out in my bed, and I sleep on the couch, unable to stand being in the same room with him any longer than absolutely necessary. His insane jealousy makes no sense to me whatsoever. We are not a couple and haven't been for a very long time, yet he calls me every name in the book when he accuses me of seeing other men.

Not that I'm the least bit interested in even trying to date. I still can't get rid of the last mistake I made.

Now he shows up and demands I move across the country with him. I'm having a hard time wrapping my head around this one. It's not like either of us wants to be with the other. That much is clear. But I believe he'll make good on his threat to kill everyone I love. In fact, I have no doubt he will.

One problem at a time, though. Before we even reach the East Coast, I have to survive the actual 3,000-mile trip with him and his buddies. That should be fun—waiting for them to pass out on the bed from the abundance of drugs and alcohol so I can grab the extra linens and sleep on the nasty floor. But I prefer the floor over touching any of them. Maybe I'll sleep in the truck...with the doors locked…under the guise of protecting our belongings.

A few hours later when I walk into the hospital for the night shift, my heart is heavy, and all my feelings show on my face. My coworker takes one look at me, and her face falls.

"What has Butch done now?" Stella puts her hands on her hips and draws in a deep breath. She already knows she won't like the answer.

After explaining the series of events and the commandment Butch issued, I watch her face for the disappointment I know will come. On one hand, I completely understand it, and I was even the same way…before I became the abused and battered victim. Life is now divided into two sections: BB and AB. Before Butch and After Butch.

Before Butch, I said no man would ever lay a hand on me and live to tell about it.

No man would ever abuse me in any way—physically, mentally, or verbally. I would leave him in a heartbeat.

No man would replace my job, my dreams, or my friends—the sacred relationships I'd always held so dear.

After Butch, I withdrew from my friends.

My dreams took a back seat.

Self-esteem was what others had, but not me.

I miss the Before Butch version of myself. But now I feel as if I'm in too deep and can't claw my way out. One thing I've realized after looking back over the past eighteen months is none of this happened suddenly. He chipped away at the very core of me little by little, bit by bit, day by day. Until the very spark that made me *me* disappeared. And I allowed him to do it.

It's my fault.

If I'd been stronger, smarter, faster…maybe I would've seen the warning signs for what they really were.

Huge signs that flashed "Bridge Out Ahead."

But his apologies were so sincere at first. So heart-felt. He was remorseful and promised those bad things would never happen again.

He'd drunk too much. He always liked to fight when he drank. Such a man's man.

He was under too much stress. Work was a constant sore spot. His coworkers or his boss never liked him. They always made up a reason to get rid of him.

Of course, that was before I found out the truth about him. Before I understood what being in a one-percenter motorcycle club really meant. When I made the mistake of calling his club a gang during a heated argument, I saw stars after he backhanded me for disrespecting his brothers.

That was the day the apologies stopped and the real threats began. Old ladies didn't leave bona fide club members. Ever. It wasn't the woman's decision whether to stay or go. She just did what she was told and lived with what she got. He warned me to be glad I wasn't a sheep—one of the women they pass around to each other indiscriminately, using at will for any hedonistic pleasure they wanted to indulge in at the moment.

Ignoring the pleas and concern in Stella's eyes, I continue updating her on my plans. "I'm turning in my two-week notice tonight. That date was the earliest I could get a moving truck big enough for my stuff plus theirs anyway. I'm so glad it has a towing hitch for my car too."

I leave Stella, disappointed expression and all, to start my rounds and focus on the emergency cases. I wish I could stop time so my shift would never end. But working in busy emergency rooms always makes the time go by faster than the slower pace, comparatively, on the medical-surgical floors. Before I know it, the sun rises and a new day dawns, and I have to face the unpleasantness of packing all my belongings.

Two weeks will pass in the blink of an eye.

The Initiation
Nick

"YOU READY FOR TONIGHT?" JACK'S SERIOUS

expression gives away his thoughts. Unusual for him after the years of handling undercover officers.

"I'm as ready as I'll ever be." I slide my arm into my cut and complete the persona of Renegade.

Turns out, the idea to convince them I was part of a Tijuana-based club was a stroke of genius on Jack's part. The Devils' ties to the Mexican cartel are already in place, but with my joining them, the full backing of the cartel is implied, giving them more muscle than they already have. An ATF agent has been working a few members of that gang over the last several years, so interagency cooperation kicked in, and my alibi was instantly airtight. With my background in prison and ties to the Mexican cartel-sanctioned motorcycle club firmly in place, I approached the Devils with an offer they couldn't refuse.

The Devils' already long reach just increased with no effort on their part. At least as far as their reputation with rival clubs is concerned. Keeping those other clubs at arm's length while the Devils conduct business is vital to maintaining their dominance in the territory. When the club president realized the possibilities I could bring, the dollar signs in his eyes were so bright, they rivaled the neon signs of the Vegas strip.

Headbanger, also known as Bobby Blalock, is the club president. He has a rap sheet longer than my leg, along with countless other crimes he's never been charged with committing. Or ordering. His officers and many other members are all too eager to carry out plans on his behalf. They're brothers in colors, but they're also all vying for the attention of one man. The one who can make or break them in the club.

Tonight is initiation for a few new prospects who are on their way to becoming full patch members. The ceremony to patch in is a big deal to these guys —it seals their identity and their place in the family.

I've been riding with the Devils for the past two weeks. Hanging out with them in the clubhouse provides a completely unique perspective on the inner workings of a notorious outlaw gang. Some of the guys have done hard time, and it's a miracle most aren't still in prison. I've had to bite my tongue way too many times already—something my director knew about me before he approved the assignment.

My moral compass always points due north. Always.

Their skewed sense of right and wrong doesn't mesh well with me. In fact, we're like oil and water at the very core. The only peace I have is when we're on the open road, the wind whipping around me, and the road rushing by under my wheels. The sense of freedom on a motorcycle is the sole only thing I have in common with these guys. It's the only time we're even remotely on the same page.

The long ride to the initiation grounds in the hot, arid desert of Southern California gives me time to get myself back into character. Jack stressed over and over how I have to be part of the group to avoid suspicion. Because of the high stakes, I've been given special clearance to break the laws I've sworn to uphold. But there are oaths I've taken, and I have no intention of reneging on them.

There are lines I refuse to cross.

There are rules I refuse to break—even for the greater good and the thrill of closing the case.

But I have to act like there are no lines I won't cross. To be convincing, I have to put Nick Tucker away and be Renegade to the bone. In my mind, I have to think of Renegade as a completely different person. It's the only way I can pull this off.

He's an ex-con, fresh out of a maximum-security prison, and that has to be my persona. As a convicted felon on parole, I can't legally cross the border to ride with my old club because the pigs will nab Renegade immediately. I can't exactly drive my motorcycle through the underground tunnels to cross the border. Of course, as Renegade, I have the contacts, so I could find an illegal way, like a fake passport or hidden in a caravan. But I'd take that risk only for a golden opportunity, a sure thing.

Renegade has talked a good game in his two weeks with the Devils. Tonight, Prez will present me with the final piece of my colors—the top rocker panel for my cut—because I scored the largest shipment of meth and negotiated the best deal for the club he's ever seen. Compliments of my DEA and ATF friends.

When I finally roll up to their private hideaway in the desert, my Renegade character is in full swing. After grabbing a couple of beers from the cooler, I stroll over to where the officers are hanging out with a few of the lifers—the men who have been part of the club for so long, they aren't required to attend all church meetings and outings anymore, but they're every bit a part of the club as any other member. They can come and go as they please, though most stay more than they leave. This is the only life they know.

"Good of you to bring me a beer, Renegade." Axle reaches for one of the longneck bottles I'm carrying, so I hand it over without a fuss. He's one of the most respected lifers in the group. His experience combined with his naturally level head makes for a powerful ally in a group of trigger-happy thugs. Despite Axle's advanced age and lack of officer status, no man in this group wants to tangle with him.

"You know I always got your back, Ax."

"Back atcha, kid." He takes a long pull from the bottle but keeps his eyes locked on mine. "Heard about that big score you got for us. I'm impressed—and I don't impress easily. Good job."

"Appreciate it, man. Just glad I could help out."

"Well, well, look who's coming our way. The new prospects are here, and they brought their offerings to the Devils with them." Nutcrusher, the club vice president, stands and rubs his hands together, eager to get down to business.

When I glance over my shoulder at the approaching prospects, my stomach drops to my knees and my empty hand curls into a tight fist.

Their "offerings" are new sheep, women being shoved into the midst of the already rowdy scene. The three prospects are each forcing a woman to walk in front of them. The women alternate from stumbling ahead a few steps to digging their heels in to try to stop, only to be shoved from behind and start the process all over again. Their eyes are wide and full of fear. Their faces are tear-stained and their hair is disheveled—and not from the ride here since they arrived in the club van.

I'm positive these three women have already been used as offerings before the new patches ever brought them to meet the brothers. Before I consciously realize I'm moving, my feet develop a mind of their own and take a step forward. Then I feel a hand on my shoulder, holding me back.

"What you see tonight will test your mettle, boy. You've never been around anything like this, I can already tell. But I guarantee, if you blow your cover now, you'll never see anything at all, ever again."

Shocked by his words, I whip my head around and meet Axle's knowing gaze.

"Use it, kid. Use everything you have to see and

do as a member to take them down. As shitty as it sounds, you can't save these women and do what you came here to do at the same time. Keep your eyes on the end goal, son, and make them pay for their crimes when it's all said and done."

"What are you talking about, Axle?" He knows. We both know he knows. But I'll be damned if I'll blow my own cover.

"I'm CIA, Nick Tucker from the DEA family. I've been on this case for a long time, waiting for my foreign target to make his move so I can take him down. I told you, I got your back."

"The CIA can't operate on US soil, Ax. Everyone knows that."

His grin resembles one connected to an inside joke. Everyone else is clueless, and one person holds all the aces in his hand. "Sure we don't. I'm on loan to whichever agency wants to take the credit for the bust when it goes down. If you're still here when it happens, maybe that'll be the DEA."

Before I can reply, the shrill shriek of a woman's scream combined with ripping fabric fills the air, making my guts churn with disgust. Any man who would lay a hand on a woman in anger or abuse is no man at all. He's a pussy who knows he couldn't stand toe-to-toe with a real man.

The crowd that gathers around the three women —to watch, to encourage, or to participate—are the worst of the underworld. Preying on the defenseless and taking advantage of those who are hanging on by a thread as it is.

"Come with me, Renegade. This is as good as this scene gets. It's all downhill from here, and I don't think you can stop yourself from intervening yet." Axle guides me away from the ruckus.

I can still hear their pleas to stop. Their screams that echo through the desert air. Their cries for someone to please help them…to make it stop.

But I do nothing.

What kind of man does that make me?

"When they finish with the girls, they'll take them back to the clubhouse, and the club doctor will patch them up. They'll use them as sheep, or they'll cycle them into the prostitution ring and run them on the streets. They're not easy on them, but they don't permanently damage them either. Headbanger has a strict rule on that part since it affects his cash flow."

"Axle, your explanation doesn't help me one fucking bit. Do you even hear yourself? Of course they're permanently damaged now. Maybe not in the way you meant, but they still are." He nods in under-standing, and he knows he can't say much more to justify what we've witnessed. "Where did they get those girls? Did they kidnap them?"

"No. They pick up hitchhikers or strays. Bring them into the family. Give them food, a place to sleep, and the protection of a notorious motorcycle club. But they expect the girls to earn their keep one way or another. This may be the first time you've ever seen this, but it won't be the last. It won't even be the worst thing you've seen by the time your undercover operation ends."

The silence between us only seems to amplify the mixture of screams and catcalls behind us.

"Talk to me, Axle. Tell me about life in the CIA. Were you in the service? Anything, man. Talk about the fucking weather. I don't care."

"This gets easier, kid. You'll learn to compartmentalize shit like this. Picture those assholes in prison orange, enduring the same fate they're subjecting those girls to right now at the hands of a big, angry brute in their cell, where they have nowhere else to run. Then make that your end goal and sole mission in life. Find what gets you through the rough spots one day at a time. Your assignment will be over before you know it. Then you can put all this bullshit behind you."

I don't see that happening.

CHAPTER 1

Savannah—Two Years Later

"We're moving you out of that apartment today. I've been waiting for this day forever. No more excuses about waiting until your lease is up." Karen slings her backpack over her shoulder and jingles her car keys in her hand. "Let's go do this."

"What if he's still there?"

"That's why my husband and his friends are meeting us. We need their muscles to carry your furniture, and the fact that they're all cops doesn't hurt either." Karen smiles broadly, knowing Butch wouldn't dare start something with them around. "You know, you're welcome to stay with Spencer and me anytime you want. For example, if you wake up in the middle of the night scared and don't want to be alone anymore. Or if you just want to have a slumber party full of alcohol and junk food. Just show up at my house and make yourself at home."

"That sounds like so much fun. I don't know how to thank you for this, Karen." The shame of my situation is almost unbearable. All the time I've wasted, being afraid of Butch and what he'd do if I said or did the wrong thing when he was around. Not living my life to the fullest, enjoying every minute of every day. Not doing all the things I've wanted to do when I wanted to do them. Not spending time with my family so I could keep them as far away from that bastard as possible.

Being controlled and dominated by a cruel man.

"You can thank me by staying away from him for good. By calling the police if he comes anywhere near you again. By asking for help if he finds a way to back you into a corner again. I will get you out—one way or another. You are not alone in this, and you are not to blame." Karen grabs my arms to emphasize her words, and I consciously avoid wincing in pain from the pressure on my bruised skin. She doesn't know the bruises are there; I've hid them well.

Guess old habits do die hard.

"You have my word. Once I'm rid of him, it will be once and for all. There will be no going back or letting him in again for any reason. I've honestly wanted this for a long time, but I never could make it work. I think this time will definitely be different. For the first time in a long time, I have hope for a better life."

"It's all yours, babe. All yours for the taking. Once we get you moved, we'll work on finding you a real man. I'm sure Spencer has at least one single, handsome friend we can set you up with."

"Oh, no. No, no, no. I'm not interested in anything remotely resembling a man in my life. I'll just borrow your husband and his friends for heavy-lifting duties and scaring away bad guys. That's as close to having another man as I want to get."

"Woman-to-woman…friend-to-friend…I have to be brutally honest with you, Savannah."

"Go ahead. I know you. You'll explode if you don't get it out."

"It's not you I'm worried about as much as it's your poor, neglected, prune-shriveled va-jay-jay. I mean, it's seriously been three years since you took it out for a sit and spin? No squats in the cucumber patch? No gland-to-gland combat? We're both mandatory reporters, and you are definitely way past neglecting the old bearded clam. I think I need to turn you in to the nearest hot policeman."

Before meeting Karen, I'd almost forgotten how good it felt to simply laugh with a friend. To say whatever crazy thought came to my mind without fear of ridicule or reprisal. To have someone on my side, in my corner, standing by me no matter where the chips may fall. Stella was the last person I was semi-close to, but my friendship with Stella was nothing like the one I now have with Karen. We tease each other relentlessly, and I always tell her she elbowed her way into my heart, never taking no for an answer.

And saved my life in the process.

Now she's adding fun, love, and laughter too. Maybe the old me will emerge like a butterfly coming out of a cocoon.

We arrive at my apartment complex and find Spencer is already here waiting for us with his own small army. He pulls Karen into his arms, a warm, sweet smile on his face as he looks at her and kisses her hello. He's not at all shy or embarrassed by public displays of affection—or showing how completely and utterly in love he is.

Watching the two of them embrace, I'd swear the depth of their love for each other is their source of strength.

Butch insisted love was a weakness. A way other people could use you without explanation or a chance for retribution. He didn't believe anything that exposed your vulnerabilities could possibly make you stronger.

Butch was wrong.

I see it so clearly now, watching my friends. They give me something to aspire to reach in relationship goals—one day, possibly. The way I feel right now, I'd never trust a man enough to feel safe with him. To give him all of me and believe he'd do the same.

Perhaps I'll find that man at some point in my life, but I plan to focus on myself first.

My goals.

My hopes.

My dreams.

I've put them on the back burner for a man who wasn't worth even a second of my time. Today is the first day of the new me.

"Hi, Savannah. Good to see you." Spencer turns his attention to me, keeping his arm wrapped around Karen's waist.

"Thank you for doing this, Spence. I don't know how to repay your kindness—and all your friends. I wish you'd let me pay you for your trouble." My gaze drifts to each of his friends standing by the moving truck—and I immediately regret it. Though they try to mask their thoughts, I see the judging stares and disgusted glances.

I can't exactly hide the black eye I'm sporting, though it has mostly faded to light green bruising.

They're asking why I've stayed so long.

They're questioning what I've done to deserve this.

They want to know why I'm so weak and spineless to let someone treat me this way.

I've experienced these reactions so many times from other people. Until they've walked a mile in my shoes, they'll never understand what it takes to be able to get out of a situation like this. Now that I've lived it, I can honestly say I didn't have a fucking clue what I was talking about when I used to pass those same judgments on other women.

"You're not paying us one single penny. We're happy to help." Spencer releases Karen and steps toward me. "Can I have your keys? Jake and I are going up to your apartment to make sure it's safe. Stay here with Terry, Jarod, and Trent until you hear from us. Then you and Karen can pack your things and we'll get you away from this asshole." Jake steps up next to Spencer and inclines his head at me as Spencer speaks.

"Sure. This one is the door key, this one is to the top bolt, and this one is the bottom bolt." I hand the keys over, feeling guilty for allowing complete strangers to stick their necks out for me. They're off duty, doing this as a favor to Spencer.

"I sure hope he's up there. And I hope he puts up a fight. At the very least, a little resistance. All I need is one good reason to take him down." Jake cracks his knuckles and sneers his lip. "I'm more than willing to pay him back on your behalf, Savannah."

Could I have been wrong? Could their expressions I took for judgment against me have been disgust with Butch instead? Have I read others wrong too?

"I appreciate the offer, Jake. But I don't want you to get in trouble because of me."

"You're looking at it all wrong, sweetheart. All he

has to do is touch me wrong one time and he's assaulted a police officer. That's a serious offense, one he'd be hauled away in handcuffs over." Jake smiles, hopeful for the chance to arrest Butch and avenge me in one fell swoop.

One can hope he's in my apartment. Right?

BOTH FORTUNATELY AND UNFORTUNATELY, BUTCH wasn't in my apartment, and he never showed up while we were there, packing and moving all my belongings out, cleaning up afterward, and leaving the complex without a trace we'd ever been there. While I would've enjoyed seeing him hauled away in handcuffs by a few of DC's finest detectives, I'll take the stealthy approach we pulled off over a confrontation with him any day.

My new home is actually in a newer apartment, but the rent is affordable, and the neighborhood is on the trendier side. This area is nice and safe. I spotted a small coffee shop down the street. Cozy and quaint, it looks like the perfect place to work on my secret project. Something I've decided to do just for myself as much as for others.

"This place looks great!" Karen walks in like she lives here—after unlocking all my locks and bolts with the extra key I gave her—and I wouldn't have it any other way. "You must've been up all night, unpacking and decorating your new place."

"I couldn't sleep. I was too excited to close my eyes."

She drops her purse on the couch, places her hand on her hip, and quirks one eyebrow up at me. "For the record, I'm letting you get away with that abbreviated answer because there is some truth to it. Don't think for one second you'll get away with that shit in the future, though."

"Fine. I was also checking the door and window locks every five minutes and thirty-six seconds. And my ears were oddly in tune with every loud engine that drove past, regardless of the hour."

"I knew I should've spent the night with you last night, even though you insisted you'd be fine. It's really too bad Butch didn't show up yesterday. I would've enjoyed seeing the guys take care of him. But that also means he has no idea where you are now. There are over six million people in the DC metro area. You could live in Virginia or Maryland now for all he knows."

"But he knows where I work. He could follow me home from the hospital." With that thought, I can't help but glance nervously around my small condo, even knowing he isn't inside it. It's a reflex, as if mentioning his name will actually conjure the man out of thin air. "And it's not like you can just move in with me, so enough of the guilt trip for not spending the night."

"Let's devise a plan in case he does show up at the hospital or spots you on the road on the way home." Karen gives me her undivided attention. "Watch your surroundings at all times. We'll alert human resources and arrange for a security guard to escort you to your car every morning. If you think anyone is following you, don't go home. Drive straight to the police station and call me on the way. I'll get Spencer and the guys on the case immediately. Stay in public sight, and never yell for help. Always yell 'Fire.' That draws more people faster than screaming for help does."

"You are definitely married to a cop."

"I need to ask Spencer about self-defense classes. I'll go with you. We can do it on our days off." The wheels in Karen's head are spinning, making plans and mental to-do lists. All to ensure my safety and security.

My best friend is the best person.

"Have a seat. I'll get us a couple of sodas from the fridge, and we'll just bask in the newness of my new little home." True to her nature, she refuses the seat and checks out my decorating skills instead.

"You have great taste, Savannah. I don't know why you chose the noble but overworked profession of nursing over interior design. You could star in your own remodeling TV show by now." Karen pops the top on the Coke can and sips as she strolls to the master bedroom. "I love how you arranged this. You need to come over to my house and help me figure out how to rearrange and redecorate."

"You want to change your bedroom?"

"Oh no, not just the bedroom. My house. I want you to redo my whole house."

"That's more than just a weekend project, Karen."

"Yeah, I know. I'm good with however long it takes. Gives me time to parade Spencer's friends around and see which one you mesh with best."

"Sit. Stop with the matchmaking. Talk to me about more important topics."

We settle on the couch, facing the floor-to-ceiling windows that let in all the natural light I could ever want, and stare at the landscape of Meridian Hill Park only a block away. A light dusting of snow covers the bare trees, shrubs, and grassy areas. The temperatures haven't dropped enough for the snow to stick to the pavement yet, and the cold wind hasn't stopped anyone from enjoying the park.

"You know I only want you to be happy and loved, right? The way Spence loves me and puts me first in everything he does. I want that happy home life for you too." Karen's unusually serious tone makes my breath catch. I swing my eyes up to read her expression. Should've known I'd only find kindness and compassion there.

"I do know that, Karen. Sometimes when I watch

you and Spence together, I'm overwhelmed by how much I wish I had what you two have. It's not envy—it's a goal I've set for myself. But whether the man for me is one of Spencer's friends or not doesn't make a difference right now.

"I've lost myself over the last three years. Butch was a different man when I first met him, though I should've recognized the warning signs and red flags for what they really were. The blinders I wore were my fault, and I accept the blame for that. But when the switch flipped and the abuse started, it wasn't just physical injuries. The mental damage he caused nearly destroyed me. Before I even consider looking at another man, I have to be okay with looking at myself in the mirror again.

"There's a fine line between love and hate. I need to find my way back across that line."

"You know I don't judge you for staying with him as long as you did. The threats, the violence, and being in the constant state of fight-or-flight takes a terrible toll on your overall well-being. But I am so thankful you're away from him now, and I'm so proud of you for finding the courage and strength to do it. Just to be clear, though, I will have you committed on a seventy-two-hour psychiatric hold if you let him back in now. You have all the support you need from me, Spence, and a host of DC's finest."

"That seventy-two-hour hold kind of sounds appealing. A little vacation. I could use a long weekend away. Can you arrange for that evaluation to be done in the Bahamas?"

"Your sarcastic humor is what first told me we'd be best friends. You know you're not going off to a Caribbean island for a mental-health check and leaving me here to work your shifts. We go mental together, or we don't go at all."

"Good to know your priorities are in order."

"Did you expect anything less of me?" A sly smile spreads across her face.

"No. In fact, I would've been very disappointed in you if you had replied any other way."

"You know me too well. There's no mystery left in our relationship…no hidden gems for you to uncover."

"I haven't met all of your personalities yet. I'm sure you have plenty of mysteries left for me to figure out."

Days bled into weeks with no sign or word from Butch. Over that time, I began to find purpose in my work again. Meaning in my life. A new direction to take and a way to use what I've been through for good. The exciting prospects of new projects, secret plans, and shifts at the hospital consumed my time. I fell into bed every day completely exhausted and thoroughly content for the first time in years.

"Have a good day. I'm off for the next four days, and I am not coming in for anyone or anything." I've already briefed the incoming day nurse on the status of each patient and completed all my charting from the night shift. All that's left is to clock out and stroll through the doors.

The snow flurries swirl in the wind outside and the skies are a gloomy shade of gray, but nothing can dampen my mood today. My neighborhood has a quaint little coffee shop at the end of the block. The scents and the scenery are calling my name. My laptop, a table with a view, and a piping hot cup of coffee are all I need to work on my life-defining purpose—a new business venture to help other women in my predicament. I'm writing a book for women in abusive relationships, and I need time and inspiration to add another chapter to the hardest story I've ever told.

My own.

No time like the present.

CHAPTER 2

Nick

"This shit is for the birds. What the fuck am I even doing here?"

The wind coming off the water of the canal is colder than I remember when I step out of my brownstone in old Georgetown. I haven't been back in DC for so long, I've forgotten how cold it can get. Lucky me. Just when I arrive back in town, the weatherman predicts we'll have the coldest winter on record. Although, we haven't even officially reached the first day of winter yet, leaving me little optimism for the remainder of the season. Guess I got a little too comfortable in the Southern California sun. With the collar of my leather bomber jacket flipped up as a shield against the wind, I shove my hands in my pockets and keep walking toward a small coffee shop in the Adams Morgan neighborhood of DC. I found it by accident one day while wandering around aimlessly, and I've made the two-mile walk there every morning since. Holiday lights, decorations, and Christmas trees line my path, adding to the festive vibe of the neighborhood.

The best thing about this quaint little shop is it's not a chain. There are no hipster kids taking up all the seats, trying to appear cool or studious. This place just serves great coffee with equally delicious food, and everyone leaves me the fuck alone. I've come here every day for the last two weeks, ordered the same drink, and walked the couple of miles back to my brownstone in Georgetown.

Routine. Order. Peace.

I order my usual coffee and move to the end of the counter to wait for my name to be called. The bell over the door chimes so frequently with customers coming and going, I've almost tuned it out. But the energy in the café changes instantly, becoming stifling from the nervous electricity arcs crackling in the air. The tingling sensation zings up my spine before I even turn my head to look at who just walked in the shop.

"Get your fucking ass up and get out of here right now!"

The shop is filled with people this morning. They're talking, laughing, or furiously typing on their phones. But they all stop at the same time. I know, because the only noise in the room now is coming from the mouth-breathing bottom-feeder causing a scene. I drop my head forward because I know—I fucking *know*—no one else will step in and stop him. They'll watch. They'll say what a dick he is under their breath. One may be brave enough to threaten to call the police, but that won't faze a motherfucker like him.

I know his type all too well. He'll get off on showing them just how fucking evil he can be. The person who will take the brunt of his pathetic display of power will be the defenseless woman sitting in the coffee shop. No doubt she thought she'd be safe in such a busy public place. But this dickhead is banking on being the only tough guy in a room full of nonfat soy latte drinkers. Not a flask of whiskey in sight.

"I said get the fuck up!"

The unmistakable sound of scraping against the wood floor followed by a chair toppling over suggests he's jerked her out of the seat.

Still, no one moves.

"Let go! You're hurting me!" Her shrill shrieks fill the coffee shop, and I close my eyes, willing the scene to go away.

But it doesn't, and she's terrified. Still, no one says a word or tries to intervene in any way.

"You don't know what *hurt* is yet. But you will after this fucking stunt."

"Stop! I have to get my laptop and my purse."

"You spend too much time on that fucking thing anyway. You must be talking to some other guy. You're such a slut. I should stomp that fucking thing into a million pieces so you can't whore around anymore."

No one steps forward to stop him or his ridiculous tirade.

She cries out in pain, and I can't take it any longer. I turn around and stride toward him, determination set in my stance and murderous rage written on my face. As if on cue, every person between him and me takes two steps back, giving me plenty of room to move. "Get your fucking hands off her before I break them off your arms and shove them so far up your ass, you'll be able to wave at people from the back of your fucking throat."

The expression on his face is priceless. He's a big guy, but then I am too. The difference is, I'm a hell of a lot meaner than he has ever thought about being. I've committed acts of violence that would make him piss in his pants like a little baby. Breaking him with one punch will be the easiest task on my to-do list for the day.

"Who the fuck are you?" His sneer and intense stare-down are meant to intimidate me.

I'd laugh in his face if I weren't so pissed off over his treatment of this beautiful, terrified lady.

"I'm the man who's going to fuck you up one side

and down the other if you don't take your hands off her right now. I won't say it again."

I know the instant he decides to call my bluff. He's gotten away with this too many times. He's been given too many idle threats by guys who didn't have the ass to back up their words. He thinks he'll get away with it again with me because his fingers on his left hand tighten on her arm and he jerks her harder toward his chest as he nonchalantly drops his right hand. She loses her balance and falls into him, causing him to manhandle her even more until she regains her footing.

His right arm juts toward me, but I see his pathetic punch coming from a mile away. That's when I take him. A quick, swift jab to his nose makes his head snap backward. The pop of the bone breaking echoes through the room, and he stumbles backward before crumpling to the ground. His hand is still firmly wrapped around her bicep, though, so I rush forward to break his hold and keep her from falling to the floor with him. Once I free her of his grip, I instinctively wrap my arm around her waist, pulling her into me, and move her farther away from him.

The small shop erupts in claps and cheers as the dickhead lies bleeding on the floor, but she buries her face in my chest to hide. Shame, embarrassment, guilt —I've seen all the emotions written in her posture and her reaction too many times to count. And every single time, it enrages me because the abused woman thinks it's her fault instead of the man who can't fucking control himself. If I never see this unwarranted shame on an innocent woman's face again, it'll be too soon.

But I'm not ready for what else I see when this lady in particular finally peers up at me.

Through the tears shining in her deep green eyes and the black streaks of wet mascara on her face, she looks up at me with admiration. Adoration. Her champion. A hero.

"Are you okay? Did he hurt you?" Somehow, I manage to ask her the most basic questions about her well-being, but she has rattled me to my core without uttering a single word.

I'm no hero. I can't even say I'm a good man anymore.

"I'm okay. Thank you for what you did, stepping in like that. I can't tell you how much I appreciate it."

I wipe the mascara away with the pad of my thumb. Dickhead has embarrassed her enough for today. She doesn't need raccoon eyes to add insult to injury.

As the dickhead tries to stand, two police officers step into the café. He wipes the blood from his face when he's finally on his feet then startles from the red smear on his hand. His angry gaze flies up to me and amps up tenfold when his eyes trail my arm around her midsection. An ugly snarl covers his face, and I pull her tighter into me out of sheer spite. My eyebrow quirks up, and a smirk covers my face.

It's a blatant dare. He knows it. I know it. I don't fucking care. He can bring his A game, and he'll still get his ass beaten down.

"What's going on here?" One of the officers takes control of the situation. His authoritative tone defuses the angry spark in dickhead's eyes.

"That guy just punched me and broke my nose." He points to me, and the officers' gazes follow his finger.

"Is that true?"

"Absolutely."

Several patrons start chiming in at once.

"That man was abusing that woman."

"He got punched in the nose because he was hurting her."

"That's not all that happened, Officer. That man saved her."

"Okay, okay. Everyone calm down until we get to the bottom of this. We need to see some ID." One officer takes the name and information of the other guy. "Butch McMahan. Is the address on your license still correct?"

"Yes, sir."

Oh, *now* he's polite and respectful.

The other officer approaches me cautiously. "You got some ID?"

"Sure, Officer." I smile and pull my own badge

out from under my jacket. "Special Agent Nick Tucker, DEA."

All the color drains from Butch's face. My smirk morphs into the first real smile I've had in a long time.

"Special Agent Tucker, can you tell me what happened here?"

"Absolutely." I give him the play-by-play of the events leading up to the altercation that rendered Bitch temporarily dazed and incapacitated on the floor. Every time I say "Bitch," he corrects me with "Butch," but I keep going. It's the little things that make me feel better. Like calling Butch "Bitch." By the time I finish relaying the events, both cops have to actively work to avoid laughing out loud.

I don't even try to hide my mirth. Bitch deserves it.

Then one of the officers checks the license of the woman still clinging to me. "Savannah Fields. Is this address still correct?"

"No. That's my old address. I moved a couple of months ago but haven't had my license updated."

"What's your new address, then?" The cop waits with his pen pressed against the paper, looking up when she doesn't answer.

"I don't want to give it out." Her eyes jerk toward Butch then back to the officer's. I immediately understand the situation.

"Let's step outside so she can give you her information in private, Officer."

"Absolutely. Better yet, I have another idea. Frank, can you take Mr. McMahan outside and finish getting his information, away from Miss Fields?"

"My pleasure. Step outside, sir. We're not finished yet." The other officer opens the door and motions with his head for Butch to step through.

When the door is closed and Savannah is assured he can't hear her, she rattles off her new address to the officer, and it's immediately committed to my memory.

"I don't want to press charges, Officer. It'll only provoke him more than he already is."

"Are you sure about that, Miss Fields? This is a clear-cut case of simple assault and battery. You have plenty of credible witnesses who are more than happy to testify to that fact, if needed."

I watch her face as she weighs the pros and cons, and I know the very second she's made up her mind. "No, I just want him to leave me alone and put all this behind me once and for all."

The problem is, I've been around men like Butch for the past two years. He won't leave her alone. He won't let this slight against him go unanswered. His pride has been wounded whether he leaves here in the back of the patrol car or not. And he will want revenge for that insult. But her mind is made up, and she urges the officer to wrap this up so everyone can get back to their business.

With the paperwork done, Bitch and the other office rejoin us in the warmth of the coffee shop.

"I want him arrested." Bitch thrusts his finger at me as he approaches, and I'm sorely tempted to break it. "He assaulted me. Broke my nose. Look at me."

"Go ahead and press charges. Savannah and I will both press charges against you too, and we'll see who walks out of the precinct and who spends the night." My blatant dare is meant to incite him again. He doesn't take much goading to push him over the edge, and I'm in the mood to have another go at him.

The cop finishes writing on his form and turns to Bitch. "Here's the deal. You can either leave now and stay away from her for good, and I mean *forever*, Mr. McMahan. Or, we can arrest you right now for assault and battery. You can try to press charges against Special Agent Tucker, but I guarantee his director will have already talked to the chief of police before we even get to the station."

Butch hesitates for just a moment, weighing his options, before he concedes. "I'll leave. I never want to see her again anyway."

The cop turns to Savannah. "Go file a restraining order against him. If he breaks it, we'll haul him in."

"Like a piece of paper can save her if I wanted to get to her."

"Did you just threaten her in front of me? Because I'll arrest you right here and now if you want to play this stupid game." The cop grabs his cuffs and advances on Bitch.

"No, no, I'm not threatening her. If you're finished with me, I'll go now."

"That would be best. Stay away from her. Don't call her. Don't look for her. If you see her out somewhere, turn and walk the other way. You get me?"

He nods then storms out the door. A collective sigh echoes through the shop when the door closes behind him. When I look down at Savannah, I'm surprised to find her still attached to me even after Butch is gone. The two cops leave soon after Savannah promises to pursue the restraining order so they can arrest his ass when he approaches her again. They know he will—they've seen the signs too many times, too.

"You okay?" I wait for her to tip her face up to me, and those emerald-green eyes hypnotize me instantly.

She nods. "I think I'm okay now. Thank you for not leaving me to deal with this mess alone."

"My pleasure, Savannah. Let me grab a hot coffee then I'll walk you home to make sure you get there safely. Can I get you anything?"

"I think I'm already jittery enough. I don't need more caffeine to add to it." She laughs nervously and glances away. "I'll just grab my things then I'll be ready to go."

With my coffee in hand and Savannah's laptop bag slung over my shoulder, she and I set off on foot. The chilly air hits us the second we step out of the café. "Good thing your place is only at the end of the block. You'd freeze to death if you had to walk much farther."

She nods and looks down, a sure sign of the low self-esteem. "I know, but I'm too fat, so I need the exercise. Butch used to complain about my weight frequently."

I place my hand on her arm, careful not to alarm her, and halt her steps. "That's not what I said at all. You're gorgeous, built, and sexy as hell. I don't give a shit what that fucking moron said—you're perfect exactly the way you are right now. From what I've seen and felt, you have all the right curves in all the right places."

Her face burns bright red and her eyes drop to the ground, but a smile spreads across her face. "Thank you, Nick. That's very sweet of you to say."

With a chuckle, I shake my head. "I've never been accused of being *sweet* before." We continue our short walk to her apartment building. "Do you mind if I come up for a minute? Before you get the wrong idea, I only want to make sure he's not waiting for you up there before I leave you alone."

"Um, sure. I guess that's a good idea, considering

he just showed up in my neighborhood today, and I have no idea how he found out where I live now."

"You're still in scrubs, so I'm guessing you work nights. Any chance he could've followed you home from work?"

"Maybe. But I was very careful, watching all around me and everything. I didn't even drive to work today. I took the Metro and walked to the coffee shop."

I can tell she's very uneasy about being alone with me in the elevator, but I know this guy isn't going to give up as easily as he said. So I take advantage of the time to learn more about the clusterfuck that just happened. "I take it Butch McMahan is your ex-boyfriend?"

"Unfortunately. It's actually a long, ugly story, but we haven't been more than acquaintances for about three years. Though, he obviously thinks that means he owns me and gets to boss me around. I know the cop was adamant about the restraining order, but it won't do any good to get one. It may even make the situation worse because Butch would take it as a dare. I don't want his temper to escalate."

I'm leaning against the elevator wall as we slowly climb to the fifth floor, watching her every move and expression, when a sobering fact hits me.

The threat of danger to Savannah is far from being over. Undercover work sharpened my gut instincts. My intuition kept me alive at times I could just as easily have died, but I heeded the warnings even when I questioned the logic behind doing so. I learned quickly not to ignore them, and right now, they're screaming at the top of their lungs at me.

Can I simply walk away knowing that?

CHAPTER 3

Savannah

*T*his enormous man moving through my apartment like he owns it is reassuring and intimidating at the same time. And sexy. Very, very sexy. That's something I shouldn't even be thinking about right now. I've sworn off men completely until I get my own shit together. I don't need another complication in my life right now. I mean, I haven't even fully gotten rid of Butch yet, despite my best attempts. I wouldn't feel right about starting something with another man with that kind of loser baggage still clinging to me.

But there's something innately calming and reassuring about Nick. He didn't even flinch over the extra time it took to open all my dead bolts and door locks—and lock them back again once we were inside. Now, I can't help but follow him around like a lost puppy and watch his every move, explaining my reasoning for decorating or furniture arrangement. He has no idea how much I appreciate his good-natured replies to my rambling. He's definitely lethal to the female population in those jeans that cling to his legs perfectly, outlining the muscular tree trunks underneath the denim fabric. And I find myself jealous of the thermal Henley stretching across his broad shoulders, thick chest, and muscular arms, clinging to his fine physique like a tattoo.

Speaking of a tattoo, I see hints of extensive ink across his chest now and then when he moves in just the right way. The tips of an elaborate design peek out from under his shirt, and I'm dying to ask him if I can see it. When we walked into my apartment, he took off his jacket and draped it over his arm, no expectations for me to pick it up off the floor wherever he decided to drop it. Unlike someone else I know but wish I didn't.

"You don't have an alarm system?" His tone is nonchalant, absent any judgment or condemnation. But I have a feeling it's anything but benign from the way he thoroughly checks and rechecks my doors and windows, as if I don't check them a hundred times a day without his help.

"No. I'm only renting and have no intentions of buying this place, so I didn't see the point in investing the money."

He nods his head, but his demeanor clearly says he doesn't agree with me. "Maybe you'll change your mind after the incident today."

When I'm silent for too long, he turns and pierces me with his amber-colored eyes that make me think of a shot of whiskey—smooth and warm, but with an extra kick that comes from out of nowhere. But something deeper in them speaks to me. I feel an instant connection to him, past the acts of kindness he's shown me.

"Maybe."

I can't tell him I don't have the extra money for a security monitoring system right now. I've already put myself in an embarrassing situation, and I'm working hard to get out of it. The investments in my future endeavors coupled with the usual moving expenses hit my savings account harder than I originally estimated, so I'll need time to save up enough money to cover more than the necessities. Living in DC is not cheap, and I'm well aware I could move to another town and get away from Butch. I could pick any small town or big city in the world, but I refuse to run and hide from a place I've grown to call home. Maybe that makes me stupid. Or stubborn. Or both. But I refuse to leave behind the best friends I've ever known just because of a poor excuse for a man.

There's definitely much more to Nick Tucker than the rough exterior and the savior attitude I've seen so far. The way he carries himself screams confidence and capability—but he also gives off enough signals to let everyone know to keep a wide berth. When he speaks, his message is short and to the point. Even on the walk to my apartment, the limited conversation we had was all about me. He seemed hesitant to share anything about himself—personal or otherwise.

Yet, he cares. Even about a stranger embroiled in the drama of domestic abuse, probable frequent flyer at the local police station, and general wimp of a woman, for all he knows. First impressions are as hard to overcome as false beliefs about women who don't flee from domestic violence.

"I have some friends in the security business. To the public, they've closed up shop and redirected their efforts elsewhere. To those of us who know them, they still provide the best security services anyone would ever need, all while keeping it under the radar. They're good friends of mine, so I'd trust them with my life, and I don't say that about anyone else. If you'll let me, I'd like to call them to install a security system for you."

"But you don't know me. Why would you do that?" No man would call in a favor like that for someone he didn't know. He only knows my name because I had to give it to the police officer. We literally just met a few minutes ago. What does he expect in return?

His eyes drop to the floor, and a dark shadow

passes over his expression. There's so much regret deep inside this man. Pain seeps out of his very essence, troubling him so much, even a stranger can see it. "You don't deserve how he treated you. You're entitled to feel safe in your own home." He shrugs his muscular shoulders, still not meeting my gaze head on. "If I can help take some of that away, I want to try."

"I appreciate the offer, but I can't let you do that. It's very kind of you to be so concerned about me, though. You have a good heart, Nick." I'm not flirting —I'm being as sincere as possible. Maybe I missed a few huge warning signs with the other guy, but my eyes are wide open now.

"I don't think your friend would agree with that assessment of me, but I'll admit to having a strong sense of right and wrong. My protective instincts have always been fairly keen, too. Sorry if I crossed the line with my offer. Sometimes I do get a little overzealous...but that's only because of what I've seen in my line of work."

When he speaks this time, those amber eyes lock on to mine and hold me captive. I almost feel bad about turning down his offer to help. It seems so important to him.

"Your friends in security, did you use to work with them?" I'm genuinely curious about Nick, but maybe I'll learn more about him by asking about his friends rather than about him directly.

"Yeah. We were all Army buddies first. Reaper started his own security company when he left the service. I worked for him for a while before I took a private security job with the software mogul Dominic Powers. Now I'm with the DEA. Reaper had his security business for several years before all the guys settled down with families, but they couldn't stand being out of the thick of things for long. Now they take high-powered but low-visibility cases."

"You mean they handle undercover work, don't you?"

"Something like that." Is that a small smile? Finally, some type of reaction from him. Amused by my amusement.

"I've always been fascinated by that type of work. I never could do it myself, but I love watching documentaries about other people who do it. It's intriguing."

That amused look is gone, replaced by a haunted expression I can't even begin to guess about.

He pulls a card out of his wallet and writes something on the back. "Here's my contact info, and my personal cell is on there. If you change your mind or if he shows up here, call me. My address is on the back if you ever need a nearby place to escape to. I'm only a couple of miles from here—in Georgetown. Don't hesitate to call or drop by if you need help."

With that, he slides his jacket over his muscular

arms and back. "Lock up behind me. Stay safe, Savannah."

"Thank you again for everything. Are you sure you don't want me to drive you home? It's getting pretty cold out there."

"No, I like to walk. Thanks anyway. Enjoy the rest of your day." Before the door closes behind him, he graces me with a full-face smile.

Straight white teeth against naturally tanned skin. Short hair that looks black on sight, but closer inspection reveals the dark brown mixture. Well-groomed beard that adds to his rugged and handsome appearance. But that real smile makes me weak in the knees.

After he's gone, I realize he never asked for my number. That really shouldn't disappoint me as much as it does. I shouldn't care whether he wants to call me or not. I certainly shouldn't wonder if he has a girlfriend, or recount that I didn't see a ring on his finger.

And I definitely shouldn't tell Karen about him.

For the next few hours, I keep myself busy writing and plotting my next couple of chapters, motivated even more by the events of the morning. The distinctive rumble of a motorcycle engine slowly moving by catches my attention. My heart races, my hands shake, and my palms sweat. Sliding along the wall to the window, I peek through the crack between the curtains and the wall without giving away my location. My breath hitches in my chest, and I stand motionless while staring down at Butch. He's stopped in front of my building, casing the scene. My only consolation is he doesn't know which apartment is mine. The tenant names aren't listed on the door buzzer for safety concerns—exactly like this situation. Still, if someone opens the door and holds it for him, he would find me all too soon.

He raises his hand, his forefinger pointed outward and his thumb extended upward, forming a mock gun. Then he slowly moves his hand across the building, pretending to shoot when he reaches each window. Though he doesn't know which one I'm in, the threat is obvious. And real—because he has no idea I'm watching, but he's taking the time to see it through regardless.

I can't breathe.

I'm never going to get away from him. He doesn't even care about me, much less love me. So why can't he just leave me alone?

His arm drops limply to his side, and his spine straightens. A large figure steps out of the shadows, slowly approaching Butch's bike. A hood covers the second man's head and his hands are in his jacket pockets, but I'd recognize that strut anywhere.

Nick is out there with Butch.

So many thoughts rush through my mind, I can barely keep up with them. Was the entire scene at the coffee shop a ruse to get me to trust Nick? Is he in league with Butch and the motorcycle gang? I can't chance moving to slide the window open, but then, I wouldn't be able to hear them from the fifth floor anyway.

Butch makes a show of turning the ignition key off and putting the kickstand down. He stands and climbs off his bike. An anxiety attack is imminent. There's no way I can fight off these two muscular brutes if they turn on me. I slide my cell out of my pocket and prepare to dial 9-1-1. If they walk toward the building, I'm running and dialing at the same time.

Butch faces Nick, his arms hanging loosely at his sides, but his fists are ready. That stance is all too familiar. Butch is about to sucker-punch Nick. Maybe they're not friends, after all. My imagination is all over the place, along with my paranoia and anxiety. Butch takes a swing, but Nick easily ducks before delivering a powerful blow to Butch's stomach, one fist after the other.

Butch doubles over in pain and drops to his knees in the middle of the road, coughing and spitting on the ground. Nick takes that opportunity to snatch something out of Butch's vest pocket then spikes it on the asphalt in front of Butch. Then I realize what it is —or was. Butch's cell phone. Nick stomps on what's left of it with the heel of his boot, further demolishing it and grinding it into dust.

Nick doesn't walk away before adding insult to injury. He smiles and gives Butch an imaginary tip of his hat. Then Nick strolls off without a care in the world while Butch tries to catch his breath and stand up straight again. He holds his side as he straddles his motorcycle then glances down at the broken pieces of his phone before putting his bike into gear and riding away.

First, I'm dying to call Nick and ask him what the hell just happened. Then I realize he never left my neighborhood when he left my apartment. He knew Butch would show up, and he waited out in the cold wind and snow for hours.

Second, there's no way in hell I can keep any of this from Karen and Spencer. She will flip her shit on me for not calling her immediately, and I'm sure Spencer will want to meet Nick. Either way, I'll be in an embarrassing predicament—Karen with her matchmaking plans and Spencer with his law enforcement brotherhood bond pushing me on a man I just met.

Lastly, watching Nick dishing out what I've taken from Butch was way too hot. I wish I'd videoed it on my phone so I could replay it a million and one times. From what I've seen of him so far, Nick Tucker is the perfect man. Did I mention he's also a fine specimen to examine?

If I wait much longer, I run the risk of facing a thoroughly pissed-off best friend, so I fish my phone from my pocket again. Funny, I don't even remember putting it back in there. When she answers, she's her usual chipper self. Until I recount the coffee shop scene. I only get as far as Butch dragging me out of my seat before she becomes unhinged.

"What the hell, Savannah? Why are you just now calling me? Spence! Spence! Where is your gun? I'm going to neuter Butch and spare the world from any chance of him reproducing any satanic spawn in his image."

"What?" I can hear the confusion in Spencer's tone, and it makes me laugh.

"Hold on, Karen. Let me finish the whole story first. You'll enjoy it."

"There's more? Let me put you on speaker so Spence can hear too. He may have better ideas of how to rid Butch of his cock and balls. Maybe some dry ice. Think that would freeze them off, babe?"

"Please don't talk about dry-icing anyone's cock and balls. It causes me physical pain. Savannah, please tell us your story so we can change the subject. Quickly."

An image of Spencer protectively covering his junk with his hand flashes in my mind, and I choke back a laugh. Then I recount everything—from start to finish—for both of them. When I reach the end of the story, I'm met with complete silence on the other end of the line.

"Karen? Spence? Did I lose you?"

"No. We're here. Just in shock." Spencer answers

first, which is odd, but the hesitancy in his voice is even more so.

"What? Do you know Nick?"

"You haven't been watching the news lately, have you?"

"No. Why? I've been asleep during the day or on my way to work most evenings."

"Nick Tucker is the agent who was involved in that shootout with the Devil's Dominion motorcycle gang in LA a few months ago. He'd been undercover with them for two years, and his cover was blown after he saved those kidnapped actresses."

"So, he's one of the good guys, then?" I knew it.

"Well, technically, yes. But Savannah, he was one of them for two years. I'm sure there were things he had to do to prove his allegiance. That's a long time to be in with one of those gangs and not be like them. He had to fit in. If they'd ever questioned his loyalty to them, they would've just killed him. He may be a federal agent, but he may not be completely harmless either. Just be careful, okay?"

And just like that, my walls go back up again.

CHAPTER 4

Nick

My morning coffee run takes me by Savannah's building. Curiosity gets the better of me, so I have to look up at her condo, but I don't catch any movement as I walk by. Within a few minutes, my favorite coffee shop is in sight, and my craving intensifies. When I step inside, those emerald-green eyes lift to meet mine, and a smile lights up her face.

What was I thinking about craving again?

"Good morning, Savannah. How's your day going?"

"Good morning. So far, so good. You?"

"About the same." I walk to the counter and order my usual, feeling her eyes boring into my back the entire time. After I waste a few minutes making small talk with the barista, I quickly turn before Savannah can avert her eyes.

Busted.

Staring straight at me. Checking me out. From the angle of her gaze, she was looking at my ass. From the way she's chewing on her bottom lip, I'd say she liked it. Without asking or waiting for an invitation, I take a seat at her table, sipping my coffee and ignoring her surprised reaction.

"What are you working on so early this morning?" I incline my head toward her laptop.

"Um, I'm...um, writing a book." Her cheeks flush, and she lowers her gaze to the table, as if she's waiting for me to ridicule her for such an absurd idea. That, however, is the furthest thing from my mind.

"What's it about?" I lean in, giving her my full attention.

"I want to help other women who are in abusive relationships, so it's about what I've experienced and what I wish I'd done differently." She searches my eyes and waits for the other shoe to drop.

"I'm impressed. That's incredibly thoughtful and insightful of you. When you become famous and hit the talk-show circuit, I'll be able to say, 'I knew her when.' You'll be my claim to fame." The truth is, I mean every word of it.

Gratitude shimmers in her eyes before she swallows hard, regaining control over her composure. "Thank you for saying that, Nick. I don't expect that will happen at all, but I appreciate the vote of confidence."

"Of course. I won't keep you from working any longer, then. Have a good one." Just as I push back from the table, a picture of me flashes up on the TV mounted over the barista bar.

"Looks like you have your own claim to fame." Her eyes remain glued to the screen as the images change.

The first one is of me in character, decked out as a member of the Devil's Dominion motorcycle club with my long, scruffy hair and scraggly beard, wearing my cut with the club colors boldly displayed on my back. The next image looks more like I do today, with my short, military-style haircut, neatly trimmed beard, and sporting a DEA jacket. The trial for the members running drugs, guns, prostitution rings, and kidnapping schemes is underway. The more attention it garners, the more my face is flashed on every TV screen across the nation.

My cover was blown shortly after the gang take-down. One of the surviving members made sure to sing like a fucking canary to anyone who'd listen—after I saved his pathetic life. An overly eager jour-nalist was all too willing to accommodate his anonymity in exchange for my name—all to get the scoop on everyone else. When the journalist ran with the story and my pictures, he annihilated any chance I have to go undercover again—ever. There's no outlaw organization in North America that won't recognize me on the spot by the time this trial is over —whether it's a motorcycle gang or an organized crime syndicate. They'd never believe I'd turned rogue either. My blood bleeds DEA and following the law to the letter, and that's the tune every reporter sings about me now.

Calvin, my director, already warned me that this do-gooder character they've made me out to be could all be fueled by the gang's lawyers…to discredit me and relish my epic fall from grace when my gang crimes are revealed. Pointing out all my flaws after making me out to be the best agent since James Bond will be part of their defense. My fall from grace will help create an ounce of doubt in the jurors' minds toward the gang members—or at least some hesitation to throw the entire book at them. My sins will be broadcast from every satellite and antennae across the nation, all in the name of discrediting me and getting those low-life thugs off the hook.

This is another reason Calvin didn't think I was ready for undercover work. The aftermath can be fucking brutal.

"I wish they'd quit running that load of bullshit. They're only trying to sensationalize the trial and get the public more engaged." I shake my head, disgusted with how slowly the wheels of justice turn sometimes, and start toward the door. "That's my cue to exit stage left. Good luck with your book."

"Hey, Nick?" The tentative tone in her voice grabs my attention.

"Yeah?"

"Do you miss it?" Her eyes roam over my face while she waits for me to answer, searching for any clue of my real feelings.

"Miss what, exactly?" I'm not sure what to make of her question or why she's so concerned about it.

"Undercover work, I guess." She shrugs unconvincingly. "Being part of the motorcycle club."

"Miss being part of those fucked-up losers? No, I don't miss that at all. Undercover work...wasn't exactly what I thought it would be. I don't appreciate that my option to participate in undercover operations has been taken from me now, but I'm still considering my options for the future. Riding a desk isn't my cup of tea."

She bites on the end of her pen, a subconscious behavior showing she's nervous about what she has to say next. "There's something else I should tell you. Um, Butch stopped in front of my building yesterday. I don't think he saw me, but I saw him."

That memory brings a smile to my face. "Yeah, I figured he would. I waited around for him to show his fugly mug. An idiot thug like him couldn't resist, not even realizing all he accomplished was showing his entire hand."

"What do you mean?"

"I knew he was tracking you somehow. He found

you here in the coffee shop after you said you moved without telling him where you went, didn't he? When he rolled up at your building, I approached him, made a few not so vague threats to his person, and took his phone from him."

"His phone? Why would you take his phone? What does that have to do with anything?" Her eyebrows draw down, her head tilts to the side, and her lips part slightly. On top of being too fucking beautiful to look at, she's so damn cute when she scrunches up her face.

"He had an app on it so he could trace you. It was still open when I snatched his phone from his cut. It was a burner phone. With a guy like him, I made an educated guess he doesn't have your number memorized. Still, I suggest changing your phone number and your email address in case he's actually smarter than he looks."

"You mean I went to all the trouble of packing and moving in secret, to a new location he knew nothing about, only to have him track me with an app on his phone? Oh my gosh, Nick. I feel so stupid. I should've anticipated something like that, but the thought honestly never crossed my mind. I can't believe you stayed out in the cold for so long, waiting for him to show just so you could make him leave me alone. Saying thank you—again—seems so inadequate. The news anchor had it completely correct when he said you're an undercover hero."

"I'm no hero, Savannah. Not at all. But I've witnessed firsthand how some sorry excuse for a man treats women. If I can help keep one of them away from you, I'll do whatever needs to be done."

"He's one of them, you know."

My head snaps back toward her fast enough to give me whiplash. "He's one of who?"

"The Devil's Dominion motorcycle club. The club president sent him out here a little over two years ago to oversee bringing a smaller gang into their circle. Things didn't go too smoothly with that assignment, though. He never told me anything, of course. But his voice is naturally loud, so I overheard everything he said about it when he came around me. He wouldn't go back out to LA because he'd failed at the assignment he was given, and he knew he'd never be promoted to an officer after that."

"He was a Devil, and he doesn't know who I am?" I can't fucking believe what I'm hearing. "And he just ditched his colors and ran?"

"Butch never watched TV—not even the news— so it doesn't surprise me he didn't recognize you. He hasn't owned a TV since he put his foot through one before we left LA because something someone said pissed him off. I kept mine off when he was around so he wouldn't break it. As far as his colors, I was never involved in that side of his life, so I don't know much about how it works. The other group didn't like the raw deal they were getting, and there were more of them than there were Devils here, so they ran Butch and a couple of his buddies off. It was after that when he quit wearing his vest with their patches. Is that what you mean?"

"Yeah, a cut is the vest, and the colors are the patches—the top and bottom rocker panels and the middle patch. Under the club bylaws, he's supposed to wear his colors every time he's on his bike. He must've tucked his tail and run when the other club refused him. Rather than make believers of them himself, or even call in the reinforcements to help him, he just dropped his colors and hid instead. He's even more of a coward than I thought. What do you know? I've given Bitch way too much credit."

She snickers at my choice nickname for him. "He may not be too bright, but don't underestimate him, Nick. He's as cruel and malicious as they come."

"I'm sure he is. But there's always someone bigger, badder, and meaner just around the corner. Let me know if he comes sniffing around, looking to cause trouble for you again. I'll make good on those threats I made."

Not that I think she will, but the offer stands. I can't stand guard outside her place day and night, but I'll gladly jump on my bike, whisk around the stalled traffic, and make a quick dash of the two miles separating us to face off with that dickhead again. All this pent-up energy and frustration have to vent somewhere.

For some reason, I'm still standing here, staring into those emerald-green eyes and those flaming strands of auburn-colored hair that are pulled back in some kind of beautiful, intricate braid. I'm sure I look like a fucking idiot. What I'm thinking about her is the last thing I need right now. My life is complicated enough as it is. After two raps on the table with my knuckles, I make my exit. "That book won't write itself, Savannah. I'll leave you to it."

OVER THE NEXT TWO WEEKS, SAVANNAH IS IN MY favorite coffee shop every morning in her nursing scrubs, sitting in the same seat, with her fingers furiously flying across the keyboard. My routine is also the same—walk in, say hello, grab my usual order, and take a seat with her while she types away on her laptop. After the first couple of days, I noticed she rarely ate, still stuck on that stupid fucking notion that she's too fat. So I started ordering breakfast to go with my coffee. She isn't fat. She is *fine*. And watching her enjoy the variety of menu items I deliver to her every day gives me an unusual satisfaction.

These visits with Savannah are not dates. I'm just getting to know the beautiful redhead with emerald-green eyes better every day. There's a difference. Besides, I'm enjoying just spending time with her. The aroma of coffee mixed with cinnamon buns and every other imaginable pastry is the icing on the piece of delicious red velvet cake sitting across from me. Plus, she's smart and funny. For the first time in a long time, I enjoy talking to someone about everyday mundane topics instead of the logistics of an undercover operation.

"So, tell me, what made you leave your private employer and join the DEA?" She watches me over the rim of her mug, blowing on the piping hot java before touching it to her mouth. I can't help but watch every movement of her lips and tongue until they disappear behind the bottom of her cup.

"The owner of the company, Dominic Powers, got married. He and his wife Sofia had a baby. Dominic hired someone else to run the company while he sat back and made the money. His home has state-of-the-art security with monitoring stations and impenetrable fences. My unique services were no longer required, not at the level I was used to providing anyway. After serving in the Army, I still had a strong conviction of serving my country, so the DEA became my new home."

"And the undercover work? Weren't you scared? I mean, if they'd found out you were a federal agent, they would've killed you on the spot." She looks at me with awe, waiting for my reply.

"They would have—and actually tried to there at the end. They almost succeeded in killing a buddy of mine from the CIA. He joined late in the investigation for a different reason, but he ended up blowing his cover to save a girl he was in love with. Almost blew my entire case, but so far, it hasn't completely unraveled. Once the trials are over, I'll be able to breathe freely again."

"I can't tell you how impressed I am with everything you've done. You've been all over the world. Done all kinds of work. Met all kinds of people. You've faced real-life situations that would make me pee the bed if I only dreamed about them. Besides work, what do you like to do?"

"I've been undercover for the past two years, until recently. I don't do anything besides work. Except go to the gym, if that counts as a hobby. I use weights to work off stress and keep in peak physical condition. Never know when you'll need that extra bit of ass to back up your threats."

She smiles and her eyes sparkle. Like emeralds. "You, threaten someone? Surely not. I can't even imagine that. You're just a big teddy bear." She puts her hand on my arm as she speaks. An innocent act to emphasize her tease, but the mere contact of her soft skin ignites every nerve in my body.

Fuck. It's been way too long since I've enjoyed the scents and sounds of a willing and beautiful woman underneath me. And I shouldn't be thinking any of the thoughts about a certain auburn-haired woman that are running through my mind. Or seeing any of the visions surrounding her that are parading through my mind's eye at the moment. "Yeah. You just keep thinking that, darlin'."

"You're still my hero, Nick. My undercover hero. Don't you ever forget it."

"No, you won't let me forget that moniker for shit." We laugh together, comfortable with the playful joking between us. "Speaking of the gym, I should get going."

"Will I see you tomorrow? Same time, same place?" There's a hopeful tone to her voice that wasn't there yesterday or the day before when she asked me the same question.

"Never know what tomorrow holds, darlin'." My standard response doesn't have quite as much conviction as it's held every other time I've used it either. Maybe we're both looking forward to seeing each other tomorrow.

Maybe a little too much. I leave with a wink and a quick wave before I say something I'll regret later. I'm not looking for romance. She's not looking for a good time. We're definitely not a match made in heaven.

Thinking of working off pent-up frustration leaves me with two options. One, start going through my little black book and seeing which friend-with-benefits still feels friendly after I've been away more than two years. Or two, go to the gym and hit the weights until I lose control of all voluntary muscle movement and regret my decision in the morning.

The gym it is.

After a quick jog back to my brownstone, I change into my dark gray sweat pants, throw on a tank top, and slide my thick hoodie over my head. After stuffing a change of clothes in my old gym bag, I'm out the door and on my way to wear myself out. Bypassing all the boutique gyms in the area, I head toward a man's-man gym—no machines, only heavy weights that take two hands to lift. No yoga classes. No Zen rooms. No safe spaces. Just free weights, free water, and freedom to work out undisturbed. Down the steps and into the basement I go, to my favorite unknown gym, The Dungeon.

Many other agents work out here from every agency identified by initials. We share a mutual understanding of how a labor-intensive workout helps more than any mandated therapy session could. Punishing ourselves while simultaneously making our bodies harder and stronger is the ultimate win-win scenario. Likely the only one of those we'll ever have in our line of work.

Hours pass as I lift weights until I've pushed my muscles beyond fatigue and into exhaustion. It hurts so good, though. My arms are made of cooked spaghetti now, and I can barely push the bar back up on the holder on my last rep. After putting my weights back on the racks, I hit the treadmill for a long stretch of my legs and my lungs. This is when I completely clear my mind, only listening to the way my feet fall on the conveyor belt and focusing on keeping my breathing consistent. The rest of the world doesn't exist for this hour. It's mine and mine alone.

It's when I'm in the shower with the scalding hot water soothing my exhausted muscles that my thoughts are overrun once again. The news coverage is still running. The nickname the anchor gave me is used every day on every station now. The way Savannah looked at me when she called me an undercover hero was the same way she looked at me when I tossed Bitch around like a little bitch doll for manhandling her.

That expression will change when the smear campaign begins.

The higher they rise, the further they fall.

And currently, they're trying to launch me and my superhero alter ego they've created into the fucking stratosphere.

Back in my brownstone, I grab a gallon of water from the refrigerator and stand in the open door, guzzling it down to quench my thirst and cool my engines. Out of nowhere, someone starts pounding on my door and frantically screaming my name. On my way to the commotion, I drop the jug of water on the table and grab my gun instead. When I jerk the door open, I find a battered and bloodied Savannah.

Her once expertly styled hair now hangs in tatters—parts of it frizzy but still in place, and other large chunks hang loose. Two large sections next to her scalp are matted and still wet with blood. One eye is nearly swollen shut, and both her lips are busted and bleeding. Her cheeks show scrapes and abrasions, while bruises in the shapes of long fingers are already forming in angry red tendrils on her neck. Some of these injuries very recently occurred because not enough time has passed for the coagulation process to begin, but others are at least a couple of hours older.

That son of a bitch.

"Nick."

Her voice breaks when she says my name, then her knees buckle under her weight. I easily scoop her up with one arm and carry her inside my home. All the adrenaline and rage flowing through my veins must flush the lactic acid from my muscles because I am primed and ready to give Bitch the beatdown of his life.

CHAPTER 5

Savannah

The sensation of strength and warmth envelops me, and I feel protected and sheltered for the first time in far too many years. Every inch of my body hurts, but Nick's muscular arms cradle me with such care, I feel as well cared for as a newborn baby. His scent is soothing too—sandalwood mixed with hints of the aroma of coffee, reminding me of the first time he saved me. Those scents are forever ingrained in my psyche and associated with Nick.

Safe. Secure. Protected. Cherished.

He places me on the soft cushions of his couch and covers with me a blanket. "Just relax, darlin'. You're safe. I'm here with you, and I guarantee he won't get through me to reach you."

With one hand on my shoulder, giving me all the reassurance and sharing his strength, he uses the other to call the police. A fleeting thought to protest getting them involved pops into my mind, but I quickly dismiss it. Butch has had way too many chances, and this time, he's gone way too far. Nick gives the police his address and a rundown of my injuries, then he pauses—the first sign of hesitancy I detect.

"Savannah, do you need to go to the hospital? Did he...did he rape you?" He's seething just below the surface, barely able to contain his anger. But it's all directed at Butch, that much I already know.

"No, he didn't. He wasn't interested in that kind of power. Tell them to send Detective Spencer Donovan. He's my best friend's husband."

Nick finishes the conversation with the dispatcher and releases a long, heavy sigh after he hangs up. "They got a hold of Detective Donovan. He will be here in a few minutes, darlin'. We'll get Butch, and he'll pay for every mark he put on you. Just rest until your friend gets here."

Sure enough, only a few minutes pass before someone knocks on the door, identifying himself as a DC detective. Nick partially opens the door and checks his identification before inviting him inside, even though I'm right here and can hear Spencer's voice loud and clear. After giving Spencer all my pertinent information and assuring both men, again,

I don't want to go to the hospital, I begin telling them what happened today.

"I'd been out for the early part of the day, running errands and shopping. When I got back to my apartment, my arms were full of bags and I was distracted, so I didn't notice if anything was out of the ordinary. But looking back, I realize now a couple of my dead bolts were too easy to turn. I remember opening the door and kicking it closed behind me, knowing I still had to secure all the locks before I put up my groceries. Before I even had time to set the bags down in the kitchen, Butch hit me from behind and sent me flying across the table. So he was already inside before I arrived home."

From there, I continue describing the attack in chronological order to the best of my spotty memory, retracing my steps, backing up, and adding to the details as flashes return to me. The punches to my face and head, the kicks to my abdomen and back, the objects hurtling through the air at me from so many directions. The indiscriminate screaming and yelling mixed with items crashing and breaking all around me. Chunks of time are missing from when I went in and out of consciousness, only to awaken to Butch's manic tirade again.

"I don't know how long the entire attack lasted— but it wasn't over with quickly. When I woke the final time, he was gone, and I didn't wait around to see if he was coming back."

"Did he give you any indication of what set him off?" I know Spencer has to ask that; it's part of his job. But there is no finding reason in an extremely unreasonable man.

"He kept saying he wasn't going to let me out of a sweet deal so easily. That it'd be over his dead body. But I have no idea what he meant. We haven't been romantically involved in years. I've made it perfectly clear multiple times I want nothing more to do with him. I even moved and didn't tell him where I was going. He was crazed, but I have no idea why."

After more questions and Nick sharing the details of the altercations he's had with Butch, I'm once again urged to go get a piece of paper that says he can't come within 500 yards of me. Because criminals always follow the law, and abusers are always remorseful enough to simply stop abusing others.

That piece of paper won't help me, no matter what laws are behind it.

If they can't get to Butch to arrest him for the assault I've endured, how will they find him to arrest him for breaking a restraining order?

Spencer promises a warrant will be issued for his arrest. If they find him, they'll take him in and hold him—until he makes bail. And I'll hold my breath and wait for that to happen. He's like a cockroach—scurrying into the dark places to hide from any light. Only coming out when something he wants is there, unsuspecting and unprotected.

Nick takes several pictures of my injuries with both an instant camera and with his phone. He understands as well as I do that this situation is far from over. But what can they do until Butch is found and put behind bars?

"Do you want me to escort you back to your apartment? I need to talk to your neighbors and document the state of your place." Spencer slides his pen into his shirt pocket, signaling we're finished here and he's ready to go.

But I'm not ready to go back there at all. The thought of it nearly sends me into a full-fledged panic attack. Without realizing I'm doing it, I shake my head.

"No, she's not going back there for a while. She's in no shape to be alone, and she doesn't have a security system. Yet. Butch could walk back in there at any time, if he even left the building at all. Look at her injuries—there's no telling how long he held her there against her will. He has stalked and harassed and abused her enough." Nick partially steps between Spencer and me, shielding me with his body even if he doesn't realize he's doing it.

"Nick, do you want to join me when I check out her apartment?" Spencer is hesitant to leave me here alone with Nick, especially after our last conversation about him.

"Here—just take my keys and let yourself in. If he's there, you can arrest him or shoot him." I pick up my small bag off the floor and hand over my keys. "I don't care if you have to go through all my things."

Spencer is obviously unsure about leaving me in Nick's care but takes the keys anyway. "I'll bring them back to you as soon as I'm finished with my reports. Call my cell if you need me before then. Will you be here? With Nick?"

"She will." Nick answers before I can and lays his hand on my shoulder, but I nod at Spencer and give him a small smile, silently telling him not to worry.

"I'm safe here, Spencer. Nick is a DEA agent. He knows how to handle Butch if he's stupid enough to come around here." Nick gently squeezes my shoulder in response.

I glance up at him, gratitude glimmering in my eyes and blurring my vision. He looks down at me, concern mixed with the inherent air of authority etched in his masculine features, then his face softens. A shadow passes over his eyes, like a rain cloud blotting out the sun on a bright day. Then he walks to the door to see Spencer out.

So many questions are answered in that one telltale sign, a rare glimpse into the man who reveals so little of himself to others. Nick lives with as many regrets as I do. They may not be anywhere near the same types of disappointments, but they still create the life-altering sense of shame that is nearly impossible to live under. I know from personal experience how the weight of past mistakes suffocates and binds until almost all hope is lost. The doubts nag and remind of all the bad decisions made in the past, badgering the mind and troubling the soul. Too many wishes to count have been wasted on seeking a way to turn back time and undo the years of unnecessary guilt.

A realization hits me from out of nowhere, sucker-punching me in the gut and stealing all my breath. That painfully deep pool of sorrow and self-loathing I just glimpsed in Nick's eyes…is the exact same hollow gaze I see when I look in the mirror.

"Savannah, you know Karen will be livid when I talk to her." Spence turns in the doorway, craning his neck around Nick to see me. "You may want to warn Nick about her, too."

"When you tell her what happened, please tell her every minute detail so I don't have to repeat any of it. Then tell her I love her…and remind her how much she loves me."

Spencer chuckles and shakes his head. "I'll be back soon, Savannah. Stay inside. Rest. We'll get him."

"Thank you, Spencer. And I love you too."

"Feeling's mutual, Savannah."

Nick closes the door after watching Spencer walk away, I presume to see what kind of car he drives so Nick will recognize it on sight next time. Unable to hold my head up any longer, I stretch out on the couch and try to find a comfortable position, one that doesn't put too much pressure on all my aches and pains and abrasions and contusions. When the door closes, I hear Nick lock the knob. Then the dead bolt. A second later, metal slides across metal, mixed the distinct sound of a chain clinking. Stupid, hot tears fill my closed eyes from the simplest gesture no one else even would've noticed.

Nick secured all the locks on his door. For me. From the short time he's been around me, he knows exactly what I need to feel safe and secure. Even though a logical part of my brain knows those locks can't protect me—obviously, as evidenced by my current state—it's an irrational need I can't do without. But those locks ease the storm that rages inside me, the one that grows more out of control when all I can fixate on is their unlocked status.

My self-doubt creeps in, and I don't want him to think I'm emotionally unstable, despite the fact that I am, actually, emotionally distraught...overwrought... frazzled...jittery. I hold my breath in an attempt to squelch the flood of sensations inside before the dam breaks, and I start blubbering out of control.

Then I feel the slightest touch on my face, so feathery and light, I question if I actually felt it. When I feel it a second time, I slowly open my eyes and find Nick sitting on the coffee table next to me, cleaning my wounds with a cotton swab. His focused expression shows his attention to detail, but the extra care he takes to avoid inflicting more pain while doctoring my injuries pushes me over the edge. Once the tears start, there's no stopping them. Like water escaping over a full spillway, rivers flow uncontrollably from my eyes.

Nick lifts his eyes to mine, startled at first—probably thinking he hurt me in some way—then realization settles into his features. He nods wordlessly in understanding. We move in tandem, each sensing what the other will do beforehand. His arms extend as I sit upright on the couch. He pulls me into his arms as I move into his lap. He cradles me like a baby, holding me close to his chest as he moves to the couch. I bury my head in the crook of his neck just before the sobs rack my body. He rocks me, whispering words of comfort as I rest my aching cheek against his chest, soaking his shirt with the torrent still pouring from my eyes.

Time passes—minutes into hours—while he comforts me. And I soak up every second of it, selfishly taking every ounce of security and reassurance he gives me. When I'm finally calm enough—and dehydrated enough—to stop the waterworks, I remain motionless in his arms and use my unique vantage point to examine him much closer than usual.

His chest is solid as a rock, yet remarkably easy to cuddle against.

His arms are thick and muscular, but gentle and comforting.

His voice is deep and masculine, full of intimidation for those who cross him. But lying here in his care, that same voice encouraged me to let it all out because I was safe with him. That voice soothed my frayed nerves and calmed my racing heart when the panic set in and the anxiety threatened to pull me under.

He's my undercover hero, even if he can't see it because of the blinders he wears when he looks at himself. But that's okay, because one day soon, he'll see himself exactly how I see him, through my eyes. I'll make sure of it. He tries to hide his soft heart and his protective nature behind a gruff exterior and threatening air. But now that I've seen the man inside, I wonder how I ever could've missed him.

"Thank you." I intentionally keep my voice soft, afraid I'll break the trance we're both in and he'll jump up, ready to leave me behind. "I'm sorry I brought all this to your doorstep. Literally."

"You're welcome. But you haven't done anything to be sorry about. I hate that this happened to you, but I'm glad you came to me. At least I know you're safe from him while you're here with me. He said he'd let you go over his dead body? I'm not seeing a downside to that proposition."

I can't help but notice how he kept his lips close to my head when he spoke. How low and sensual his voice sounded, like a velvety-soft caress over my skin.

How his thumb lightly strokes my lower back, slowly back and forth, as if he's my attentive lover.

Maybe this is the most inappropriate time to entertain such flights of fancy. But Nick isn't the one who hurt me. He isn't the one who left me for dead. He isn't the one who has threatened me day in and day out over the last few years.

Nick is the one who saved me…not only from Butch, but from myself. If I look hard enough, maybe I can see myself with him in the future.

CHAPTER 6

Nick

The beautiful redhead in my arms reminds me of so many women who paraded in and out of the club headquarters in LA. The majority of those women wanted to be there—on some level anyway. They endured abuse and were passed around freely among the brothers, like a water canteen for a group of men stranded in the desert too long. They weren't allowed to complain. They couldn't say no to any demand. And they didn't have a choice of which man had his turn next. Had they had any alternative other than living on the street in a cardboard box, I'm sure they would've jumped at it instead. But the relative safety of being inside a notorious outlaw biker gang hangout was better than what most of them already had faced on the outside.

My imagination is incapable of seeing Savannah in a place like that, though. Her entire disposition is the complete opposite of every sheep or old lady I met in my two-plus years undercover. She's the epitome of my dream woman, but she's definitely here in the flesh. Her plump, round ass fits perfectly in my lap. Her waist is small enough for my arms to wrap around at least a couple of times. Her long, red hair is thick and smells of vanilla and violet, especially so close to my face that I can't avoid it. Even with the now clotted injuries to her scalp, the scrapes, bruises, and puffy contusions on her face, she's the most beautiful woman I've ever seen. Or held.

But this can never be. The thought I'm having of holding her forever is really just wishful thinking, never to come to fruition. I have to admit, it's a really great dream, though.

She apologized for bringing her problems to me, as if I'd want her to go anywhere else at this point. Helping her is not a hardship for me. Doing what's right is every bit as much a part of me as my fingerprints are. This is what identifies and makes me who I am, what distinguishes me from everyone else out there. In some small way, maybe I also wonder if helping her will absolve me of some of my other sins...the laws I broke while undercover...the women I didn't protect because my cover came first. The ones I allowed to suffer so I wouldn't be killed for being a DEA agent.

"I don't want to impose on your generosity, Nick. You've been too good to me as it is. When Spencer gets back from checking everything out, I can go back to my apartment."

She can't see my smile from the way she's cradled in my arms, so I don't try to hide it at all. There's no conviction in her voice. If she actually wanted to stay in her place alone, she would've insisted. She would've stated she was going back, not left it up to me to decide for her. She doesn't want to impose, but she doesn't get that she's not an imposition to me. At all. Time to make a believer out of her.

"You're not going back to your apartment tonight. Or tomorrow. You can go back after you've healed and after we've had a top-of-the-line security system installed. For the record, I'm fairly blunt about what I think and what I want. If you ever impose, I'll tell you straight up. If I tell you I want you to come to me if you need help, that's exactly what I mean. And when I say you're staying here with me, where I know for a fact that you're safe, your pretty little ass isn't going anywhere. Got it?"

I can feel her smile against my chest at the same time her tense muscles relax again, her body melting against mine. "Got it, Nick. Thank you again. Thank you, thank you, thank you."

"While you're here, I expect you to make yourself at home. If there's something you want in the kitchen, it's yours. If there's something you want to watch on TV, you're welcome to the remote. If you need anything from the store, just tell me. We're thick as thieves, you and I."

"Then you have to give me some way to earn my keep around here." She raises her head from my chest to look at me. I hope to hell she can't read minds, because that offer is way too fucking tempting to turn down. "I'm a great cook. Let me feed you while I'm here."

Not exactly the same thing I thought she was offering, and I like my original thought better. Still, a home-cooked meal is not something I'll easily turn down.

"Deal, with a couple of exceptions. Don't even think about doing anything tonight. Probably not tomorrow either. You've been through hell. And if you don't feel up to cooking any other day you're here, then don't. No expectations. No tit for tat. You are a guest who's making herself at home here. Feeling at home means if you don't want to cook, we order takeout. Plain and simple."

"I can work with those stipulations." She smiles— or tries to. The bruises on her cheeks and the busted lips make it difficult for her to accomplish a full smile.

Seeing her injuries ignites the fury in me all over again. If I could get my hands on Butch, Savannah would never worry about him hurting her again. Fucker ghosted two weeks ago—not a sighting, not a word, nothing. Then all of a sudden, he's lying in wait for her inside her apartment. For all he knew, she could've died from her injuries after he left her unconscious on the floor. After spending a couple of hours every day with her over the last two weeks, I've gotten to know her fairly well. What makes her tick. Things she likes and doesn't like. Dreams and aspirations she has for her life.

She's not a casualty of a case I'm working while undercover.

A knock at the door pulls me from my murderous thoughts. Visions of Butch strung up by his balls, screaming in pain in a shrill, high-pitched voice retreat to the back of my mind. I'm sure it's Spencer at the door, coming back to deliver Savannah's keys. At the moment, I'm considering leaving Detective Donovan outside the door just so I don't have to move Savannah off my lap. We're both very comfortable in our current positions, and I felt her breath catch before she released it in a disappointed sigh. She thinks she's sly, this fiery little minx in my arms, but I can tell she wants more than friendship from me.

I'm not sure I'm capable of giving more.

I'm also not sure she's truly ready to want more.

Still, neither of us offers to move to answer the door. She's also considering her options, and that makes me want to grin much more than it fucking should.

"I should probably get that. I'm sure it's your

detective friend stopping back by. He was already worried about leaving you here with me. We shouldn't cause him more concern by pretending we don't hear him at the door." My lips are against her hair as I speak, brushing along the shell of her ear. She leans closer into me. My arms tighten around her. My brain knows it should make me get up, but my fucking body is revolting against letting her go.

A louder and longer bang on the door signals Spencer's increasing frustration. "Savannah, are you in there?"

"Why don't you go take a hot shower? Use the one in my bedroom—it has a walk-in shower with a seat. Use the seat. I don't want to go in there and find you passed out on the floor. There are clean towels on the heated rack. Yell if you need anything at all."

"God, yes, that sounds like heaven. I think I will take you up on that." She looks up at me again. "I can't thank you enough. For everything."

"No reason to thank me, darlin'. It's my pleasure."

After I help her stand and make sure she's steady on her feet, I go to the door and let Spencer in. Savannah is already in my bathroom, adjusting the hot water for the shower when he walks into my living room. I can always spot a career cop—their eyes scan everything in the room, unabashedly looking at every single item in their surroundings, taking in the scene and processing it on the spot, whether it's considered rude by normal standards or not.

"Savannah okay?" His eyes assess me now, and I already know what he thinks of me. It's clear as fucking day.

"She will be. She had somewhat of a breakdown after you left, but I think she got most of it out."

"I packed a few of her things I thought she may want. I've had to do similar for Karen before when she got stuck working double shifts at the hospital because of the weather and stuff. Where is she anyway?" He hands me a small duffle bag with a few articles of clothes and toiletries then glances over my shoulder, toward the hallway.

"She just now went to take a shower."

Spencer nods, maintaining eye contact, and puts his hands on his hips. "At the risk of sounding cliché, this is the part where I warn you about not hurting her. She's a good person, and she doesn't deserve to be treated the way she has been."

"No one deserves that." My voice is flat, and my statement is blunt for a reason. While I wholeheartedly agree Savannah doesn't deserve this, I adamantly believe no one else does either.

"Of course not, but I'm not here for everyone else. I'm here for her. I don't know what your intentions are, but I know you were undercover with the same gang Butch is in. Since I don't believe in coincidences, I'm more than uncomfortable with your budding relationship with my wife's best friend. So maybe you can explain how you just happened to get mixed up with a woman who was mixed up with a gang member from the very gang you just spent two years riding with."

"Detective Donovan, I'm a trained DEA Special Agent. Now, maybe you don't understand the grueling nature of our training or what it takes to become a Special Agent, but I can assure you that not a fucking one of those low-life fuckers were friends of mine. I put my life on the line every fucking day just to take them down. I didn't risk everything I've worked my entire career to build, spend two years of my life gathering intel and putting up with their bullshit, just to choke when they're finally going to trial for their many, many crimes."

He has the decency to show his embarrassment over his idiotic blunder. "You're right. I'm sorry, man. Savannah has just been through enough hell, and I'd never forgive myself if she went through even more because I didn't ask the tough questions."

"Don't sweat it. She needs friends like that. I'm glad she has you."

He fishes her keys out of his pocket and extends his hand to me. I take them and put them on the coffee table in plain sight. "Thanks. Find anything interesting in her apartment?"

"Yeah, but you're not going to like it."

"Let's hear it." I stiffen my spine and school my features. Undercover expressionless mode activated.

"He left a note there—for you. I had to turn the actual note in for evidence, but here's what it said."

He holds out his phone, so I take it and study the picture of the note Bitch left me at Savannah's apartment.

You Fucking Undercover Pig—

How are my sloppy seconds? You think you can take her from me before I've released her? You know the rules—none of the bitches leave the club before a Devil says she can. I'll be back to collect my property…and you'll show the world what a piece of shit you are.

Signed,

Suck My Dick

"What a charming letter. He really missed his calling. I'm thinking he could get a high-level gig writing greeting cards." I hand Spencer's phone back to him, unconcerned with Butch's insignificant threat against me. But his continued threats against Savannah do concern me because he's already shown he will carry those out without hesitation.

"Has Savannah said anything else about Butch's comment regarding not letting his sweet deal go?"

"No, she hasn't talked about it at all, actually. The

trauma of everything he did hit her at once. I've literally sat here for hours and held her while she cried it all out, reassuring her that she's safe and I'll keep her that way. She hasn't mentioned anything else about his ranting and raving."

"I don't know what he meant." A siren's voice replies from the hallway behind me.

When I turn to look at her, I realize exactly how true my initial thought is. She's freshly showered, with wet hair hanging in long, natural curls. She has a towel wrapped around her neck, partially covering her shoulders. But that's not exactly what's captured my attention and refuses to let me look away. One thing I didn't consider when I suggested a shower is what she'd wear afterward. Seeing her in one of my T-shirts and a pair of my boxer briefs is fucking hotter than I ever could've imagined. And I can imagine a lot.

Bruised and battered or not, Savannah Fields is stunningly beautiful. So much so, she takes my breath away just looking at her.

"Okay, just checking. I'll keep digging for additional information. I've issued a BOLO for him. If any of our guys sees him, he'll go away for a long time. I brought your keys back, and I have a message from Karen. She will be calling you later so you'd better answer on the first ring, and she's subject to stop by here at any time of the day or night to check on you."

Savannah smiles, the appreciation for her friend warming her from the inside out. She glows with love for Karen—the one friend I've heard all about during our daily meetings over coffee. "Tell her I'll call her tomorrow morning when I wake up. I've had a very long and painful day. I'm taking some ibuprofen and going to bed soon. Now that I've had a hot shower, I'll pass right out."

"Not until you've eaten first. Then I'll tuck you in and let you sleep till noon tomorrow if you want." I raise one eyebrow in mock challenge.

Her familiar laugh is music to my ears. "Fine. Let me rephrase. I'm eating first, then going to bed."

Satisfied Savannah is indeed as well as she can be under the circumstances, Spencer leaves before I head to the kitchen and start cooking. Chicken alfredo is my specialty, and pasta cures anything that ails. After she finishes a plate of food, complete with garlic bread and a glass of wine, her eyes start closing on their own.

Scooping her into my arms, I carry her to the guest bedroom and tuck her into the bed. She's out as soon as her head hits the pillow and the blankets cover her body. I watch her for a moment, sleeping peacefully after such a terrifying day, and make her a solemn vow.

"For you, I will try my damnedest to be the undercover hero you deserve."

After making sure the front door is locked,

cleaning up the kitchen, and scrolling through the channels, searching for anything that will take my mind off the horrors Savannah endured today, I finally give up and head to bed. After a quick hot shower to rinse off, I climb into my bed and stare at the ceiling until sleep finally overtakes me.

An hour later, I wake to the sensation of the hairs on the back of my neck standing on end. Someone is in my room, moving toward me. I curl my hands into fists, ready to tear into whoever was stupid enough to pull this stunt. I watch the dark figure move to the foot of my bed, then bump into it. A hand reaches out and feels the way around to the opposite side of the bed—a small, dainty hand. When she reaches the head of the bed, she gently pulls back the covers and gingerly slides into bed beside me. Then she moves over until she's pressed up against me, her head finding a comfortable spot on my chest and her arm draping across my abdomen.

Within seconds, her breathing slows to an even, easy pace as she rests peacefully with my arm wrapped around her.

My breathing, however, is anything but slow and easy.

CHAPTER 7

Savannah

When I open my eyes after the best sleep I've had in years, I realize there's a very hard body under my cheek. My eyes roam the length of that fine, chiseled body until they locate my arm. My hand is splayed out on his stomach, precariously low and definitely inappropriately placed for someone I've only known a couple of weeks. A man who hasn't shown the slightest interest in kissing me, much less being molested by me in my sleep first thing in the morning.

The problem is, now that I've realized where my hand is resting, any sudden movement will be overtly obvious. And embarrassing. This requires delicate and deliberate extrication. Preferably before he even wakes and realizes the full magnitude of my blunder.

If I pretend to stretch, maybe?

No. I can tell without moving more than it takes to breathe that my whole body is sore—much more so than when I went to bed last night. Engaging all my muscles at once for a good, full-body stretch would be excruciating.

The longer I lie here, arguing with myself, the longer my hand rests in a dangerous location.

Then there's the whole topic of "'What are you doing in my bed?' for $500, Alex." Not that I think Nick would mind since I had awful nightmares despite being tired to the bone. Snuggling next to him kept the monster away all night. I wouldn't have slept a wink without him after the first dream woke me.

I'm just going to make sure he's still asleep, then gently lift my hand from his...nether regions. As easily and slowly as I can, I lift my head to look at his gorgeous sleeping face.

And find whiskey-colored amber eyes looking directly at me. Wide awake and wide open, with amusement and something else shining brightly in those golden flecks. That something else is need and desire. Oh God, definitely desire, if the involuntary rising of my hand is any indication.

"Good morning, darlin'. Sleep well?"

"Best sleep of my life. You?"

"Can't complain. At all. Slept really, really well."

"Guess you're wondering how I got in here." I smile sweetly—on purpose.

"Not at all. I watched you sneak in and crawl into bed with me."

"Oh. Really? I had a bad dream."

"I figured. It's fine—I don't mind that you came in here with me. If that's what you wanted, all you had to do was say so."

I feel like there's an intentional double meaning to his offer.

Hand still rising…still rising…

Followed by awkward silence and actively searching for somewhere to set my gaze upon. Anywhere but at my hand.

Do not look at the hand.

This isn't uncomfortable at all.

"How do you feel today?"

The sudden loss of complete silence in the room startles me, making me jump. Even though it sends pain throughout my entire body, the jolt to my system does accomplish removing my hand from his dick. At least I don't have to make up an excuse to stop touching him now.

"Umm, really sore. Really, really sore, to be honest. It even hurts to breathe normally."

"I'm going to take this moment to point out the obvious." He pauses and I hold my breath, afraid of what he'll say next. "You're an ER nurse. You know better than anyone if you should go get checked out. My non-medical expert opinion is you should've let me take you to the hospital last night. But since you didn't, I'm offering to take you now. Breathing normally shouldn't cause you pain."

"Here's a little secret you may not know, Nick. Nurses are terrible patients. We hate being on the receiving end of medical care. It is better to give care than to receive care, in our expert opinion. Last night, I wasn't mentally prepared to go to the hospital. I mean, I work there, and I don't want my coworkers seeing me like this."

"Savannah, I completely understand what you're saying." His voice is tender, understanding. That doesn't mean I don't hear the "but" that's coming next. "But guys who abuse women are counting on you to hide what they do. No evidence, no crime. By hiding out and suffering through the injuries on your own, you're actually shielding him."

"You're right, Nick. On one hand, you're exactly right. On the other, the people I work with every day will think of me as being weak. They'll ask why I've tolerated his behavior, they'll question what I've done to deserve it. They'll look at me differently every day for the rest of the time I work there."

He sits up and turns his upper body to face me. "Your friends will want to help you. They may be hurt that you didn't turn to them for help, but they will stand by your side and defend you. The backbiters who aren't your friends can go fuck themselves. If you're really that concerned about what others will think of you, don't tell them about anything except this time. He's a crazy ex, so they can keep an eye out for him. They will not blame you for this, darlin'."

"All right." His point is valid, and if Karen were in my situation, I'd tell her the same thing. Taking my own advice isn't an easy pill to swallow, though.

He drags his hand down his face, releasing a long sigh between clenched teeth. "I'm sorry, Savannah. I don't mean to push you into something you don't want to do. Tell me what to do, from an emergency room nurse perspective. If a woman showed up, presenting with your same symptoms, would she need medical attention?"

"You play dirty, Nick." There's only a hint of a smile on his lips, but it fully reaches his eyes. He knows he's won. "If she were my patient, I'd recommend she at least have X-rays of her ribs to make sure there was no danger of a broken rib puncturing a lung."

He nods, probably expecting as much. I have a sneaking suspicion he's at least had field medical training. Not as extensive as my training, of course, but enough to patch up a friend and get them off the battlefield when necessary. That's what he's trying to do with me—patch up his friend after I've limped off the battlefield, worse for wear.

"Do you think that patient will let me take her to have her ribs checked out now?" He cocks his head to the side before allowing that stunning smile to overtake his gorgeous face.

"Maybe…after she eats breakfast, since they won't let her have anything once she gets there."

"You've just given me a great idea. I think I have a bright future in hostage negotiations since undercover work is out of the question now. Breakfast is coming up in twenty, so you have time to get dressed while I'm cooking."

"Just so we're clear, I won't forget how you twisted my arm. I will use your tactics against you one day, and you won't have a leg to stand on. You'll have to give in to my every whim."

"One day?" He chuckles and stands, looking like a real-life Adonis in snug-fitting black boxer briefs… and nothing else. Chiseled chest. Trim waist. That sexy V low on his abdomen. Muscular legs. He is absolutely the full package. "Pretty sure we passed the 'one day' mark a while back."

He walks off toward the kitchen, while I stay in his bed to watch him leave. Holy hell. He looks just as good from the back as he does from the front. These thoughts shouldn't be running through my mind, and I feel guilty for even entertaining the notion there could be anything between us. All this baggage that still haunts me isn't fair to bring into any new relationship. Although, I do have to admit, Nick handles Butch and all his bullshit better than anyone I know, myself included. The truth is, I don't think I deserve Nick or anything he's doing for me out of the kindness of his heart.

But the more time I spend with him, the harder I find it to think of not having him in my life.

When I hear him taking pans out of the cupboard, I reluctantly move to get out of bed. Fighting for every inch, I finally reach the side of the bed and clench my jaw before attempting to stand. I've managed to roll over onto my stomach, thinking incorrectly that would make it easier to slide off the bed, and every inch of my body is on fire from the short distance I just covered.

"Can I help?" Nick asks from the doorway.

In my defense, I'm not normally a constant crybaby. But I've cried more in front of him than anyone else in my life. Tears of frustration and pain sting my eyes because I know I can't even get out of bed without his help. Had I not stayed with him last night, I would be in a world of trouble today.

"Okay." I manage to mumble a reply without completely breaking.

He grabs a top sheet from the closet and folds it in half a couple of times. From the opposite side of the bed, he gently pushes as much of it underneath me as he can. "I'll help you roll over onto the sheet—slow and easy—but tell me if anything hurts too much. Okay?"

I nod, unable to speak because of the ball of emotion that's stuck in my throat.

With gentle hands and a reassuring tone, he helps me to roll over on my back, straightening the part of the sheet that was under me as I roll. He uses both sides of the sheet as support under my back to lift and move me to the edge of the bed. When I sit up and slide my legs off the bed, that's also with Nick's support. Once I'm sitting erect and the tips of my toes are touching the floor, he's kneeling down on one knee in front of me, watching my reactions with eagle-eye precision.

"Talk to me, Savannah. Are you in a lot of pain? Did I hurt you?"

I shake my head. "You didn't hurt me at all. I was just thinking I'm actually in a lot worse shape than I originally thought. If you hadn't been here last night...if I hadn't stayed here..."

"Don't think like that. I'm here, and you're here with me. We'll do this together. You need time to heal, and you need help while you heal. I won't leave you alone. You can stay here as long as you need to. When you're ready to go back to your place, I'll make sure you feel safe doing it. I won't abandon you." He reaches up and cups my cheek in his big hand, his natural body heat warming me inside and out.

Like a frightened puppy craving human attention, I lean into his hand and close my eyes, soaking up the connection I feel building between us every minute we're together. Whether a relationship builds fast or slow, the pace doesn't define its depth. This bond I feel with Nick didn't develop immediately. We didn't experience the whole "love at first sight" phenomenon, but my feelings are dangerously close to that. I can't say he feels the same, but I can say I pray that he does. Or will, eventually.

And that scares me.

Straightening my spine, I inhale carefully and open my eyes, finding his still closely watching me. "That was a good idea to use the draw sheet. You have more medical experience than you admit."

"You never know, I may have a few more tricks up my sleeve."

"Let's see if one of those tricks is helping me to stand. I hope once I get up, I'll be able to walk on my own. You never realize how much you use your abdominal muscles for every little move until you can't use them at all."

"Put your arms around my neck. When I stand, use me to help pull yourself up. I'll wrap my arms around your waist to hold you steady, but I don't want to put too much pressure on your sore areas."

I do as he says, and at the last second, his hands slide under my behind to help push me upright. Leaning back a little, I give him a playful side-eye glance. "Did you just cop a feel on an injured and defenseless woman?"

He grins, and mischief shines in his eyes. "No more than you did when you thought I was still asleep this morning." He waggles his eyebrows, both play-fully and seductively, and I hide my face in his neck.

"Stop trying to make me laugh. It hurts!" I say,

through both my laughter and pain. His deep chuckle rumbles in my ear in response.

"I took a chance that your ass wasn't hurt as badly as your ribs are. Hopefully that was a good guess."

"Yes, it was a great guess, and surprisingly helpful. Thank you, Nick. You're the best man I've ever met."

He goes completely still, making me worry I've crossed an unknown line, but he doesn't release me. There's such a fine line between right and wrong sometimes. When I move my face from the hiding place against his neck, I pluck up the courage to meet him eye-to-eye. The expression on his face nearly shatters my heart into a million pieces.

It's pure, unadulterated, palpable gratitude.

He searches my eyes and face, not asking the question that's on the tip of his tongue. The one I see in his eyes, though he tries to hide it.

"I meant every word, Nick. You're brave and you're strong. You're thoughtful and considerate. You take care of me and show me how to take care of myself. You're easy to talk to but refuse to let anyone run over you. You're funny and sweet, but serious and mean when you have to be. I don't know one single man who would've done everything you've done for me—or even a fraction of it. You are, hands down, the best man I've ever known."

He opens his mouth to speak but stops himself before it's too late. He shakes his head while keeping his eyes locked on mine. "You never cease to amaze me. Thank you for saying that."

That look—the one he's giving me now—the one that tells me he desperately wants to believe me, steals what little breath I have in my lungs. He needs to believe me. But he's not quite there yet. That seals my heart's fate. It's not about "fixing him." He's perfect exactly the way he is now. My heart is now focused on helping him see the many wonderful qualities he possesses, the traits I've seen since day one. For me, this is more than the good friend mission I originally set out on. I know, beyond a shadow of a doubt, I've already fallen for him.

"The bag Spencer brought over for you is in the bathroom. But let's make sure you can walk alone before I go cook your breakfast."

After I take a few steps, I assure him I'll be okay alone in the bathroom and promise to yell for him if I need anything at all. With the door closed behind me, I glare at the commode and silently contemplate how I'll manage the whole sitting maneuver alone, while knowing there's no way in hell I'm asking Nick to help me out with *that*.

Though it takes much more out of me than it should, I manage to use the vanity to help brace myself as I sit and stand again. Rifling through my bag, I find my brush and a few hair bands. Thank you, Spencer! With my hair pulled up in a high, messy bun, my teeth brushed, and my comfy yoga pants and long-sleeved T-shirt on, I feel somewhat human again.

Nick has a tasty breakfast waiting for me when I finally join him in the kitchen. Instead of eating at the table, he puts our plates on the bar so I can slide on and off the higher stool easier. It really is the little things that matter the most.

We take my car to the hospital so I can use my employee parking decal and retrieve my badge I left in the glove compartment when I drove to Nick's last night. Bypassing the triage desk, we walk in through the ambulance bay and straight into the secure area. It's a relatively slow day, so one of the doctors is behind the desk, catching up on his charting when I approach.

"Holy shit, Savannah! What happened to you?" His eyes immediately move to size up Nick, the brawny brute standing behind me.

"Can you check me out, Dr. Wattress? I think I may have a couple of cracked ribs, but I just want to be sure they don't move and cause more damage." I reach back and grab Nick's hand, wordlessly conveying he's here to help me.

"Of course. Let's get you into a room and see what's going on with your injuries." He chooses an open exam room and ushers Nick and me inside. He gives me a gown to change into and closes the curtain, giving me a little privacy. I slide the curtain back to let them know I'm ready. Technically, I'm supposed to remove my bra and panties too, but that's not happening. They were hard enough to get into the first time.

Nick immediately notices the bed is too low for me to comfortably sit down, so he moves to the far side and raises it until the height is just right for me. Every move I make, he's right there to help me.

"Who did this to you, Savannah?" Dr. Wattress asks when he begins checking my injuries.

I'm quiet for a heartbeat too long, so Nick answers for me. "Her ex who can't seem to take a hint. She moved to get away from him, and he found her again."

The doctor looks up at Nick, anger rolling off him in waves. "When you get a hold of him, don't bring him to my emergency room for treatment."

"Understood, Doc. If I get my hands on him, he's more likely to need a good mortician than a physician."

"Nick has been taking good care of me, even though I haven't made it too easy on him." I smile up at Nick, but that quickly changes when the doctor touches my ribs. "Ouch!"

"When did this happen?"

"Yesterday."

"And you're just now coming to see me?" Dr. Wattress shakes his head, clearly not pleased with my decision-making skills. "You definitely have a few broken ribs, I can tell you that without X-rays.

There's really no danger of them moving or puncturing anything if you follow doctor's orders to the letter."

"She will." Nick's confident reply makes the doctor smile. "Just tell me what they are, and I'll make sure of it."

He goes through a list of dos and don'ts with Nick. Ice packs. Ibuprofen. Cough if I feel the urge, to help reduce the chance of pneumonia—just hold a pillow against my side to lessen the impact. Six weeks off work, taking extra care the first two weeks. Move around as much as I'm able, to help keep fluids moving freely. Come back immediately if I reinjure my ribs or have any shortness of breath.

All things I could've told Nick before we got here, but he wouldn't have taken my word for it after our hostage-negotiation discussion.

The doctor writes a prescription for a stronger pain medication to use at night to help me sleep through the discomfort and tells me he'll submit the medical documentation for my required time off. Back in the car an hour later, Nick picks up my prescription for me before driving us back to his place with a triumphant smirk on his face.

"What are you so happy about?" I ask teasingly.

"One, I was right about a lot of things. Two, I really like that doctor. And three, you have to stay with me for the next two weeks so I can make sure you follow his orders to a T."

"He didn't say I had to stay with you for the next two weeks, Nick."

"Yes, he did. Would you like to go back and ask him?" He glances at me over his shoulder, hoping I'll accept his dare.

"No, because you two will just conspire against me."

"Like I said, you're staying with me for the next couple of weeks so I can make sure you behave. Doctor's orders."

Funny thing is, "behave" isn't the first word that comes to mind when I think about spending two weeks with Nick at his place.

It's not even in the top ten thoughts.

CHAPTER 8

Nick

*W*ith Savannah resting comfortably on my couch, I retreat to my bedroom with the intention of making a few calls. Butch's ability to access not only her building but her apartment is a huge red flag, one I can't quite put my finger on at the moment. I know for a fact that she has multiple locks on her door and uses every one of them. The sinking feeling in my gut tells me Butch went to great lengths to get to her—but not because he's distraught that she dumped him.

He's after something else entirely.

I casually stroll back into the living room where Savannah is watching the news and fighting to keep her eyes open. Taking a seat on the coffee table across from her, I pick up her keys Spencer left and hand them to her. She looks at me then down at her keys, confusion and apprehension clear in her expression.

"Are any keys missing from your key ring?" I intentionally keep my tone light and my demeanor calm. There's no need to cause her even more alarm if I'm simply being hypervigilant. As usual.

Her eyebrows draw down, and her eyes crinkle slightly in the corner, as much as she can with the swelling anyway, but she goes through each key on the ring as I asked. "No, they're all here. I don't keep the building's garage door key on here anymore since I've been taking the Metro to work lately. It's still in my car from when I drove over here yesterday."

"Where did you have it before that?"

"Hidden inside my apartment. Why?" She lays the keys down beside me and gives me her full attention, preparing for a long explanation.

"Just a hunch I'm working on."

She's silent for a minute, waiting for me to continue, but that only results in us staring at each other. "Nick, that's not enough. I need more than that."

"Does Butch keep anything in your car? Did he ever use it?"

"No, to both questions. He was always on his motorcycle, and he always insisted I drive my car instead of riding with him. Said it ruined his image to have someone riding bitch. That was fine with me—I didn't want to stay in the places he went any longer than I absolutely had to anyway. He went to the seed-iest parts of town he could find. There were always other gang members around with half-dressed women who I'm sure were strung out on drugs."

"But he insisted you go with him to those places? Did he make you hang around very long?" I'm getting a clearer picture, and I don't like it at all.

"No, not long at all. It was usually to change the bandages on his friend's wounds…or to look at what-ever new rash someone had." A chill runs up her spine, and she shakes involuntarily in disgust. "After I'd played doctor and helped as much as I could, I got the hell out of there. Tell me what you're thinking. What has he done to my car? Did he put a tracker on it?"

"I don't think he has anything that high-tech. But I do think he's after something specific, more than getting his rocks off by beating up a woman."

Pulling my cell out of my pocket, I call Calvin at the agency and ask him to send a low-key forensics team to my townhouse. Savannah's eyes grow wide with fear.

"What are you doing? What's going on, Nick?"

"It's best to wait until they get here. Do you have Spencer's number in your phone?"

"Yes, I do." She pulls up his contact info, and we wait for him to pick up. "Hi, Spencer. Nick needs to talk to you."

She hands the phone to me, and I tell him about

the team on the way to my apartment then ask if he can join us since he's involved in the assault and battery charges against Butch. He promises to be here within minutes. He obviously understands the urgency, and Savannah feels the increasing pressure from all the stress. In case my gut is correct, I can't tell her anything just yet and possibly taint the findings.

But I'll do whatever it takes to protect her.

"Just trust me. I would never do anything to hurt you, and I won't let anyone else hurt you either. I'm doing all of this to protect you."

"I trust you."

Though she has every reason never to trust another man in her life, she freely gives it to me. That realization is humbling. A knock on my door stops me from saying something neither of us is ready to hear. The feeling is there, on the edge of the proverbial cliff, but I'm not ready to take the leap off it just yet.

Tim, another Special Agent I've known for quite a while, is standing on the threshold. His team waits a few spaces down by the unmarked forensics van with the gear stowed inside, ready to get to work. We shake hands in a friendly reunion and a quick catch-up of what we've each been doing since we saw each other last. While we're chatting, Spencer pulls up and joins us. After I introduce them, I turn my request to Savannah's friend.

"Spencer, I need you to stay in here with

Savannah and me while Tim does his job. We'll need a third-party witness to verify whatever Tim finds hasn't been tampered with by either Savannah or me. Every step of this is being done by the book to protect all of us in the long run."

"You got it. I'll go in and keep her company now." Spencer leaves Tim and me alone to finish our conversation in private.

"What do you need us to do, Nick?" Tim looks puzzled and intrigued, ready to dive into the job at hand.

"Cover every inch of Savannah's car. Don't leave anything unchecked. But try not to look like a DEA agent searching the car. Act like you're a mechanic or something—leave the hood open." I explain her prior relationship with Butch, his ties to the Devils, and the recent events. "I don't think he's found what he's looking for, and my gut tells me whatever it is will be found in her car."

"The Devils are about to go to trial, you're the main undercover officer for the DEA, and you're involved with the ex-girlfriend of a club member? Have you lost your fucking mind, Nick?" Tim stares me down, looking at me as if he has no clue who I am.

"Did you hear a fucking word I just told you? I met her in a coffee shop—while he was manhandling her. You think I'd just stand by and let that shit happen, especially after everything I've seen? I told her she had a safe place to get away from him if she ever needed it. Well, step inside the door and take a look at her. She fucking needed it, man. He could've killed her." My voice gets louder with each passing second. My blood boils while rushing through my veins.

Tim curses under his breath and steps around me. He opens the door, walks inside, and comes back out with a bottle of water. "I see what you mean. Any chance she's in on this with him to help the Devils? To get any information or intel on you?"

"Zero chance." I place my hands on my hips and wait for him to drop the subject.

"Don't say I didn't warn you. When you tell Calvin the whole story, he'll ream you a new asshole, and you know it."

"Let me handle Calvin. You handle searching the car. I'm going inside now so I can't be accused of trying to hide any evidence you may find."

"If there's anything there, the Devils' lawyer may accuse you of planting it."

"Anyone who'd believe I'd plant something, especially on someone I consider a friend, is a moron."

"Yeah, well, the world is full of them, my friend. Any spin they can put on the story to make the good guys look bad is a good spin."

Maybe he's right—maybe I'm damned if I do and damned if I don't. But my conscience will be clear, and I'll be able to look at myself in the mirror without questioning which lines I'll cross today.

Savannah is sitting up on the couch with a pillow pressed to her side when I walk back into the brownstone, leaving Tim and his team to do their job. She has a blanket draped over her lap, and she's nervously biting her thumbnail. Something hitches in my chest —a twinge of life I haven't felt in a very long time. Years. I refused to let myself get close to anyone while I was undercover. There was no way I'd trust anyone in that world with my real identity and no way I'd start a relationship under false pretenses. Plus, when shit went down, she would've been the first target on their hit list.

Since I've been back in DC, I've had zero interest in anything except getting back to my normal self. Putting the past couple years behind me and letting go of all the guilt over what I didn't do about the crimes I witnessed. Trying to reconcile the man I thought I was before the assignment began with the man I had to be while undercover. When I condemned them for lying and dealing underhandedly, the mirror told me I was doing the same things they were. When I couldn't wait to bust them and send them away for life for the crimes they committed, my conscience reminded me about all the times I watched or participated in those very crimes.

Being around Savannah brings a breath of fresh air to my stale existence. One I didn't even know was missing until getting better acquainted with her. When I look at her injuries, I vacillate between wanting to dedicate my life to showing her how a real man should treat her and wanting to rip Butch's head from his body and shove it up his ass.

The struggle is real.

But when she looks at me like that—like I hung the fucking moon and stars—I can't help but think my former self is making a full comeback, pushing the corrupt man inside me out of the way. Maybe she's exactly what I need in my life. Someone to take care of, someone to help, someone who will listen when I share the details of my days—the good, the bad, the ups, the downs.

Someone to love.

Someone who can love me.

Not that she's ready for a relationship. She hasn't even been able to get rid of the last guy. I doubt she'd appreciate me adding more stress by trying to start something new. Bad timing and all.

"Nick?"

"Yeah?"

"Are...you okay?" Her eyes narrow as she cuts them sideways at me.

"Fine. Why?"

"Well, because you've just been standing there staring at me. Not saying anything at all."

"Have I?"

Staring at her isn't a hardship on me. Looking away from her is.

When I don't elaborate, she stands, pushing the pillow harder into her side as she moves. I start to protest, but she shakes her head. "The doctor said I need to move around frequently, remember?"

I nod, smiling while letting her have that one.

She walks to me, pain in every step, but that doesn't stop her. When she reaches me, she places her hand on my chest and peers up at me, her emerald-green eyes searching mine. "What's going on out there that has you so distracted?"

"There's a team of DEA forensic agents searching your car for drugs or other contraband."

Reading people and gauging reactions are skills I've spent years training and refining. Knowing when they're lying, when they're holding out, and when they're about to pull the gun they have hidden in their back waistband has saved my ass too many times to count. Studying Savannah's face and reaction to that news tells me everything I need to know. She doesn't have a clue why we'd look for anything in her car.

Sometimes I wish I could still be that naïve…that trusting of other people.

But not today. Today, I'm glad I'm listening to my instincts, so when I take Butch out of the equation, he's out for good with no possibility of ever hurting Savannah again. In any way.

"I don't understand. Why would you think I'd have drugs, Nick?" Pain flashes in her eyes. Hurt because I'd think so little of her.

"Savannah, I know better than that. I don't think you'd do that at all. But I do think Butch has hidden them in your car, and I think he was so pissed off over not being able to get into your building's garage to get them, he broke in to your apartment to look for the key. Then he attacked you when you walked in on him in the act."

After helping her back to the couch, I order delivery for all of us. My friends will be hungry when they've finished with her car, and I need to make sure she eats more than enough to keep a bird alive, too. By the time the food delivery is expected, Tim and team join us inside the living room, smiles from ear to ear covering their faces. The delivery guy shows up just behind them, so I throw a couple of bills in his direction and tell everyone to help themselves after I fix Savannah's plate.

"The good news is," Tim begins, "I can't tell you much about what we found. And that in itself should tell you enough about what we found."

"There's a calling card?" I hold my slice of pizza in midair, waiting for the confirmation I've been dying to hear.

"Definite calling card. Enough that I can guarantee Savannah can't be held responsible under the constructive possession laws." Tim beams, knowing the significance of his find.

"I'm sorry—I have no idea what that means." Savannah's eyes dart back and forth between Tim and me, waiting for a better explanation.

Tim takes pity on her. "What I'm saying is, I know without a shadow of a doubt you had no idea what was hidden in your car, so you can't be held responsible for possession."

"Did you leave everything exactly as you found it?" Not that I doubt his ability to do his job, but I'm leaving no stone unturned in this maneuver.

"I'm insulted you even thought it was necessary to ask me that, Tucker."

"Just making sure. Calm your tits, Tim. Now, Savannah, tell me every move you'd normally make in your car before you started taking the Metro to work. Where did you go? How long did you stay there? Where did you park? Don't leave out any detail, no matter how small you may think it is. Do you think you can do that?"

"Sure, I can do that. Then what happens?"

"Then we wait."

CHAPTER 9

Savannah

"What's a calling card?"

Now that we're alone, I feel more comfortable asking Nick all my questions that weren't answered earlier. Not that the other men would've minded, but they were so involved in the logistics and planning of every detail of the upcoming operations, I didn't want to delay their conversation by asking them to explain all their jargon to me.

Besides, now I have even more to talk about with Nick. More reasons to stay right beside him. More reasons to stare at his handsome face and finely built physique. The way he looks at me when we talk has changed. When we first met, I saw mostly pity in his eyes. That bothered me more than I would admit.

Now, I see admiration in those whiskey-colored

eyes. I also see desire—and not only when I accidentally molest him in the bed. I caught him watching
me several times when we were eating pizza earlier.
When Tim tried a little too hard to get to know me, I
was secretly thrilled Nick immediately shut him
down. Not in a jealous, possessive way, but his reaction was enough to let me know he didn't appreciate
the intrusion.

Maybe there's hope after all.

"A calling card is the signature way drug distribu-
tors package their shit for the street dealers to sell.
The major players are arrogant, and they want
everyone on the street to know who's running the
show. Butch is in over his head, so I'm going to help
him drown."

"I feel guilty getting you involved in all this, you
know? I've caused you so much trouble in the so little
time you've known me. You must think I'm one big
walking disaster."

He surprises me by kneeling in front me, gently
cupping my face in his big hands, and holding my
gaze with his intense stare. "No, Savannah. In fact,
I've never thought that, and you're not allowed to
think that either. You don't have a clue how amazing
you are, do you?"

This smoldering attraction I've been fighting just
lit up in a fully involved five-alarm fire.

Without thinking, without overanalyzing, without
asking for permission, I lean toward him and press

my lips to his. Gently at first, in case he doesn't recip-rocate, but he takes control after about a second. He slides his hands around my head, threading his fingers through my hair as they glide. I can tell he's being so easy with me, treating me like a porcelain doll. But I can't feel my injuries at the moment. I can only feel the sensation of every nerve ending firing at once and my body being set on fire, all from his tender touch and simple kiss.

When his tongue swipes across my lips, my resulting gasp gives him full access to claim my mouth. I lean back on the couch cushions and wrap my hands around his neck, pulling him with me so that he's partially lying on me. Though I'm sore and have bruises covering most of my body, the weight of his body on me feels like heaven. The warmth of his hands on my skin and the velvety smoothness of his tongue send chills over my body, fanning out like ripples in still water.

He breaks the kiss first, ever so slowly, and presses his forehead against mine while we both try to slow our racing hearts. I can feel his pulse jumping in his neck, and it makes me want to kiss him all over again. With a look, a touch, a gesture, Nick Tucker makes me feel beautiful, desired, and needed.

"That was the hottest fucking kiss." His words are a strained whisper, full of longing and a thirst for me. I know, because I feel it all the way to my soul.

"It definitely was. Now I need a cold shower before I combust."

He smiles, releases a small chuckle, and gently kisses my cheek. "Believe me when I say it kills me to stop this. But if you kiss me like that again, I'm afraid you'll have a lot more broken bones after I throw you over my shoulder, haul you into the bedroom, and bend you in more ways than a pretzel."

"Oh my God. Why do I get the feeling all the extra broken bones would be so worth it?"

"Savannah, you're really not helping, darlin'. The situation is hard enough as it is." He waggles his eyebrows at me, and the butterflies in my chest not only take flight but break out into an impromptu *Riverdance* production.

"Just so you know, I feel it too."

"I don't see how you couldn't feel it since it's lying on your leg right now."

We both break out laughing, and I immediately regret it. Grabbing my trusty pillow, I push it into my broken ribs for support and alternate between laughing and howling "ow" repeatedly.

"Okay, so we both needed that laugh. And maybe we should let the current broken bones heal before we break new ones. I'm not sure I'm up to it today, after all." I stroke his cheek, feeling the words but refusing to say them now. It's too soon. No one feels—*that*—this soon.

"It's nice, being able to joke with you. But know

this about me, Savannah. There's only one part of you I'd ever break—and that's any desire you may have for another man. I'll make sure that's completely obliterated, to the point that even looking doesn't appeal to you."

"I believe you, Nick…because I'm already there."

"Darlin', I'm so glad to hear that." Then his smile falters, and a concerned expression takes its place. "But don't feel pressured to say that. You don't owe me anything in return for my help, and the last thing I want you to think is I expect any kind of payment."

"I'd never think that about you, Nick. And I hope you know I understand the difference between gratitude and what I actually feel for you."

"You have no idea how happy I am to know we're on the same page. You get some rest while I get some work done. I'm running the logistics on this operation, so I'm going to make sure the plan is airtight before we make the first move. Yell if you need anything at all."

"Can you bring my laptop out of my bag? I have a few things I want to look into myself."

"You got it."

While Nick is at the kitchen table, eyeball-deep in maps, routes, and plans, I boot up my laptop and start researching how to volunteer in various positions with our local women's shelter. After what I've been through and how much help I've been given because of nothing more than the kindness of strangers, volunteering to help others in similar situations is the least I can do.

When I find the website, I fill out all the forms and consent to a background check. I'm looking forward to putting a different spin on my circumstances and crossing that fine line between fear and courage. Even though putting myself in front of others and sharing my story scares me, I feel I need to step into the spotlight and make myself more vulnerable before I can fully be strong again. Trial by fire. Actions speak louder than words. Every cloud has a silver lining. All the inspirational sayings that are meant to encourage and inspire swirl in my head, but even without them, I know I'm making the right move.

Just as I open my document to continue working on my book, with a new chapter inspired by recent revelations, my phone rings, and I realize I neglected to call my best friend first thing this morning.

"Hello?" I know exactly who's calling, but I'm still trying to figure out a way to defuse the situation.

"Don't act like you don't know who this is or why I'm calling, Savannah Fields. How dare you let me find out from one of the day nurses that you showed up in the emergency room with broken ribs! If you weren't already injured, I'd be over there kicking your ass right now."

"That's actually the only part of me that doesn't hurt."

"Spence said Nick is taking good care of you." Her tone changes, letting me know she's not actually mad at me for anything. Worried about my well-being, but not mad. "I'm glad someone is. You know you could've stayed with us if you needed a place to hide."

"Staying here with Nick is actually working out to my benefit. He knows how Butch operates, and he's working on a plan to make sure Butch stays out of my life forever. When I first came here, it was because I was too terrified to go anywhere else, plus his brownstone was closer than your place. But I'm staying because he takes such good care of me, Karen. He keeps the nightmares at bay." I describe what happened last night and this morning—sneaking into his bed and waking up in a compromising position.

"After all that, he still had to help you out of bed?" Karen laughs heartily at my expense, but I don't mind. My pillow is tight against my ribs, so my occasional outbursts don't hurt as bad. "Well, if all that hasn't scared him away, nothing will, my friend. Sounds like you have a keeper there. Spencer has even given his seal of approval, and you know that doesn't come easily for him."

"We're both taking things really slowly. I've brought a lot of shitty baggage with me. It's a little hard to start something new on solid ground when it feels like quicksand will swallow you at any time."

"You know what your problem is, Savannah? You

don't give yourself nearly enough credit. Butch is shit, but he's not your shitty baggage. You got away from him. What he continues to do is all on him—not you. Don't take the blame for any of his bullshit anymore. Make him own what he's done, and you own the brave things you've done."

"Thank you, Karen. You know I needed to hear that. I love you."

"I love you too. Now when do I get to meet Nick, hook him up to a lie detector, and play 150 Questions with cords that deliver electric shocks for every lie?"

"Stop making me laugh! It hurts!" She laughs in my ear. "You can meet him, if you behave. Besides, he doesn't lie. He's brutally honest, so I don't think you'll need to use the electricity on him."

"He sounds too good to be true. I'll be the judge of his honesty. But not tomorrow. You may not have considered this, but the third day after an injury is always the worst, so I'm afraid you'll feel worse tomorrow. So, can we get this on the books for the day after tomorrow? I'm off, Spence is off, and you're there. Perfect timing." I'm almost positive Karen has our entire evening already planned out in her head.

"That's good with me. Let me check with Nick to make sure he's okay with it, though."

"Check with Nick about what?" Speak of the tall, handsome, irresistible devil, and he appears out of nowhere. He sits on the couch beside me, fingering the long curls of my ponytail while he waits for my answer.

"My best friend wants to meet you. She's bringing her own lie-detector machine, complete with an electric chair to shock you when you lie."

"I have no reason to lie, but she's welcome to use mine if she doesn't want to lug hers across town." One side of his mouth lifts in amusement as he winks at me. "The day after tomorrow is good with me. We can eat here if you're not ready to go out to a restaurant by then. But if you want to go out, it'll be our first official date. Your call, darlin'."

"Date, huh? You wouldn't be embarrassed to take me out like this? All busted up with black, purple, and green bruises everywhere?"

"Nope. Not at all. You're still just as beautiful to me."

"Oh my God, Savannah! If you don't marry him by tomorrow, I just might!" Karen yells into the phone loud enough for Nick to hear her.

"You're already taken, Karen," Nick yells back with a chuckle. Then he looks dead into my eyes and adds, "And so am I."

Karen's excited squeal nearly bursts my eardrum. At least she's breathing, because I can't right now.

He leans over and presses his soft, plump lips against mine. He trails his fingertips along my cheek, barely touching me but leaving his invisible brand on my skin. Marking me…as his.

Our eyes remain locked when he pulls back. A knowing smirk crosses his face while I fight to maintain my composure. When I'm finally able to speak again, I confirm our plans with Karen. "We're definitely going out to a nice restaurant. Nick and I are having that first date."

After we eat dinner together, I'm so tired I can barely keep my eyes open. Nick helps me up, and we walk toward the bedrooms together. He smiles down at me when we reach the hallway. "Where are you sleeping tonight?"

He knows the answer. He just wants to hear me say it.

"Smartass." I walk into his bedroom, his responding chuckle rumbling through his chest. I secretly love how relaxed and comfortable we are with each other. Now I can see—and feel—what was lacking in every other relationship I've ever attempted to have.

If I feel this strongly about him after only a couple of weeks of spending time with him, getting to know him inside and out, I can't imagine what a few more weeks will do. He helps me into bed then takes his spot beside me. He wraps his arm around me protectively when I lay my head in the crook of his shoulder. Warm, safe, and protected, I close my eyes and sleep soundly all night.

The next day is, unfortunately, as Karen predicted and I expected. Everywhere I wasn't sore yesterday hurts today. Everywhere I was sore yesterday is worse now. Nick looks down at me before we attempt to get out of bed. "Well, darlin', how do you feel today?"

"It hurts to blink. Can I just stay in bed all day?"

"Afraid not. The doctor said you need to keep moving throughout the day, remember? No pneumonia allowed. Besides, that would just make your muscles hurt longer. Come on, I'll help you out of bed. You can shower first. Maybe the hot water will help. Then we'll go by your apartment and get more of your things to bring back here. Plus, I want to look around for myself."

"You're sure we'll be safe if he shows up while we're there?"

"You and I will be perfectly safe. I can only wish he'd show up while I'm there. Please, God, let him show up."

CHAPTER 10

Nick

Showered, dressed, and fed, Savannah says she feels a little better than she did first thing this morning. We're on our way to her apartment now. How Butch got inside still bothers me. Time to bring up the touchy subject with her again.

"Darlin', I really don't like the idea of your apartment not having more security than it does. I'm in no hurry for you to leave my place, but when you do move back in to your condo, I'd like to know it's under the safest possible conditions."

"It sounds like you have a very complex system in mind. I spent my extra money on moving, buying a new laptop, and taking marketing classes for my book. Now I'm not able to work overtime for a month and a half, so it'll be a while before I can do anything extra like that." She looks out the window as she explains, not wanting to make eye contact with me.

"You never know when a great opportunity will just fall into your lap."

"What have you done, Nick?"

"Me? Nothing. Nothing at all."

We arrive at her building, and I feel the anxiety rolling off her and crashing into me before we even exit my truck. She looks up at the building and inhales a haggard breath. Though the sudden expansion of her lungs and ribs causes a jolt of pain to cut through her, the fear of going inside overrides it.

"Hey, look at me." I speak softly to get her attention without startling her.

Her gaze shifts to meet mine. All color has drained from her face. Her green eyes are huge, and her pupils are dilated. She looks at me, waiting for the strength and courage to leave the relative safety of my vehicle.

"He will not touch you—not one hair on that beautiful head of yours. If he's stupid enough to be here again, he'll leave in a body bag before I let him lay one finger on you. I've got you, darlin'. You have nothing to worry about."

"I worry about you, too, Nick. I worry that Butch will find some way to take you away from me."

"Not even a remote possibility, darlin'. Can we go up and get your clothes now? I'm really looking forward to our date tomorrow night. But if you'd rather go naked, we can do that. We'll be the talk of the town."

She rewards me with a small smile for that. "Okay, let's go up there and get it over with."

Before we reach the outer door, another resident is leaving and holds the door open for us. He's a younger guy, barely out of his teens, and obviously thinks he's being helpful. He doesn't have a clue how his politeness could cost someone their life.

Strike one.

Inside the elevator, she's practically glued to my side as we watch the floors tick by on the lighted panel. Taking a second to glance around, I notice there are no security cameras in the elevators, and there were none in the entryway.

Strike two.

I wrap my arm around her, and she molds her body against mine. I'm enjoying how she seems to fit against me like the missing piece of a jigsaw puzzle a little too much. When the elevator stops and we stroll down the hallway together, a sense of dread settles in my gut from out of the blue. This time, it's not over concern about her apartment not being safe enough —I'm facing the fact that she has her own place and will be leaving mine soon.

Years of being alone have suddenly caught up with me, and I don't want to be alone anymore.

She stops at her door and begins unlocking the dead bolts, and I take the time to inspect the door closely. There are light scratches around the locks and the bolts, other scratches in the paint where the door meets the frame, indicating someone worked to pick all the locks and gain entry into her condo. She just arrived home at the worst possible time.

Yet none of her neighbors heard anything, called the police, or came to her aid.

Strike three.

The door to her condo swings open, but she stands motionless at the threshold, staring inside at the mess left behind. From where we stand, I can see her overturned dining table and a few broken chairs surrounding it. Shattered glass from broken vases litters the floor. The groceries she'd bought are scattered throughout the room.

"I'm with you, babe. Right beside you every step of the way. Let's go inside."

She nods, but her actions are almost robotic. Dealing with the aftermath of the attack brings back too many terrible memories, but this must be done one way or another. For me, I wouldn't have it any other way than being right here with her to help her work through the pain and fear. When she slips her hand into mine, I realize she's putting her full trust in me yet again to protect her. I'll be her undercover hero, in whatever capacity she needs.

I step inside first, and she follows in my footsteps, staying close to me in case a monster steps out of the shadows. With my other hand, I unholster the gun on my hip and hold it at the ready. When she looks up at me, she appears to be a little more comforted than just a moment ago. She knows I meant what I said about Butch leaving in a body bag. If it comes down to him or her, there's really no choice to be made.

"We're going to check every possible hiding place in each room first to make sure we're completely alone. Then while you pack, I'll straighten up, so you don't have to look at this mess anymore. Are you ready?"

She nods again, this time more animatedly, letting me know she feels more secure. After I lock the door behind us, we move from room to room together, checking in every closet, behind every door, and under every piece of intact furniture. Butch was frantic in his search, hitting every room and leaving a path of chaos and destruction. Satisfied that we're alone and no one will get past me to hurt her, she releases her death grip on my hand and walks into her closet to begin picking out the additional items she'll need. I grab her suitcases from the top shelf and lay them out for her easy access. While she's busy with that, I set out to clean up and make her home feel as close to normal as possible.

When I've finished righting her furniture, picking up shattered debris, and sweeping up broken glass in the other rooms, I move back into to her bedroom. She's sitting at her vanity table, staring at her still-bruised face. The swelling is down considerably since she first showed up at my door, but it's nowhere near gone. Neither are the discolorations around her eye, on her cheeks, or on her neck. Those are the visible injuries. Under her shirt, the bruises on her ribs and back are worse, as I suspected they would be before they get better.

It's on the tip of my tongue to say, "What's on your mind, gorgeous?", but I know she'd assume I'm only attempting to distract her from her current thoughts. I'm not—all I see is her beauty shining through—but I hold my tongue anyway.

"Last room to clean up. Do you need any help packing your clothes and one million and one shoes?"

"One million and one? Does one of my feet not get a shoe?" She can't stop the small grin that breaks free despite her resistance. "I think I've packed every-thing I'll need. To be honest, I didn't leave much here —most everything I have is coming with me. Except my scrubs, of course, since I won't be working during the next couple of weeks."

"You can work all you want." I wait for her to give me the side-eye before continuing. "On your book. While sitting on my couch. Safe in my house."

"I should've known there was a catch." She shakes her head, but I don't miss the smile she attempts to hide. She secretly enjoys all the doting she's receiving. And maybe I'm enjoying giving it more than I've realized before now.

Over the next few minutes, I straighten up her

bedroom to erase all traces of Butch's presence. Putting the mattress and box spring back on the bed frame and picking up the mess Butch left behind doesn't take long. When I've finished, I zip her suitcases closed and pull them with one hand.

"Shall we?" I offer my other arm to her, and she wraps her hand around it, pulling close to me again.

When we reach her living room, she stops and looks around. "This is amazing, Nick. I thought it would take hours to make a dent in the damage he did. It's almost back to normal, minus the broken furniture I'll have to replace now."

"We'll come back another day, and I'll take all the garbage out. I didn't want to leave you up here alone to get everything out of here today. At least you can walk through here without stepping on anything now." She squeezes my arm and leans her head against me.

"Thank you, Nick. What would I have done without you?" Her voice is a little watery, clogged with emotion, so I simply kiss her on the top of the head in response.

We leave the building without incident, and I help her climb into my vehicle for the short drive back to my place. Glancing over at her in the passenger seat of my truck, I can tell this short excursion has worn her out, probably more from the emotional aspect than anything. She leans her head against the back of the seat and fights sleep as I take my time, slowing at yellow lights and actually coming to a full stop at the stop signs.

When I pull into my driveway and kill the engine, I almost hate to wake her to get her inside. But the chilly weather starts to permeate the interior of the truck almost immediately, preventing me from sitting here and staring at her for too long.

"Are we already back home?" Her eyes are still closed, and her voice is heavy with sleep, but she knows where we are. *Home.* Funny. I've never thought of my brownstone as home until she said it.

"We're home, darlin'. Let's get you inside so you can finish that nap under your blanket."

After getting her settled on the couch, I grab her suitcases from the truck and put them in the bedroom. Then I take my spot at the kitchen table and review the plan to nab Butch for the umpteenth time. Now more than ever, I want him out of her life. For her safety, of course. But for more selfish reasons I've only just realized.

When she said she didn't know what she'd do without me, it struck a chord deep inside me. One that, now that she rang it, can't be unrung now. Will she still want me when he's no longer a threat? Will her feelings for me diminish when she's free to live her life again?

Or will she be ready to pursue something more serious…more permanent?

While she sleeps, I decide to make that phone call

I've been putting off for far too long. I feel partially responsible for Butch even having the opportunity to get to her. Had I followed my gut and insisted on helping her, she wouldn't be all beaten up, sleeping on my couch right now. Then again, had I interfered when she didn't want my help, she might not have spoken to me afterward. Now, I think she'll understand both my motives and the dire need for the additional layer of security.

"Hey Reaper, it's Nick Tucker. Long time since we've talked, my friend."

"Nick Tucker, it has been way too long. What can I do you for?" Noah Steele, my former employer and longtime friend, is one of the best men I know. He's never too busy to help out a brother in need.

I explain Savannah's situation and ask for his expert help to safeguard her condo. He's particularly interested in hearing about Butch and his ties to the Devils. Noah and his team were there to help during a tight spot when I was undercover. Knowing what those fuckers were capable of, Noah jumps at the chance to help us out.

"Consider it done, Nick. I've got a couple of men in the area I'd trust with my life. If Silas is back in DC, I'll ask him to swing by and try to break in after they're done. If he can't get inside, no one can."

We talk for a while longer, chatting about the crazed news coverage over the notorious outlaw gang and all the nicknames the media outlets have given me, over and above their favorite—the Undercover Hero.

"Special Agent Adonis is my personal favorite." Noah laughs out loud at my expense.

"Yeah, yeah. Whatever, man."

"Brianna said to tell you she likes Undercover Stud Muffin, and she thinks you should change your business cards to match it." Noah is still laughing, and I hear his wife's laughter join in on the roast in the background.

"Tell Brianna I said hello." I will never live this down for the rest of my life.

"Undercover Panty Charmer is Bull's favorite."

"Okay, that's enough running down all my nicknames. I'm sure each of you can add even more humiliating titles to the already long list, but I've really had enough of the whole press thing now."

I'm thinking I should've just gone to Home Depot and bought a home monitoring system to install on my own.

"My guys will be there by the first of next week. Is that soon enough?"

"That's great. She's staying here with me for a couple of weeks anyway. That'll give us time to try out the new system and let her get used to it before she goes back home."

There's that word again.

Home.

"Speaking of Silas, when will you know if he's in town?"

"I can try to get a hold of him right now if you need him."

"If you don't mind, that'd be great. I need an extra hand from someone I know I can trust for my side project with Butch. We're all hands on deck as it is, but I can't leave Savannah unprotected, and I'm sure as hell not letting her tag along. Thanks for your help, Reap."

"Anytime, my friend. I'll send Silas in your direction if he's back on US soil. If not, we'll figure something else out. I won't leave you hanging."

We disconnect and I step into the doorway, checking on Savannah. She's still sleeping soundly on the couch, wrapped up in the blanket, and I ask myself which moment it was that made me fall so hard for her.

CHAPTER 11

Savannah

*B*ad decision #856 of this week alone is insisting we go out on a real date instead of having dinner in my pajamas at Nick's house. And the personal flaw I can't seem to move past is my stubborn nature, and that's preventing me from telling Nick that clothes hurt my ribs even more than breathing does. But our first date is important to me. It feels like we need this milestone to say we have the beginnings of a real relationship, not just a fly-by-night passing.

I can hear the conversation with my mother now.

"So where did Nick take you on your first date?" Asked in the standard judgy-Mom tone.

"To his kitchen, where we had pizza and breadsticks while relaxing in our pajamas. Then we cuddled in his bed

until I fell asleep with my cheek on his chest and his arm around me to keep the monsters in the dark from getting to me."

"That's not a date, Savannah. That's a booty call."

"No one says 'booty call' anymore, Mom. It's called 'Netflix and chill,' and we didn't even watch Netflix. It was an awesome first date, though."

That's not exactly the most romantic version of how I've pictured our time together. Then again, being in near tears from the clothes squeezing me in the wrong places isn't exactly romantic either. Even though the temperature is far too cold for me to wear my soft cotton pullover dress, that's exactly what I've decided on. My thick wool overcoat should help shield me from the whipping winds, no longer than the minute or two we'll be outside. I'll just hurry as fast as I can in my current state to get from the truck to the door of the restaurant.

Changing clothes takes me an entire ten minutes because every time I move, it hurts more than the last. I'm so screwed.

When I finally sit down at the mirror to put on a little makeup, I realize I need a lot of makeup to hide the rainbow of colors my face is currently sporting. Dabbing carefully, I apply plenty of concealer and foundation, then I even out the tone with a dusting of loose powder. A little blush then some nice eyeshadow round it out.

And, ta-da...all my bruises are still visible.

They're just very well accessorized with other colors now.

Finally dressed, complete with full makeup and my hair styled in a way other than a ponytail or messy bun, I realize there's absolutely no way I can walk in heels tonight. I grab my thigh-high boots from my available selection of shoes. They're low-heeled, so I don't have to worry about tripping over air and hurting myself even worse.

When I finally emerge from the bathroom, Nick whistles a long, low catcall as his eyes drink me in. I feel them skimming across my skin, like light touches from his fingertips all over my body. My insecurities melt away, and excited butterflies flutter in my belly, ready for the first date I've had in...years. That real-ization would actually make me sad, if not for the handsome and sexy man leaning against the door-frame, watching my every move with hungry eyes and waiting to whisk me away for the evening.

"You look absolutely gorgeous. I'll be the envy of every man in there tonight. Maybe I should just keep you at home instead, so I don't get into any fights when someone tries to steal you away from me." He leans over and kisses me softly, and I briefly consider taking him up on that offer.

"There's no man alive who could take me away from you, Nick. But we should get going before you talk me into the idea of just staying home. Karen is looking forward to meeting you after everything she's heard about you from Spence and me. If we're a no-show, she'll hunt us both down, and it won't be pretty when she finds us."

"Only if you're sure you feel up to it. You sleep with me at night, remember? I know you're nowhere near healed yet, no matter how much you pretend you're better off than you really are."

"You know, it's a little scary how you can see through me sometimes. You're right, I'll probably pay for it later tonight. And when I say I will, I mean you will, too. But…"

"But?" His eyes twinkle like stars in the dark sky. He knows I was about to admit to something that would embarrass me.

"But tonight is important to me. It's our first date. Even though we've spent a lot of time together, and even though I'm sort of even living with you, tonight kind of feels like our beginning."

He smiles, understanding shining in his eyes, but he slowly shakes his head. "No, darlin', tonight is not our beginning. Not for me anyway. We began the first day I laid eyes on you, when you captured me with those gorgeous green eyes. Then every morning when we met for coffee and you shared your hopes and dreams for the future with me. Our first official date may be tonight, but I've been yours for weeks now. Now that we've gotten much better acquainted, I know my feelings for you won't ever diminish."

"Nick." His name comes out on a whisper as I

place my hand on his cheek. Tears well up in my eyes, and I fight the intense emotion rising inside me and prevent them from falling. "You have no idea how much that means to me coming from you. But there's something we should talk about before we go any further. You may change your mind about me."

"Darlin', I don't care about your past or anything you think must be the worst thing in the world. I can guarantee, whatever you have to share isn't as bad as some of the things I've had to do. I'm not even worried about what you want to tell me. But since it's important to you, I'll be glad to listen. Then we'll get back to our regularly scheduled lives."

"You make love feel so easy." I didn't mean to just blurt out the words, but I couldn't hold them in any longer. He makes me feel so much—so many feelings that are new and exciting. Hope blooms inside of me like a rare flower in a barren desert.

With lightning speed, he cups my face in his hands and covers my lips with his. With the sweetest, softest kiss, he sets my body ablaze and liquifies me where I stand. He pulls back, emotion swimming in the amber depths of his eyes. "I love you, Savannah. It may seem too soon to some. Others will think it's because of the situation we're in, but they're all wrong. It's you—the woman I've spent mornings, days, and nights with—who has captured my heart. I'm not some young kid who's never had a real relationship. I've made my share of mistakes. But this I can guarantee you, I will never want another after you. If you walk away from me tomorrow, or after fifty years of marriage, no one else will ever have my heart."

Thinking I'd get out of here this evening without messing up my makeup or my clothes was a silly wish. I'm blubbering like a baby, tears of complete joy that I wouldn't trade for all the smiles in the world if it meant I never heard those touching words of love from Nick Tucker. Those were meant for just my ears, never to be heard by another woman from his lips. I couldn't create a better man if I tried, even with a genie and a million wishes.

When we finally arrive at the restaurant, Nick pulls up to the front door and hops out of the truck. He comes around to my side and helps me slide out without too much jarring. "Wait inside where it's warm, darlin'. I'll park the truck and be right back."

My undercover hero.

Karen and Spencer are already inside when I walk in. They'd put our name on the list for a table and are waiting for Nick and me at the bar. Karen is sipping on a glass of water when I step up beside her and wrap my arm around her shoulders.

"I've missed my best friend. I thought for sure you'd show up at Nick's brownstone to see us."

Her head whips around in my direction, and she nearly jumps out of her seat. "Savannah! I've missed you too! Believe me, I was already headed out to the car with my keys in my hand when Spencer stopped me. He assured me you were in good hands before pressuring me to let Nick handle your care." Her eyes scan my face and neck, noting each and every contusion, abrasion, and swollen spot. The green, black, red, and purple marks of the bruises are impossible to hide, no matter how hard I tried. But even if I'd had stage makeup that can hide full-body tattoos, Karen would still be able to find them. She lowers her voice and continues. "Spence told me that asshole did a number on you this time, but he didn't accurately describe the severity. Dr. Wattress should've kept you inpatient."

"No, he shouldn't have either. I know it looks bad, but I am on the mend. I have the best caregiver. He even dropped me off at the door while he parks the truck and walks in the cold alone."

"There's your undercover lover now. There's no mistaking his face—it's on the news every day." Karen smiles at Nick as he approaches. He walks directly to me, greets Spencer with one hand while the other wraps around me.

"You must be Karen." Nick accepts her extended hand. "Nick Tucker."

"It's nice to finally meet you. I've heard all about you. Thanks to the news, I guess everyone knows your every secret now. I was looking forward to grilling you with my prepared questions, all 150 of them." Karen breaks out into a full-face grin before she laughs, letting Nick know she's only teasing.

"Don't believe everything you hear on the news. Fake news is a real thing, Karen. They've reported shit about me that I've never even heard of, so it makes me wonder what else I've believed without knowing the full truth. Besides, if I were really a superhero in disguise, Savannah would've already told you." Nick looks down at me and winks.

The hostess calls our name, and we follow her to the table. Over the next couple of hours, the four of us enjoy our meals, the company, and the ambiance of the restaurant. Not that Nick's place isn't great, but sometimes a girl needs to get dolled up and go outside. Even though staying home with Nick was more than appealing, I'm so glad we forced ourselves to leave and head out with friends tonight. We laugh, though I try to keep mine to a light chuckle. We make silly toasts in jest of each other. And we celebrate a momentous occasion.

"I'd like to make a toast, and there's no one I'd rather share this with." Karen raises her glass, so the rest of us follow suit. "We just recently found out... Spencer and I are going to be parents. I'm pregnant!"

My resulting yelp really, really hurts—but I wouldn't take it back for the world. My best friend is going to have a baby, and I couldn't be more thrilled for her. She rushes around the table to hug me, knowing I move like a senior citizen at the moment.

With my arms around her neck, I squeeze her tightly and whisper my congratulations.

"I'm so happy for you, Karen. I love you. You'll be the best mom ever."

She wipes tears from the corner of her eyes and retakes her seat. "Thank you. It was definitely a surprise—we weren't trying at all. My grandma always said no child is an accident. A surprise, maybe. A blessing, always. But never a mistake."

"I was wondering why you weren't drinking wine. I thought it was in solidarity with me since I can't have any with my pain meds."

"That's exactly what it is, Savannah. I love you so much, I'd deprive myself of wine just because you can't have any."

"You're such a liar. You'd drink the whole bottle by yourself and leave me with none if you could."

After stuffing ourselves with the best Italian food DC offers and topping that off with the most decadent dessert on the menu, we say our goodnights and prepare to leave. Nick, being Nick, won't let me out of the restaurant until he's pulled the truck back to the front door to pick me up. Though I don't expect the special treatment, I do love the way he takes care of me. The special touches he adds that show he's put extra thought into the details.

He really is the best man.

Mom will be so impressed with him, she may

even try to take him away from me and keep him all to herself.

That thought makes me chuckle to myself.

When the full-size truck rolls up to the curb, I hug Karen and Spencer good night, congratulate them again, and promise to make plans to just hang out—in comfortable clothes—again very soon. With that, Nick helps me into the truck and takes me home.

Home.

I keep using that word when I refer to wherever he is. It just feels so right.

Back inside his brownstone, he helped me change out of my dressy clothes and back into my oversize T-shirt and comfortable yoga pants. He slid his fingers along my skin, checking my wounds while sharing his love. Every place he found a bruise, he left hot kisses to help it heal faster. Where there were abrasions, he lovingly stroked my skin, telling me the places would heal without leaving a single scar as a reminder. I only wanted help to change because holding my arms over my head to take the dress off alone was too much to ask after a night of sitting upright, talking, and laughing. But he gave me so much more than I asked for—he realized what I needed and gave it all to me freely.

Though the doctor said to move around, all the excitement of the night zapped all my energy. We retreat to the couch to unwind from the festivities and chat about Karen's surprise news. With all seriousness, I turn to face him and take his hand in mine.

"Nick, you should know this about me. If it changes your mind about us, I will not think less of you. Just please be honest with me, that's all I ask."

"Always will be. You can tell me anything, darlin'."

"I've had female problems as far back as I can remember. Skipped periods, extremely painful cycles, so much irregularity since puberty. I've had some tests done in the past, and it doesn't appear I'll be able to conceive. My body just doesn't work like it's supposed to, so babies probably aren't a possibility for me. Ever."

I wait with bated breath for his response. What man would want a woman who can't have children?

"I'm still waiting for whatever it is that makes you think I wouldn't want to be with you anymore. Was that it?"

Thinking he's obviously teasing me, my eyes fly up to meet his, and I'm already fighting back hot, stinging tears. But there's no jest in his expression. There's no falseness in his eyes. Once again, my undercover hero just reduced the entire mountain down to a molehill.

"Yes, that was it. No kids, Nick. We can't have a family. No little Nick Juniors running around the house. No one to carry on the family name and traditions."

"That's not what you just said. You have medical issues that prevent you from getting pregnant. That's fine. That doesn't mean we can't still have a full life and a large family if that's what we decide we want. All that matters to me is I spend every day with you. You are the best part of my life, Savannah. Anything extra is just the cherry on top."

I'm blubbering. Again. Crying like a baby. Tears of joy streak my perfectly applied makeup. Black mascara pools on my fingers with every swipe. I can only imagine how much of a mess I must look like right now. "I love you so much, Nick. I never thought I could love someone so much, especially not so fast. And I swear I won't spend the rest of my life crying like an idiot...but after everything I've been through, my emotions are a mess. I either shut down completely or cry uncontrollably. It's embarrassing."

"Never be embarrassed with me...and never feel as if you have to hide any emotion from me. Sad tears, happy tears, sappy tears. They're part of you, and I'll take all of you I can get." He leans over to kiss me, and I'm completely lost in this wonderful man beside me, until I hear my name being announced on the local evening news.

"In this shot, you can see Special Agent Nick Tucker out with his new leading lady. But we have serious questions about the nature of their relationship, and who Nick Tucker really is, behind the scenes. In this closeup picture, you can clearly see that Savannah Fields, Special Agent Tucker's new flame, has

bruising all over her face and neck that is consistent with domestic abuse."

All I can do is gape at the television.

"And, with the new allegations surrounding Special Agent Tucker and the crimes he committed against women on behalf of the Devil's Dominion motorcycle club, we have to ask the hard questions. Did the undercover outlaw gang life change Nick Tucker, the pride of the DEA? Is he physically and mentally abusing Savannah Fields? Were his crimes while undercover absolutely necessary in order to complete his mission, or did they conveniently hide his true colors behind the safety of his badge? We have more from eyewitnesses at the restaurant tonight who claim they overheard Miss Fields referring to the source of her injuries as none other than Nick Tucker himself. More news, coming up next."

CHAPTER 12

Nick

*F*or the next ten minutes and thirty-seven seconds, I stare dumbfounded at the TV, listening to the news anchor drone on and on. About me. About my sins. About my crimes. The long litany of offenses bringing back every haunting memory as she reads each one off the teleprompter, speaking as if she knows every intimate detail about me.

Hitchhiking females kidnapped off the street, brought into the fold, and forced into prostitution.

Involvement in skirmishes with rival gangs, resulting in injuries and deaths.

Women bought, sold, traded, or just plain given away within the club.

Sheep, those who didn't belong to any one biker, forced into street-level drug dealing on behalf of the club.

Rampant physical and sexual abuse against any woman without a "property of" patch...and even some with the patch, with her man's consent...from any and all members, at any time they choose, in any way they want.

Every tick of the second hand makes the bile in my stomach churn even more. Any thought I had of leaving those deeds under the rug, neatly hidden from the light of day, is completely obliterated now. My chance to confess to Savannah and try to help her understand the circumstances I faced while under-cover was just annihilated by a partially fake news report. The report of the crimes committed by the Devils was true. My part in those crimes was not true. Not that I can completely absolve myself of all the violations I allowed to happen, but I'd still prefer she heard it from me first.

Time to face the music.

"Savannah." Her name leaves my lips before I dare to look at her, knowing the disappointment I'll see on her face will gut me. I feel enough like a failure as it is. My gaze swings over to hers just as she wraps her hand around mine and squeezes it.

"Nick, I can't believe they're comparing you to all those bikers and accusing you of doing this to me. You're nothing like those men. You'd never hurt me. I'm calling them to set the record straight. This is bullshit."

"Wait, darlin'. Hold up a minute. No, I'd never hurt you, but I didn't stop those guys from hurting all those other women. I'm just as guilty as they are—I watched them commit all kinds of unspeakable acts, and I did nothing. For two years, I was complicit in every crime they committed against those women. At first, I walked away from the scene so I wouldn't say anything. But I could only do that for so long before they started to question me."

"Nick—I know all of this. Don't you think I know you had to do things while undercover that you wouldn't normally do? I'm glad you did, no matter what it was at the time. Thanks to you, those violent men are off the streets. They're going to pay for their crimes. What you did was for the greater good—you were looking at the long game, no matter what it cost you in the short run. That takes more than guts and courage, Nick. That takes commitment and sacrifice.

"You're *nothing* like them, no matter what you had to do to seem like you were one of them. I know that, and I think deep down, you know too. You have to forgive yourself. I know that's easier said than done, but it's eating you alive and keeping you from being truly happy. You deserve as much happiness as anyone else. Even more. You gave up two years of your life to keep the rest of us safe from men like that. How many people would be willing to do that, much less put their life on the line every day of those two years? If the Devils didn't turn on you, a rival gang could have. Or a drug cartel. Or anyone else."

"Why does it sound like such a good idea coming from you?"

"Which part sounds good? What am I getting credit for?"

"Convincing me to forgive myself and let it go. That I deserve at least that much after all I gave up over the last couple of years. For the record, the biker life is not the life for me. I learned I enjoy hot showers, soap, and soft beds on the regular." At last, I can start to joke about serving hard time with a biker gang.

"I'm glad to hear that. So, can I call the news now and tell them they got the story all wrong? That it was actually one of the Devils who did this to me—not you?"

"Unfortunately, no. Somehow, I think they'd find an even bigger story in the fact that the ex-girlfriend of a former Devil is now living in my home and going out on dinner dates with me. The spin and sensationalism of that story would eclipse the false accusations that I beat you."

"Oh shit, Nick. I didn't even think of it that way. What if that does get out? Will you be in trouble? I mean, I can explain everything—how it all happened."

"No one will believe it was all a coincidence, darlin'. If they don't turn on me, they'll turn on you and accuse you of using me to get your boyfriend out of trouble. Or some other bullshit about us fighting over you and you getting caught in the crossfire. There are so many possibilities of how that narrative could go."

We settle back on the couch, Savannah taking her time to find a comfortable spot snuggled next to me. The news is too depressing—and infuriating—so I change the channel and find something we will actually enjoy. Just when the chaos seems to die down and we can enjoy some alone time, my cell phone rings. This late at night, that's never a good sign. I grab it off the coffee table and stare at the name on the caller ID for a moment before deciding to get it over with now instead of later.

"Calvin. What can I do for you?"

He starts yelling immediately, loud enough for Savannah to hear every word he says, even with the phone pressed against my ear. He rants and raves about my very public relationship with her, already knowing who she is but not realizing we were letting the rest of the world in on our little secret just yet.

"Do you know how this looks, Tucker? You're dating the former girlfriend of a member of the very gang we're prosecuting. How fucking stupid are you? Don't tell me you couldn't keep your dick in your pants for a few months longer to give us time to send these assholes to prison! How can you not see this is a conflict of interest?"

"How can it be a conflict of interest when she was never part of the gang? Her ex-boyfriend has been here over the last couple of years, not even an active member of the Devils after his assignment fell through. And I didn't meet her until they'd already been arrested—under a multi-agency cooperative effort, by the way, and the charges had already been filed. This is standard spin-doctor bullshit, sir. My relationship with her doesn't change the crimes they committed. They tried to murder a federal agent, for fuck's sake!"

"You should know as well as anyone that perception is key when it comes to how the public will view this. And right now, what everyone will see is that our lead undercover agent is sleeping with the fucking enemy."

"What do you suggest we do, sir? Hold a press conference? Do a few interviews?"

"Did you fall and bust your fucking head? No. You don't publicly say or do anything else. Get her out of your house and lay low until this shitshow blows over."

He hangs up without waiting for a reply from me. Just as well, he wouldn't have liked what I had to say anyway. Savannah isn't going anywhere—at least not until the security system is in place and she's mentally and physically ready to go back to her apartment. Not a moment before. And definitely not because my director thinks he can direct my personal life. After I turn off my cell phone for the night, I wrap my arms around Savannah and resume watching the movie with her.

Like nothing happened.

Because nothing did. Nothing wrong anyway. Everything between us is right. Right as rain.

Before long, Savannah is sacked out in my arms, sleeping soundly after the excitement of our first date. I chuckle to myself over that term. Not because of how much it meant to her, but because of how backward our relationship is. We started living together before we ever had our first date. We were eyeballs-deep in love before we officially had dinner out together. And we were planning our future together before I met her best friend.

But why not?

Nothing else in my life has been traditional or had any semblance of normalcy. My time in the service was spent under constant fire, enemies around every corner waiting for the opportunity to wipe me from existence. When I worked for Steele Security, I was under similar circumstances, but on a much smaller scale. My private security time with Dominic Powers brought danger and near-death experiences. Now that I'm older, it's nice to enjoy the simple pleasures in life and not wonder who's lurking in the dark, waiting to blow up my Humvee with an IED.

I'm finally at a place in my life where falling in love is a perk, not a burden.

Savannah stirs in my arms, and a light moan escapes her lips. I look down at her, expecting her to wake and ask me to take her to bed. Instead, she tightens her grip around my waist and adjusts her head to a more comfortable spot on my chest. Another first for me—sleeping with a woman without fucking all night then sending her packing in the morning. Relationships were never in my bag of tricks before I met her. One-night stands that turned into full-weekend romps between the sheets were. Occasional friends with benefits—only the ones who weren't looking for more—satisfied my itch.

But I threw that little black book in the trash. With her around, I know I won't need it again.

Fuck if I don't need a cold shower right now, with her warm body pressed against mine. The way she wraps herself around me when we sleep is a complete turn-on—even unintentionally. When she's healed and able, I have so many plans to ravage her perfect body, count how many times she screams my name in one night, and wipe her memory clean of any man she knew before me. She doesn't realize the depths of my feelings for her yet. But she will.

Soon.

"Darlin', I need to take you to bed." That's the fucking understatement of the year. I need to do a whole lot more than that, but for tonight, holding her in my arms will have to do.

"Mmm, do we have to move?"

"I'm afraid so. If I leave you lying here like this all

night, you'll be even sorer in the morning. You need to stretch out, my love."

Her eyes flutter open, and she cranes her neck to look up at me. "My love?"

"That's right. You are, aren't you?"

Her beautiful smile lights up her sleepy eyes. "I am. And you're mine."

"No question about that, darlin'. I'm all yours." After working my way out of her grip, I help her up, and we walk hand in hand to the bedroom. She steps into the bathroom to wash her face, and I climb into bed, keeping the covers turned back until she's held closely in my arms again. When she finds her comfortable place again, I release a long, relaxing breath. Now I can sleep.

"Nick?"

"Yeah, babe?"

"I know you said you didn't care about my past and didn't need to know any of it, but there is something else I want to tell you. Something I think you need to know."

"Okay. Hit me."

"When I first met Butch, I didn't know what he was. He rode a motorcycle, but a lot of men ride them. They're not all criminals. But it didn't take too long to realize exactly what kind of man he was, and our relationship, if you can even call it that, deteriorated quickly. A few weeks ago, when I moved to get away from him, it wasn't because we'd just broken up and I had to find somewhere else to live. He and I haven't been…together…in more than three years. He showed up now and then when he ordered me to go somewhere with him. But we haven't been in an intimate relationship since long before I moved here from LA. You know how the gang treated women… so I didn't want you to think I was one of their sheep."

"Darlin', I never thought you were one of their women. But I have to tell you, I'm more than a little pleased to know it's been a long time since you were last with him. On the other hand, thinking about being the last man you'll ever be with will keep me up all night now. Visions of your beautiful body underneath mine, screaming out my name until the neighbors call the cops, and watching you fall asleep in the afterglow of your multiple orgasms will haunt me all fucking night."

"Thanks for that visual. Like I said, it's been more than three years since I've had sex. Now we'll both be awake all night with no way to cure what ails us. How much longer will it be until my ribs are healed again?"

"Considering it's only been a couple of days since they were injured, five weeks, five days, and three hours. I can figure out the exact number of minutes when all my blood returns to my veins. Since I'm a nice guy and a very giving lover, I'll put you out of your three-year misery first. Lie back, darlin'. I'm going to take care of you right now. There's just one thing I need you to take care of for me, though."

"What's that?" Her words come out breathy, the excitement building inside her as I fold back the covers and slide down her body.

"You have to count how many times you scream my name for me. I'll be a little preoccupied down here and may miss one. If you lose count, I'll have to start all over again."

"Oh...my..." Then my tongue goes to work. "*Nick!*"

"Mm-hmm...that's what I want to hear. That was one. Keep going, darlin'. The night is still young. You're so fucking sweet."

CHAPTER 13

Savannah

Our first date changed our relationship in so many ways. When Nick met my best friend and they actually got along, I knew he was a special man. When his boss basically ordered him to stop seeing me, or at least being seen in public with me, and he refused, I knew he meant it when he said he loved me. But when he said he was adamant about erasing any other man from my memory, I thought it was mostly macho talk.

Until he proved it to me. Over and over. All night long. Until I begged him to stop because I couldn't take anymore. He was more than pleased with himself, and I was more than pleased with his performance. I did feel guilty because I didn't get a chance to perform for him, but when I moved to try, he wouldn't let me.

"Not until you're well, darlin'. I'm a big boy. It won't kill me to wait a few more weeks until I know it won't hurt you. Trust me, the *forty-six times* you screamed my name was more than enough satisfaction for me."

I actually did keep count. Not because he ordered me to—although I momentarily contemplated "accidentally" losing count so he would have to start over —but because I was genuinely curious too. Turns out, forty-six was technically past my limit, but he wanted to see if we could make it to fifty. My body couldn't take it...and neither could his neighbors, because they started banging on the wall and yelling for us to shut the hell up.

We fell asleep, completely exhausted, after an uncontrollable laughing spell.

In the days since then, we've grown so much closer. We talk about everything—no topic is off-limits—he wants to know my thoughts, he wants to hear what I think, and he wants to share everything with me. What a novel idea—a relationship is a partnership is a relationship. I love this connection we have, where even the silence is comfortable and the atmosphere is nurturing.

These are the thoughts that I cling to as we drive to my apartment to meet his security friends. They're going to install new protective measures, including meeting with the superintendent about making the main entry and the enclosed garage more secure. Nick says they're very persuasive men, and when the super sees the extent of my injuries after a lunatic broke in and managed to get up to the fifth floor undetected, he thinks the building's board of directors will invest in additional measures.

That's all well and good, but in the back of my mind, I know it means I'll be moving back in to my condo soon. Alone. Without Nick. Sleeping single in my queen-size bed. No hard body that scares the monsters away and keeps me warm all night to cuddle against. I'm well aware that I'm too old to react like such a juvenile over the situation. I'm also well aware that staying at Nick's brownstone was only a temporary solution to help me until I'm healed enough to be on my own again.

That doesn't make leaving him any easier.

He must sense my apprehension as we near the building, because he squeezes my hand before bringing it to his lips. "Don't worry, darlin'. I'm here with you, and I'm not going anywhere. They will fix the breaches—to my satisfaction—one way or another. You won't fight this battle alone."

That's not the battle I'm concerned about fighting alone, but I hold my tongue. One step at a time. It's not as if he's kicking me out of his apartment and his life. Two weeks is more like a vacation, not a marriage. Apparently, I just become attached way too easily, and I'm definitely attached to Nick.

"For fuck's sake, did you see that?" I shield my face with my hand, wishing I had a wide-brimmed hat to hide under.

"Yeah, they've been watching us for a while. It's aggravating, isn't it?"

Another aspect of his job hits home with his reply. His sixth sense is much more honed and refined than mine. I only noticed the person snapping pictures of us as we passed because the sun reflected off the chrome on the car and caught my eye. But Nick knew we were being followed and photographed well before I realized it. We'll be fodder for the local news again. I never thought I'd say this, but I'm starting to miss all the political mudslinging between the opposing parties that kept them busy before Nick and I became household names.

"Your director will be thrilled to see all these pictures on the news tonight."

"Babe, I'm not worried about it, so you shouldn't be either."

"I feel responsible. If I'd gone to Karen's house instead of yours, none of this would be happening."

"There was a reason you came to me, Savannah. We're meant to be together. I never believed in fate and finding that one person I'm supposed to be with until I met you. Now I can see everything that happened, happened for a reason. If that means my director gets pissed and yells at me again, I can guarantee it won't be the last time. He'll get mad about something else after this blows over. That's his job—staying on his agents' asses to keep all of us in line."

"You're pretty laid-back for a Special Agent. I thought you were all type A personalities."

"Oh, I am definitely type A. I've just learned how to control it when needed, and how to release it when I need to let all hell break loose on someone."

We arrive at my building, and he pulls into one of the surface-level parking spots in front of the building. He gets out of the truck and walks around to my side. I sit still, not because I expect him to treat me like a porcelain doll, but because the memories of this place are so vivid, I can still taste the blood in my mouth. That old anxiety I thought I'd left behind, with Nick's help, starts building in my chest and threatens to emerge as a strangled scream. I push it down, focusing on my breathing as I work to calm my racing heart.

Then I feel Nick's hand slide around my waist, keeping his grip loose but letting me know he's there. I didn't even realize he'd opened my door yet. "Darlin', tell me if you can't do this. I'll take you away from here right now, and I'll handle this myself. At first, I thought it would help if you heard the changes we're demanding, but now I'm not so sure anymore."

Somewhere in my logical mind, I hear his words and process them. He'll take me away for now, but the changes will still be implemented. The security will still be put into place. I'll still move back into my condo alone. Whether it's today, tomorrow, or next week, I will have to face the fact that I'll be here alone again at some point.

Maybe I should've realized this sooner, but the weight of my thoughts changes my view of everything. I've allowed Butch to rob me of my independence, of my freedom, of my right to live in my home without fear of him. If I don't woman up, go in there with Nick, and make my own demands heard, I'm essentially allowing Butch to win. He wins at ruining my life, making me completely dependent on someone else for my sense of security, and taking away what I've worked for my entire life.

"No, I'm ready. Let's do this. I'm glad you're here with me, but they're going to listen to what I have to say, too."

Nick smiles, genuinely and warmly, before kissing me softly. "That's my girl. I knew that feisty fighter in you would regroup and show up sooner or later."

"She's here now, and she's ready to kick ass."

When we reach the main door, a large, imposing figure steps into view just inside. Nick feels my hesitation in my faltering steps. "That's Silas Steele, Noah's brother. He's one of the good guys. Noah said he'd call Silas to see if he was in town to help us out with Operation Bitch."

"Was he undercover with you?"

"No, but he helped resolve the case in his own way. He's an officer with the CIA, so he's very skilled at interrogation techniques and extracting needed information from people. Since my case involved international arms dealers, the DEA was able to pull in Silas to help through interagency cooperation. The fact that he's the brother of one of the best friends I've ever had didn't hurt either."

"If you like him, then I'll like him. Butch should take off running in the opposite direction if he sees you two men walking toward him."

Nick chuckles darkly beside me, the low timbre of his laugh rumbling through his chest over the mental images of Butch tucking tail and running. "Nah, we don't want him to do that. We want him to stand and fight so we can end this once and for all."

Nick opens the door for me, and I step into the lobby of my building. Silas smiles at me, instantly changing his appearance from daunting and intimidating to warm and friendly.

"You must be Savannah. My brother Noah told me all about you. Seems you've captured the heart of our elusive Special Agent Friskme. Millions of women claim to have drugs hidden somewhere on their person, so he'll frisk them until he finds the contraband."

"Not you too, Silas." Nick shakes his head. "Noah, Brianna, and Bull already gave me enough shit over the pet names I've been given."

"Dude, the comments on social media posts about you are gold. Pure gold. I've laughed my ass off. You should've known better than to let your cover get blown by one of those shitheads. You'll find no sympathy here."

"Yeah, you just remember you said that, Silas Steele. What goes around, comes around, my friend."

Silas laughs, shrugging off Nick's warning like it's nothing. "Noah's men are already upstairs. You can fill me in on the plan to lure this Butch character in so we can trap him and kill him."

"Silas. Really? You sound like Shadow. Is that how the CIA trains you? Just kill everyone who gets in your way?"

"Yep."

Silas's reply makes me laugh, even though I doubt he's kidding. When we exit the elevator on the fifth floor, two men are standing outside my door. Since neither Nick nor Silas flinches, I assume these are the two men we're here to meet. Silas reaches them first and extends his hand toward the one nearest us.

"Roman, how are you?" He claps one hand on Roman's shoulder, while shaking hands with the other.

"Good. I didn't know you were back in the States. When did you get home?" Roman replies to Silas, giving me a moment to silently assess him. He's not as thick as Nick, but he's tall and muscular, nonetheless. His hair is a lighter brown, and he has that playboy vibe some men just naturally exude. But his eyes are kind, showing the good guy underneath.

"You know I never let anyone know my travel plans ahead of time. My whole family sics Liz on me when I do." Laughter fills the hallway, all at Silas's expense.

Nick turns to me to explain. "Liz is a friend of Noah's wife, and she has taken quite a liking to Silas. Even though she's old enough to be his mother."

"She wants to be a super spy with me and regularly makes my life hell when she's around. No one tell her how much I secretly love her, though." Silas grins then turns to the second man. "Brad, it's been a long time, brother. Are you here with all the latest technology gadgets for Savannah's condo?"

"Hey, Silas. You know I am. When I'm done, she'll be better protected than Beyoncé and Fort Knox combined."

"I like Brad," I chime in. "Brad is my new best friend."

"Savannah, I hope you don't mind, but we've already broken in to your condo several times, trying out new ideas and testing our equipment. We also took out all the broken furniture and the garbage for you. Everything is as good as new in there now." Roman holds out a set of keys toward me, and I immediately notice how few there are on the ring.

"Don't worry. We added a biometric lock that only opens for you and a digital lock that triggers a complete security shutdown if the wrong numbers are attempted too many times. We have cameras in the hallway and elevators now, and everything is monitored from a central, secure location with facial recognition technology. You also have a new secure door and a panic alarm inside."

"You and I are going to be BFFs too." The men laugh, amused by my commentary.

Brad asks for my hand and places it on a scanner in a large metal case. After he scans my entire hand into the system, we try out the biometric locks. I'm like a kid in a candy store with all the new gadgets and upgraded security. Locking my door will be much more fun with these new toys than my old, no-tech dead bolts.

"Have you already had words with the super?" Nick asks, looking between Roman and Brad.

"We did. When we were able to get into the lobby without any trouble at all, we paid him a visit. He was more than a little taken aback when we walked into his 'secure office' with no forewarning. Then I explained what happened to Savannah, and I may have insinuated I'd be back to visit him if anything else happened to her. After that, he was very receptive to our suggestions and upgrades. He even assured us he'll take care of getting funding approved through the board of directors. Seems the owners are sensitive to being sued over breach of contract after they lost their last lawsuit." Roman's smile is downright devious, but if that's what it takes to create a cone of protection around my building, I'm all for it.

"So, are you moving back in to your condo tonight, Savannah?" Silas asks, genuinely interested and not just fishing for information.

"No, she's not." Nick replies for me, and I cut my eyes up at him, raising my eyebrows in silent question. "What? It hasn't even been two weeks yet, and your doctor has you out of work for six weeks. You're still under my direct care and supervision right now."

"Man, you'd be better off just admitting you don't want her to leave than trying to pull the old 'doctor's orders' routine." Silas laughs and playfully punches Nick's arm. "Admit it, you are wrapped around her little finger, my friend."

"I have no reason to deny it. She knows it. I know it. You know it. Every news outlet in DC knows it, even though they accuse me of beating her up. Still, it's only been about a week since she was hurt initially, and I'm not taking any chances with her being reinjured."

"Fine, Undercover Lover—which is my personal favorite nickname, by the way—have it your way. Everyone go inside so I can find the holes in your security system. Savannah won't get to use it any time soon, but the next tenant will be thrilled with all the upgrades."

Silas urges the four of us inside so he can get to work on breaking in, cracking the codes, and just playing the bad guy in general. Every time Silas finds a way in, Brad and Roman tweak whatever failed, until the very last try. When Silas pops up behind me from out of nowhere, I simultaneously scream and jump, then grab my side as I try to catch my breath.

"Where the hell did you come from?" When I'm finally able to speak, I search my surroundings for a hidden door.

"I broke in to the condo next door and crawled through the heating duct right into your condo. This building has huge ducts." Silas smiles broadly, proud of his ingenuity.

"Adding motion sensors to the heating ducts now," Brad replies, unimpressed.

"At least now I know this place will be locked up tight." Nick steps behind me and wraps his arms around me. "That doesn't change the fact that you're not leaving my home or my bed yet."

I rest my arms on top of his, squeezing in response. "You don't have to tell me twice. You've spoiled me. I can't sleep without you now."

"Good to know my evil plan is working."

"You know I'll eventually have to come back here, right? I mean, as attached as I am to you already, you'll want your space back."

"Let's just take it one day at a time. We're in no hurry. Besides, even if you decided to stay here tonight, that doesn't mean I can't stay with you. Or that we won't see each other again. It just means half of my bed will be really cold and lonely without you in it."

Becoming attached to Nick is easy.

Falling in love with him was inevitable.

Feeling at peace with our relationship, regardless of what we face, is pure bliss.

Silas, Roman, and Brad finish demonstrating every feature of the new system they installed in my condo. Roman showed me how the cameras monitor every floor and elevator via an app on his phone. The lobby doors will be replaced with stylish yet ultra-secure doors that only the residents will be able to open.

Then they leave with promises to let us know when the doors are installed. Nick, of course, refuses to let me stay in my condo without him until those doors are in place.

Then again, he did offer to help me christen every room and leave good and long-lasting memories in place of the old ones once I'm completely healed. That's one more offer from him I simply can't refuse.

CHAPTER 14

Nick

"Can you just get back to the fucking topic at hand? I swear to God, I will shoot you myself if you change the subject again." I sit back, cross my arms over my body, and glare at Silas.

Fucker just laughs at me as if I'm a fucking comedian.

"Man, you are in an extra pissy mood since Savannah left you. News flash, brother—she just went back to her own condo. The one that's only two miles from your brownstone. You could run if you wanted and be there faster than driving in DC traffic. You two haven't known each other long enough to live together permanently yet. It's not like she broke up with you and went running back to Butch." Silas smirks at me, like he gives the best relationship advice in the world.

"What do you know? You're a fucking spy. You lie for a living. When's the last time you had a serious girlfriend?"

"Seventh grade. Worst four days of my life. I thought we'd never break up."

"That's it. I'm shooting you and putting us both out of our misery." I glare at him, giving him my worst—or best—intimidation stare. Bad thing is, he knows me too fucking well, so it only makes him laugh harder. "Can we get back to finalizing the plan to take out Butch once and for all?"

"Yeah, yeah, okay. Spoilsport. I was thinking, maybe we should invite Liz for this op. Butch wouldn't stand a chance against her."

He's really testing my nerves today. "We're not letting Liz in on our plan. No fucking way. She stays with Noah and Brianna and their kids, wherever they are. And that's not here, in harm's way, with a convicted felon, one-percenter, biker gang criminal who has no qualms about hurting women. You must miss Liz. You keep bringing her up."

"Just trying to lighten the tension in this room, brother. You're a different man without Savannah here to level out your moods."

Funny thing, I never realized that very fact until the words left his mouth. Before Savannah, I was angry all the time and hated the world, hated what

I'd become. Then she brought light and love and fresh air into my life and made me a better man without conscious effort. She made me *want* to be the best man I possibly could be—for her. Since she went back to her condo and I don't have her with me all the time, I've regressed to that moody, unapproachable bastard.

Time to snap out of that shit.

"You're right—I'm being ridiculous. My bad, man. Knowing he's still out there, regardless of how well protected she is, makes me nuts. The thought of not getting to her in time haunts me."

"Her condo has the best security in the world. It's better protected than the White House."

"But she's not always in her condo, is she?"

"I know she hasn't gone back to work yet. What's she been up to?" I'd swear Silas is stalling for some reason, but talking about Savannah does make me feel better.

"She started volunteering at the family crisis center to help other domestic abuse victims. She loves it. She's manning the phones right now, talking to women who are looking for a way to get out of a bad situation. She spends a few hours a day there. No physical work, but she leaves both completely drained and full of excitement."

"That's great. She's making a difference for others and helping herself at the same time. Have you decided when you're going back to work?"

"I haven't decided what I'm going to do yet. I can't go back to undercover work since everyone knows my face now. And with Savannah in my life, I wouldn't want to do that anyway. It definitely doesn't suck that I have more than two years' worth of my salary saved and all my accrued time off just waiting for me to burn through it. My director ordered me to take off the mandatory eight-week decompression time after the long-term operation ended, so I'm just waiting for some huge epiphany to fall out of the sky and smack me on the head."

"I'll keep that in mind."

Someone knocks on my door, and I lift my gaze to Silas's. "Are you expecting someone, Silas?"

"Just Roman and Brad. They said they'd be glad to lend their expertise on this job."

After I let Roman and Brad in, the four of us sit at the table and review every aspect of the plan, consider every possible failure, and identify potential contingencies. When we're satisfied that we've covered all the bases we can possibly think of, I pass out a round of cold longneck beers, and we settle in front of the TV.

"You really should sit this one out, Nick." Roman takes a swig of his beer. "You're technically still on administrative leave, the trial is heating up, and you probably need to stay with Savannah in case anything goes wrong with getting Butch. She wouldn't feel safe with anyone else. Plus, she'd be worried about you the whole time."

"As much as I hate to admit it, I know you're right. I can't jeopardize the trial with an unsanctioned undercover operation. And I damn sure can't risk Savannah running out on one of you to try to help me. She's likely to pull some shit like that, too." I chuckle, thinking about how she has nightmares without me beside her in bed, but she doesn't give herself enough credit. She wouldn't hesitate to face that very monster head on if she thought she could help me.

"So we're good to go for tomorrow night?" Silas asks.

"We are absolutely ready. Butch doesn't know Savannah is off work, so she'll drive her car to the hospital tomorrow night. She'll go in one door where Nick will be waiting for her, and they'll exit through another door so Butch won't see her leave. Her car will stay parked there, and we'll watch it all night if needed. The van Brad will record and monitor everything from is already in play, so it won't seem out of place.

"Butch's head will be on the chopping block soon if he doesn't move that heroin, and he knows it. That's why he went crazy trying to get to it. The Mexican cartel that the Devils were in bed with isn't a forgiving bunch." Roman finishes off his beer and grabs another from the refrigerator. "I almost want to hold on to the packages and let them deal with him."

"Tell me about it. If we ever found his body, it'd be in pieces strewn to the four corners of the world. I don't know which would be better—knowing he's dead, or seeing him behind bars." At this point, I'm thinking six feet under would be best so the fucker can't come back at all.

We finish by agreeing on the time each man will be at his assigned position, then I head to pick up Savannah from the shelter. Men aren't usually allowed to know or visit the secret location, but since I'm a federal agent, I have automatic clearance. Still, I wait in the truck for her to emerge from the building so no one is anxious about my presence. She'll be finished with her shift soon, and I can't wait to hear about her day. Her excitement over helping others has grown after every time she's volunteered. Watching her blossom and become more confident in her abilities are added benefits for me. She smiles and laughs more. No topic is left off the table, and she shares her entire day with me. Her passion for the difference she's making makes me miss my own.

Before long, she steps out of the front door, sporting the brightest smile when she spots me parked close to the road. The single-story building is mostly tan with light, mint-green accents, nothing spectacular that would draw the eye when passing by on a daily basis. There's no obvious sign advertising the services, and that's the entire point. It's unassuming and boring, not creating unnecessary attention to the people seeking solace inside. A high fence encloses the lot behind the building, with English ivy covering the slats and obstructing the view of the yard. From Savannah's description, I know there's a playground and space for outdoor activities for the kids and mothers to enjoy without prying eyes.

Behind her, the center's director emerges from the building, walking at a brisk pace toward my truck. She's a big woman, much taller than Savannah with large bone structure and muscular build. She keeps her blond hair short, letting her natural curls maintain her hairstyle for her. She motions for me to roll down my window before she even reaches the truck.

"Good afternoon, Miss Linda. How are you?"

"You know you're not allowed to be here."

Well, hello to you too.

"Actually, I am allowed to be here, and we've already covered this." I flash my badge, showing I'm a federal agent and officer of the law, and follow it up with an intentional smirk.

"Maybe you should just find somewhere else to park and wait for Savannah, or she could drive herself. It's not as if she needs a babysitter or hand-holding. Your sitting out here in your truck day after day may cause others to park here. We don't want anyone loitering around the building where women and children are hiding from estranged spouses."

"I'm not loitering, Linda. And my truck doesn't draw attention any more than your car parked right over there does. As far as Savannah driving herself, she's not my prisoner by any means, if that's what you're insinuating. She's a grown woman who can make up her own mind, go where she wants to go, and do whatever she wants to do. For reasons I'm not at liberty to discuss with you, I'm giving her a ride back and forth for the time being."

Linda purses her lips, clearly not happy with not having the last word in our battle of wills. If she thinks for one second she's entitled to boss me around, she has another think coming. She turns and walks away, her shoes smacking the ground with annoyance with every step. Savannah and I cut our eyes at each other before busting out in laughter.

"Hello, darlin'. How was your day?"

"It was good until the last few minutes. I made a new friend today. Hopefully you'll be able to meet her soon. She's really sweet."

After helping Savannah into the truck, I slide back behind the wheel and start to drive. "That'd be great. So, she's a resident there?"

"Yes. Her name is Miranda Petrovio, and she's hiding from an abusive ex. She said they were never married, but that didn't stop him from trying to own her. He's apparently a really bad man, even worse than Butch. She's still too scared to say much about him, even to me, and she's extra careful around windows. Makes me wonder if I'm not being careful enough. I mean, I know I live on the fifth floor, but I don't have blackout curtains and thick fabric shades. When I leave any building, I look around to see if he's waiting there, but I do go out and live my life."

"You never know what Miranda has been through or how he's brainwashed her. It'll take time to deprogram her mind from the abuse. You know I want you to be careful, but not to the point where you're a shut-in. That's no kind of life for anyone."

"Remember last night when you mentioned taking me to the shooting range and teaching me a few things?"

"Sure do."

"Maybe we can take her with us one time. I thought maybe it would be good for her to get out with people who will look after her and teach her self-defense at the same time."

"Maybe. Let's see if she'll even meet me first." And from there, I can make a judgment call on whether it'd be a good idea. Reading people is part of my job, and I'd definitely want a good read on her before I put a gun in the hands of a total stranger, especially around Savannah. "Tomorrow night, do you want to stay at your place or mine?"

"What's special about tomorrow night?"

"We're moving forward with the plan to nab Butch. It's time to get him off the streets and off your back."

"Let's stay at my place, then, and put the extra security measures to work. We can even hit the panic button and seal all the windows and the bedroom door. No one in or out until I unlock it."

"Darlin', I'm fine with staying there if it makes you feel safer. But we'll have to do without the panic-room setting. Besides, I was hoping you'd let me have another go at him."

She laughs, though there's little humor in it. "Oh, I know you'd love that. But I'd probably be a nervous wreck."

"You know, your lack of faith in my skills is a little insulting. I've manhandled him twice now without a single scratch on me. What makes you think he could take me in a fight?"

"It's not that, Nick. He doesn't hold a candle to you in any way. But he also wouldn't hesitate to kill you if he had the chance. He has no conscience and has no issue with fighting dirty. He didn't see you coming the other times, but if this goes south tomorrow night, he'll be the one coming for you. And coming for blood in any way he can get it. So it's more that I know how evil he really is, and I don't want to risk losing you."

"I know exactly what kind of man he is, and he doesn't scare me, babe. But for your peace of mind, we'll stay at your place. Anywhere I'm with you is fine with me."

I finish telling her the details of our sting opera-

tion and the part she'll play. The *only* part she'll play
—drive her car to the hospital with Spencer tailing
her, watching her every move. Then she'll walk inside,
where I'll be waiting to escort her right back outside
and whisk her away to safety with me.

"Are you saying I'll be your prisoner?" she asks
teasingly, throwing my words to Linda back at me.

"Nope. We're going to your condo. I'll be yours."

"Oh, I really like the sound of that."

"We're going to my place right now because it's
closer. There are some sounds I really like to hear you
make, too. Very loud sounds that piss off the
neighbors."

"Have I mentioned 'Undercover Lover' is now my
favorite?"

My lead foot presses harder on the gas, speeding
through the streets and swerving around cars moving
too slowly. I can't wait to get her home.

CHAPTER 15

Savannah

*D*riving to the hospital again after what seems like a long time away feels surreal. Before the last couple of weeks with Nick, the Metro was my primary means of transportation. Now that I know what's hiding in my car, I sort of wish I were back on the subway train instead. But this is the plan to arrest Butch once and for all. Spencer lags several cars behind me, leaving enough space to avoid being spotted.

My eyes keep darting to my rearview mirror all on their own, watching for a big, burly man on a motorcycle to come roaring up beside me.

So far, so good.

When I reach the hospital, I park in my usual spot and take my time gathering my coat and bag before

exiting the car. I'm trying my hardest to do everything as ordinarily as possible in case I'm being
watched. It's a strange feeling, wondering if someone
is right behind me, waiting to harm me. Or worse.
Then I feel him before I see him. I feel his eyes on me
and his strength flowing toward me.

Nick is hiding just inside the hospital doors,
waiting for me to join him, watching me with his
eagle eyes as I make my way across the parking lot.
He's barely visible to me, but I know it's him, and that
gives me courage to keep moving. He gave me tips
before we left his place to help me act and react
normally, rather than trying to focus on being
normal. I'm not sure his tips sank in, though, because
I feel very obvious. Then I see him smile at me and
nod his head, and I feel better about…walking
normally.

I've mastered walking. Go me.

I bite my lip to keep from laughing out loud at
myself.

Once I'm inside the hospital and away from the
glass doors, Nick folds his arms around me, pulling
me into the familiar warmth of his chest, and I melt
into him. The sandalwood scent of his cologne
envelops me as much as his embrace does, reminding
me of the day we met in the coffee shop. Even
though only a couple of months have passed since
that day, the changes I've embraced have made me a
different person. I'm not a former soldier like Nick,

ready to take on an entire motorcycle gang with my bare hands. But I'm not the trampled-down delicate flower I once was either.

Volunteering in the crisis center has opened my eyes to a lot of facts I never considered before. When those women feel beaten down or foolish for putting up with the shit they tolerated for years, I point out how strong they were for leaving when they thought they had nowhere else to go. When they are ashamed for allowing their kids to see the environment they endured, I remind them of how they fled with the clothes on their backs and nothing else, just so their children would have a better life one day.

Those women helped me realize how the changes I implemented in my own life have made me a stronger person. The mirror they put in front of my face doesn't show the hollow-eyed, scared woman I used to see. Not that I want to run into Butch in a dark alley or anything stupid like that. But his threats and taunts won't keep me under his thumb ever again.

"You've been working long enough tonight. How about I take you home now?" Nick leans down and kisses me, making me forget everything else in the process.

"Excellent idea. It has been a long night, and my feet are tired from being on them for so long." I smile up at him, playing along and loving our comfort level with each other.

"By all means, allow me to sweep you off your feet then, my love."

"Trust me, you already have, Nick."

Once I'm securely tucked into his truck, he drives back to my condo where the extreme security system awaits. Maybe the extra measures are overkill with a highly trained DEA agent locked inside with me, but I haven't quite reached the point where I'm comfortable with completely throwing caution to the wind yet.

Thankfully, Nick knows how to pick his battles, and this isn't one of them.

Nick puts his cell phone in the dash holder and sends the phone call through the truck's speakers. "Everyone on the line?"

Silas, Roman, Spencer, and Brad all respond to let Nick know the conferencing worked.

"Talk to me, Spence. Did she have a tail on her?"

"No sign of Butch on his motorcycle, but I did identify a car following her from her building to the hospital."

"There's a woman inside the car, no sign of anyone else with her. She's circling the parking lot for the third time now since Savannah walked inside," Brad adds.

"What make and model car is she driving?"

"It's a black Honda CR-V. Older model, around 2001. She's parking now. Let's see if she gets out."

The silence on the line kills me as we all hold our

collective breaths, waiting to see what move the mystery woman will make.

"She's wearing a cut with a Devil's Dominion rocker panel and 'Property of' patch. She's not very bright, wearing such easily identifiable clothing while picking up enough heroin to send her to jail for life for intent to distribute." I can just see Roman shaking his head as he speaks. "She's circling the car, trying a little too hard to be nonchalant. She has no idea what she's doing."

"And yet, she's doing it for Butch anyway. He doesn't care if she gets sent to prison for life or some rival drug dealer offs her in the parking lot. As long as he gets his stash and saves his own neck, no one else matters." Nick's fingers curl around the steering wheel, his knuckles turning white from the tight grip he has on it. "I've seen it too many times over the last couple of years. That P.O. patch means nothing when it comes down to choosing between the woman and the money. It's always the money for them."

Staring at Nick, I realize how true his words are and how he's the complete opposite. No amount of money would buy his allegiance or replace who he loves. He would give up everything else in his life for the sake of love and honor.

"She's going for it. She's on the ground, working her way under the wheel well to find the package. Once she has it, she'll take it back to Butch, and we'll have his exact location no matter what hole he

slithers into. They won't find the tracker for a while."
Brad's proud of his contributions, and I have to agree
I'm infinitely appreciative of his work.

"And now she's on the move with it. Silas, you got
her?" Roman asks.

"Absolutely. Stay on your toes, men. The game is
afoot."

I'm thankful to have the package of heroin out of
my car, but now I have so many questions. Without a
doubt, the answers will haunt me. I reach up and hit
the mute button on his phone.

"Nick, she knew exactly where to look, didn't
she?"

"Sounds like it, darlin'."

"So, this isn't the first time he's hidden drugs
somewhere in my car and let me transport them for
him." I don't even have to phrase it as a question.
The truth has already sucker-punched me in the gut.

"No, babe. In my experience, you were trans-
porting drugs for him every time he made you go
somewhere with him or told you to meet him out.
There's a reason why you always had to drive your
car and never ride on his bike. Every biker's old lady I
knew while undercover rode with their man and
proudly wore the 'Property of' patch on their back."
He glances over at me, gauging my reaction.

"All these years, I've worked my ass off to save
people's lives...and he used me to move drugs that
will kill them. Had I been caught with them, I

would've lost everything—my nursing license, my job, my apartment, my car, my freedom—and I wouldn't have had a clue until it was too late."

Nick nods, understanding my inner turmoil all too well, but also knowing words won't really comfort me right now.

"Nick?"

"Yeah, babe?"

"Can I shoot him when we catch him? It would save us a lot of trouble in the long run and save the taxpayers a lot of money on the trial."

"As much as I want to give you everything you want, you know I can't agree to that, darlin'."

"I know… I probably wouldn't be able to pull the trigger either. But it felt good to say it anyway."

Nick laughs and nods. "I'm sure it did. Almost as good as it felt hearing you say it, I bet."

"She's heading south, getting on the interstate." Silas's voice breaks the silence in the cab, bringing my thoughts back to the task in front of us. "Twenty dollars says she heads to Washington Highlands. He probably found a vacant rowhouse to assert squatter's rights in."

"Or he's taken over her house and lets her do all the work for him. What a man." Roman sounds as if he'd like to shoot Butch himself. He'll have to get in line.

We arrive at my building, and Nick takes the call off speaker until we reach my door. Once inside, he hits the speaker button again and puts the phone on the counter. Silas is still following her, changing lanes and taking exits only to get right back on the interstate. He's singing along with the radio as he drives and occasionally interrupts the song, giving a full description of his every move. The comic relief is just that—relief, in this very stressful situation.

"Everyone owes me twenty dollars when I get back. We're exiting the interstate and heading straight to Atlantic Street, Southeast. I called it."

Everyone hurls insults at Silas, telling him he's full of shit if he thinks he's getting any money from anyone. I can't help but laugh at the brotherhood and camaraderie these men have. Silas parks a couple of blocks away from where the Honda CR-V stops at a rowhouse, also called by Silas. The woman looks around nervously before darting inside with the package tucked under her arm.

We disconnect when Silas says he'll call back when there's something to report. After a couple of hours, the phone rings, and I nearly jump out of my seat.

"Talk to me, man," Nick says when he answers the phone.

"Our boy Butch is here. Do you want me to snuff him out now so we can call it a night?"

"What the hell is it with you CIA guys? When I worked with Shadow, he wanted to kill everyone too."

"It's just cleaner that way, Nick. No offense to anyone."

I'm still not really sure if Silas is kidding or not when he says things like this. If I had to guess, I'd say he's serious. Deadly serious.

"We need to arrest him, Silas."

"Yeah, well, that may be your agency's stance, but it's not mine. I don't have the authority to arrest him. But I do have other skills that will come in very handy should you change your mind. He's here with a group of his biker buddies, all piled up in a small, run-down rowhouse. From the records search, looks like the woman owns it and they all just moved in on her. So what's the plan now that you won't let me just take them all out at once and be done with it?"

"Leave it. When he starts cutting that heroin, he'll come find us. I want to nail him to the wall on more than just an intent to distribute charge. I want to make sure he never steps foot outside of a prison again."

"And which charge do you think would do that?"

"The premeditated attempted murder of a federal agent, for starters."

CHAPTER 16

Savannah

ick's words send shivers down my spine, and I'm pretty sure my heart just stopped beating. "What did you do?"

"Technically, I didn't do it. Tim did. But the gist is, Tim took the real heroin and replaced it with a look-alike substance. Once Butch realizes it's fake, and it won't take him long, he'll know it was me, and he'll come for his real heroin. He's on the line for a lot of money, and he's looking to make a lot more considering how much they hid in your car. He'll cut other substances into it and make the stash at least three times bigger."

"How about that? You do have a devious side. I never would've thought it, Nick. Learn something new every day." Silas chuckles on the line, but I don't find anything funny about the situation.

"Thanks for your help, Silas. Stay close—I'm sure you'll hear from me again soon."

"You got it, brother. I won't be far away. Call anytime."

Nick pockets his phone while keeping his intense gaze on me. "You have that worried expression on your face again."

"Maybe I'm just not used to what you do for a living. I know you've been in much more danger than this before. Doesn't mean I have to like it."

"Can't say I'd react any differently if our roles were reversed. Don't even give it another thought. I'll be fine, and several very good men have my back."

Nick's phone chimes with an incoming text, so he glances at the screen. "Roman just parked your car in the garage. I'll go meet him to get your keys back."

"For the record, I know you're only doing that so you can change the subject when you get back."

"Ah hell, I was hoping it'd take you longer than a few weeks to figure out my tricks."

"Yeah. No."

He walks out into the hallway laughing, leaving me standing here alone with a gigantic smile on my face.

I love that man.

He's back just as quickly as he left, and I realize

that I didn't rush to lock the door behind him. For the first time in years, it slipped my mind.

"Your car is safely parked back in the garage under the building. Now, we wait."

The next few days pass by without incident. Although Nick was surprised Butch hadn't made a move yet, he also wasn't alarmed. Then Nick received a call neither of us expected, and most of the bravado I'd built up immediately evaporated.

"I'm afraid I have some potentially upsetting news, darlin'."

I stop what I'm doing and give him my full attention. "What is it?"

"My director called and said it's time for me to come back to work. They think it sends a better message if I'm on the job when the trial kicks off next week. I'd hoped to extend my time off until Butch is out of the way, but unless he makes a move this weekend, that's not going to happen."

"Well, we knew that was a possibility. You can't take off forever. Although, it would be nice to be independently wealthy and never have to work again, wouldn't it?"

"Let's keep playing the lottery. Maybe we'll win and retire to our own private island one day."

We settle on the couch, cuddling and watching TV, when the news shows pictures of Nick and me again. Their love affair with him is long over, and they spout his crimes while he was undercover every chance they get. The gang members Nick knew are next up on the screen, claiming entrapment and accusing Nick of ordering them to commit the crimes they're accused of, as if he were the president of the club instead of Bobby Blalock.

"It's pretty obvious why Calvin wants me back now. My absence makes me look guilty." He sounds so gloomy, like he lost his best friend.

"Hey." I turn to face him. "There's nothing we can't get through together. You've been my rock since day one, before I even realized it. You saved me when I wasn't able to save myself. Now let me be your rock. When you feel like everything is at its worst, think about how much I love you. That's one thing you'll never question or doubt."

Gravity draws me to him with the force of colliding stars, the same stars that burst behind my eyelids when his lips press against mine. With a single stroke of his tongue across mine, I'm pulled under his splendid spell, never to be released again. An immediate urgency consumes us as the excitement low in my belly grows. Butterflies flutter in my chest, threatening to bubble up out of my throat at any second.

Summoning my inner strength, the last of my reserves, I break our kiss to look deeply into Nick's eyes, conveying my message without saying a word. At first, there's a slight hint of confusion in his expression, but it quickly changes to understanding. And anticipation.

"You're sure?"

"Positive."

"I don't want to hurt you, darlin'. I know your broken ribs are still painful."

"Then make love to me slow and easy, Nick. But when you take me, know that you take all of me. All my love. All my heart. Don't break it."

"That is one thing you'll never have to worry about, darlin'. I'd never break your heart."

Moving down the hall on cloud nine, my feet never touching the floor, I'm back in his embrace the second we step into my bedroom. Sensual kisses on my neck heighten my eagerness. Smoldering licks of his tongue increase my impatience. Then our souls connect, and the final missing link is fused inside us, a bond we created that will never be broken.

The sweat drips off his brow as he holds my gaze, and I let him see all of me. All my insecurities. My inner questions. With every move and every breath and every expression, I show him how much I love him and need him and want him. When the dams break and my heart is laid bare to him, I see in his eyes the same love that has consumed me. As I call out his name and every muscle in his body tenses, the only thought I have in my mind is that this incredible man loves me as much as I love him.

He'll be here tomorrow...the same as he is

tonight. He'll stand beside me, no matter what troubles and trials the future brings. He'll be my best friend and my lover and my world. But more than that, I'll be his too. Equals in love. Partners in life. Soul mates forever. As we descend from the highest high, spiraling toward the bottom below, I don't fear the fall. Nick will be there to catch me because he's falling with me.

"Did I hurt you, darlin'?" He strokes one cheek with his thumb and leaves sweet kisses on the other.

"No, babe, you didn't hurt me at all. I've never felt as amazing as I do right now."

"I love you, Savannah."

"I love you too, my undercover lover."

He chuckles in the dark, then silence overtakes us, and we fall asleep in each other's arms. Completely happy. Completely in love. Completely complete.

Now that the soreness in my body is improving day by day, I have so much more energy, and I'm ready to dive back into life headfirst. Nick and I spend the weekend together, strolling the electric streets of the Adams Morgan neighborhood of DC. One of the rooftop bars draws our attention Saturday evening, so we climb the stairs, and the hostess seats us under an outdoor heater. Between the heat radiating from above us and the way we're completely bundled up in parkas and hats, we're able to enjoy the sights and scenes of this popular area. Add the free-flowing alcohol, and I'm feeling no cold and no pain after a couple of drinks.

Music plays through the outdoor speakers, loud enough to enjoy but not enough to distract our conversation. Nick and I spend hours, talking, drinking, and munching on appetizers—simply sharing our entire life stories. Funny childhood stories. Embarrassing teenage tales. He tells me about some of his cases he worked before going undercover. I share stories of some of my more interesting emergency room patients. For the hours we spend on the rooftop just talking and laughing, I completely forget about anything else.

Nick pays our tab and we leave the bar, walking home since it's not far and plenty of people are still milling around. Restaurants and trendy bars are abundant in this neighborhood—and it's always been relatively safe. Still, I'm hugged up to Nick as we walk, my arm around his waist and my body pressed against him while his arm wraps around me. Without warning, he stops walking and pushes me until my back is against a tree. The bare limbs jut out above us, covered with tiny white lights like stars twinkling in the night skies.

His lips gently caress the sensitive skin of my neck, from my ear to my collarbone and back again. Then he moves to the other side and repeats his ministrations. Even in this cold air, my body is heating to the boiling point. I can see my breath hanging in the air like small puffs of smoke escaping from my overheating core. This is pure heaven and hell…and I wouldn't change it for anything in the world.

When he moves back up to my ear and whispers to me, the cold instantly seeps into my every pore, and pure terror replaces all other sensations.

"We're being followed, darlin'. I'm not sure who it is yet, but I don't think it's Butch. Stay close to me. If I tell you to run, get inside a restaurant or a bar and call the police. Do you understand?"

I nod robotically. "Yes."

"That's my girl. Let's just walk casually. They've been watching us for a while and haven't tried to approach us. That tells me they're tailing us to find out where I live, probably tied to the case somehow. But I'm not taking any chances with your safety to find out who they are."

We start walking again for a few steps before a taxi passes us. Nick flags it down, and we dash into the back seat, heading in the opposite direction of the men following us. When we drive by, Nick gets a good look at their faces, shock and annoyance clear in their expressions.

"Where to?" the cabbie asks.

Nick gives my address, and we ride the rest of the way in silence. Nick, in quiet retrospection. Me, in complete terror. Who would be following us if not Butch?

Late night activities led to sleeping in Sunday

morning. After brunch, we spend the rest of the day lounging in my condo, purposely doing nothing more than spending time together. We venture out of bed once or twice, making refueling runs to the refrigerator or the door for delivery. Nick takes his time worshiping my body and making me feel cherished. My ribs only hurt now when touched, but he's still extra careful to avoid doing anything that would cause me pain. But he makes sure he does anything and everything needed for my pleasure. My body is spent, and a smile is permanently affixed to my face now. Not that I'm complaining. Late Sunday night, Nick leaves for his apartment, knowing he has to be at work early in the morning.

My condo is too quiet without him here, but I'll survive. I always do somehow. Sleep finally overtakes me, and I wake to the chiming of my alarm clock. I'm volunteering early at the crisis center this week. Most of my time is spent on the phones, helping convince battered women to flee to safety. But since I've been on the mend, I've spent more time restocking the residents' rooms with soap, shampoo, and towels. While it may sound as if I'm little more than a maid, the benefits I reap from it are so much more valuable to me.

Miranda is quickly becoming a friend I desperately want to help. In the short time since I met her, she has opened up to me more than anyone else at the center. She hasn't shared much about her life before, but I do know she was treated more like property than a person. Her ex was a cruel man who enjoyed demeaning her in front of others. Because of the humiliation he subjected her to, she finds it difficult to look others in the eye.

But she's opening up to me, and it's a beautiful thing.

When I walk into the center, Linda is reprimanding one of the staff members for allowing her boyfriend to drop her off at work. The younger girl, Patty, counters, saying she wouldn't be able to show up for work at all without a ride, but Linda isn't having it. I understand both of their points all too well. Working in the emergency room, I have no choice but to show up for work, even during inclement weather, whether I have reliable transportation or not.

"If you need a ride tomorrow, call me. I don't mind swinging by to get you or coming in earlier." I smile at Patty as I walk around them.

"Thank you, Savannah. If you're sure you don't mind, I may have to do that."

"I don't mind at all."

I start making my rounds—as a nurse, I can't think of it any other way, it seems—and refill the used goods in each resident's room. When I reach Miranda's room, she's chewing on her thumbnail and pacing the floor. Her eyes are cast down, staring at the floor as she walks back and forth, and she hasn't noticed my presence in her room yet.

"Miranda, are you okay? What's wrong?"

"One of my friends was killed. I just found out." She stops in her tracks and looks up at me, her eyes haunted. "I will kill myself before I let him take me back to hell."

CHAPTER 17

Savannah

"Miranda, don't say that. I'm so sorry about your friend, and I wish I could help take away that pain. But you're safe here. He doesn't know where you are. Even if he somehow finds you, I won't let him take you anywhere."

She drops her hand from her mouth and rushes to me, throwing her arms around my neck and squeezing. Her voice quivers almost as much as her body shakes. "Thank you for saying that, Savannah. You're the only friend I have left in the world now."

"Even if that's true, you still have me." I write down my cell phone number and my address for her, telling her to call anytime she needs me. "And if you ever need to run from here, run to me. You know, Nick did the same for me. He gave me his address after he witnessed

Butch harassing me, and I had to use it. I showed up at his place out of the blue, beat-up and bringing trouble with me. Not once has he ever made me feel like a burden to him. And you're not one to me either."

She wipes tears from her eyes as she turns away from me. "I think he murdered my friend to try to find out where I am. I couldn't put you in that kind of danger."

"If that's true, then you need to call me before anyone else if you feel you're in danger. Nick just upgraded my apartment with state-of-the-art security. He wouldn't be able to get in to hurt either of us, trust me. If I found out he hurt you when I could've helped, that would kill me, Miranda."

She nods, even though she's not fully ready to commit yet. "Okay, you win. Thank you again, Savannah."

Right now, she doesn't want to appear ungrateful, so she agrees. But if push comes to shove, at least she knows where she can escape to safety. If she'll only swallow her pride and let me help.

"Do you want to talk about your friend? Is there anything I can do to help?"

"Believe me, you're already helping. I appreciate you more than you know. I really need time to process everything, though. I found out about it just before you got here, so my head really isn't on straight right now."

"I completely understand. If you need to talk later, you know how to reach me." I hug her before continuing on to the next room, but she stays on my mind the rest of the day. Unable to attend a friend's funeral out of fear her ex will find her, on top of suspecting that same man murdered a close friend in a desperate attempt to find her.

That has to be pure torture. I couldn't imagine being kept away from Karen and Spencer. Miranda has to feel utterly and totally alone in the world right now. I know all too well people have multiple facets to their personalities, but she has been nothing but sweet to me since the day I met her. My heart breaks for her.

As I make my way toward the front of the large building, pushing my now-empty supply cart, sounds of terrified screaming and angry shouting slow my steps. Something terrible is happening, and all the women and children are panicking.

"I said shut the fuck up!" Gunshots ring out, echoing throughout the building and bouncing off the walls.

My feet come to a complete stop, and my lungs freeze in my chest. I feel every shot in my soul, because I know that voice. And I know he won't hesitate to kill every person in this building, woman or child, as long as he gets what he wants.

And what he wants is me.

"Savannah, what's going on?" Miranda steals up beside me, making me nearly jump out of my skin.

"My ex is here. He followed me somehow." I think for a second, trying to figure out what to do. I hand Miranda my unlocked cell phone. "Call Nick Tucker. Tell him Butch is here and what's going on. I'm going outside to draw Butch away from everyone. As soon as he steps out the door, pull the emergency alarm and lock down the facility."

"Savannah, you can't do that! He'll kill you!" The fear on Miranda's face mirrors my own, but I can't put an entire building full of women and children at risk when they've already given up everything they had for a modicum of safety.

"I'm so scared I can't think straight, Miranda. But I do know one thing. I can't live with the death of innocent people on my conscience. The other people here shouldn't have to suffer because of me. Please call Nick, right now. Tell him I said to hurry...and that I love him."

With brisk steps, I move to the emergency exit and push the bar, setting off the alarm. At this point, I'm betting we need all the help we can get, as fast as we can get it. The alarm will alert the monitoring company, who will call to verify there's an actual emergency. When no one from the center answers, they'll dispatch our local fire department and police units as a precaution. While the response time won't be terrible, it's also not immediate, but it's all I have at the moment.

Moving around the side of the building, I make my way to the very front parking lot. The building is close enough to the road to draw more attention from passersby. Anything that could possibly help. When I reach the end of the line, I stand frozen in my spot, shaking from head to toe. My hands are cold, my mouth is dry, and I'm second-guessing my decision with every second that ticks by.

Then I realize the building is eerily quiet.

The alarm is off.

There's no screaming coming from inside.

Dear God. What has he done?

"Butch! I'm out here! Come out here and face me like a man!" I scream at him as loud as I can. The force exerted against my ribs sends shock waves of pain through my body, threatening to bring me to my knees, but I push the swells of nausea aside. I can't focus on that right now.

He steps to the front door, smiling at me with an evil grin that sends cold chills up and down my spine. "Well, I'm here, you fucking bitch. What are you going to do now?"

Before I can answer, he jerks a child from behind him and presses the barrel of the gun to the young boy's head.

"Nice fucking try by pulling the alarm, you whore. You must be even stupider than I thought you were. One call from the alarm company and I killed that shit on the spot. If any of those stupid whores inside suddenly tries to get smart, little Jamal here will pay the price. So, let me tell you the same thing—get your stupid fat ass inside right now, or I'll shoot him in the fucking head right in front of you."

I didn't account for this scenario at all. In my mind, he left everyone else alone and just came after me. After all, that's what he wants, right?

"Now!" His screamed command jolts me from my inner turmoil, making my feet move toward him independently of all conscious thought.

When I get close enough to him, he pushes Jamal back inside then grabs my arm, jerking me as hard as he can. I scream out in pain, but that only serves to satisfy him even more. He shoves me through the doorway and locks it behind us. Everyone who was unfortunate enough to be in the center is hunkered down in the entertainment room, lined against the wall three deep. Tears stream down every person's face—women and children alike. All the terror they've endured in their lives is conjured in one person.

Butch.

And I brought him here.

"You have me. Let them go."

"Don't you dare try to tell me what to fucking do, bitch. No one is leaving. I'll shoot them all, one by one, right in front of you if you pull that shit again." He walks over to a mother of three and points the gun at her head. "Should I show you right now?"

"No! No. I believe you. I believe you!" I put my hands up in the universal gesture for stop, as if the subliminal message will do any good with him.

"I don't think you do." He swings his arm around, leveling it at Linda, and pulls the trigger. She crumples to the floor, her eyes wide open and fixed in a death stare. The room spins around me as terror-filled screams reverberate off the walls, each one hitting me like a thousand sharp knives.

Butch walks to me, unaffected by his heinous deed, and roughly grabs my face. "Call that under-cover pig you've been fucking and tell him to bring me my shit right now. My real shit. If he shows up here with that fucking talcum powder bullshit, everyone in here will eat a fucking bullet for dinner." He releases me with a snap of his wrist, making my head jerk violently.

"I-I don't have m-my cell phone on me to call him. I n-need a phone." My reply is stammered; I can barely get the words out. I don't want to draw atten-tion to Miranda by telling him I already asked her to call Nick for me. That may be just the excuse he needs to kill her too.

He looks at me with contempt and skepticism. "Who doesn't have their fucking cell phone in their pocket these days?"

I run my hands over my pockets, showing him they're empty. "I'm serious. I don't have it with me."

"Here, Savannah. You can use mine." Miranda stands and extends her hand to me, returning my cell without giving away our prior plan.

My hands shake uncontrollably, but somehow, I manage to dial the phone.

"Put it on speaker, you two-bit whore. I want to hear every word."

"She doesn't need the speaker. You can hear me just fine from right here." Nick steps into the room with his gun drawn and his sights set squarely on Butch's chest. His eyes drop to Linda's lifeless body lying on the floor, and I know his hatred for Butch has surpassed his previous contempt.

I end the call and slip my cell back into Miranda's hand before giving her a slight push toward her place in the crowd of people crouched on the floor. Out of sight, out of mind is my hope. There's little chance I'll come out of this unscathed. Knowing Butch's savagery, I shudder to think what he'll do just to inflict pain on me. My biggest fear at the moment is he'll use Nick for that very purpose.

But seeing Nick in action, completely at ease in his element, makes me think we may all have a chance to walk away.

"Well, well, well, if it isn't the undercover pig himself. You got balls showing up here like this. Alone. Thinking you can just waltz in here and take over because you wear a fucking badge. We all know you're just as bad as any so-called criminal you arrest. You were one of us—that means you did every dirty little deed we did. And now you're a fucking rat pig, so that makes you even worse."

"I know exactly who and what I am, Bitch. I'm a DEA Special Agent. I was undercover to stop a bunch of badass wannabes who didn't have the guts or brains to make it on his own. You're a pathetic loser and you know it. When you leave here today, it'll be in either handcuffs or a body bag. When I leave, it'll be in my nice vehicle, going back to my nice home, and lying in bed next to my fine girlfriend. Now drop your fucking gun before I put a hole in your chest big enough to drive my truck through."

Butch smirks and my blood runs cold.

"You put your gun down…or I'll blow her fucking head off right here, right now. Do you want to see her brains? I bet they're as pretty as she is." Another Devil steps out from behind the open door, giving up his hiding place behind me. The cold metal of his gun digs into my temple while his rough hand squeezes my neck. "Maybe I'll fuck her first and let you watch. Hard decision."

Tears well up in my eyes. Hope is fleeting, and I can feel every ounce of it draining from my body. I trust Nick, but two against one, using me as leverage, is a no-win scenario. A sudden, loud crash behind me makes me jump. A split second later, I'm on the floor in the middle of flailing arms and legs. When I finally work free of the tangled limbs, I'm beyond relieved to see Silas has the other Devil in a full-body lock, sporting a wide grin on his face.

"Are you okay, Savannah?" Silas asks. All I can do is nod. I think I'm okay. "Good. Be with you in just a second. Let me help this troubled young man go to sleep."

Glancing over at Nick, I see he's engaged in a brawl with Butch, taking out his frustrations on him one punch at a time. Butch staggers backward and Nick follows, delivering one punishing blow after the other. As I watch Nick in action, the thought crosses my mind that he could easily knock Butch out with a single punch, but he's enjoying beating the shit out of him too much to do that. When Butch falls flat on his ass, Nick stands over him and reads him his rights.

Nick reaches to grab his handcuffs, but they're on the ground a few feet away after falling out during their brawl. One of the ladies huddled nearby crawls toward them and pushes them across the tile floor. When Nick reaches to grab them, Butch capitalizes on Nick's off-balance position to push free and run. Nick jumps to his feet, fast on Butch's tail. In the blink of an eye, I take off running after Nick.

"Savannah, no!" I hear Miranda scream as I run, but the words don't register. I know Butch. He'll kill Nick first, then he'll come back and kill the rest of us.

When I burst through the front door of the building, Nick and Butch are squared off against each other again. Nick has his gun drawn, cars are stopped on the side of the road, and the onlookers all have their phones trained on the men. Instead of calling for help, they're videoing the showdown happening in the parking lot.

"You're just in time, little whore." Butch's gaze swings from me to Nick just before he draws a gun from the side of his motorcycle. "Say goodbye to your double-crossing pig. I hope he fucked your brains out last night…because it'll be his last time."

CHAPTER 18

Nick

*A*n ugly sneer crosses his face then he pulls the trigger.

The painful scream that follows turns my blood to ice and stills my heart. He never intended to shoot me —Savannah was always his target.

And that bullet found its mark.

The thumping rumble of a motorcycle leaving the scene registers in the back of my mind as I rush to her side, holstering my gun and withdrawing my cell to call an ambulance. Blood is already pooling on the ground underneath her. Dark blood, almost black, covers her abdomen. In a matter of seconds, she goes from loud, shrill screams of pain to low, quiet whimpers.

She's already lost a lot of blood.

I rip her shirt open and wipe away the blood covering her skin, trying to find the wound so I can apply pressure and slow the loss. When I finally locate the hole, she's even quieter than just seconds before.

"No, Savannah! No! You hold on. Do you hear me? Don't you dare fucking give up on me now!" I jerk my shirt off my back and use it to put pressure on the wound.

The plethora of sirens from police, EMS, and Fire/Rescue vehicles coming from behind me bring little relief with them. The entry hole is low in her abdomen…lower, in her pelvic region. The internal damage a bullet does in that region is catastrophic. I've been in this line of work long enough to know that without a confirmation from a doctor. The ride to the hospital will be the longest ride of our lives.

Multiple sets of tires screech to a halt, and a host of men and women descend on us from every side, hauling every piece of medical equipment they have. I'm pushed out of the way to make room for all the emergency procedures they need to perform to try to save her life. I pray it's enough to keep her going until they can get her into the operating room.

The paramedic calls out her stats before issuing medical directives to the others, letting them know what he's doing and what he expects them to do. I hear terms like bilateral IVs with fluid bolus, run them wide open, and hypotensive. I know enough to understand none of that equals good news about her condition.

"This will be a load and go. Get those bilateral lines in right now. Let's move fast, ladies and gents." The paramedic in charge points to two EMTs then down to Savannah's hands.

"What's her name?" The paramedic swings his gaze to me, and it's then that I realize I've dropped to my knees at her head.

"Savannah Fields." I'm running on autopilot. I have no idea how I even answered him with a coherent response. If asked, I couldn't even tell him my own name at this very moment.

"Hey dear, can you tell me your name?" His voice is loud, nearly shouting at her, and he rubs her shoulder to get her attention.

When she moans in response, my heart nearly leaps out of my chest. "Savannah."

"Savannah, do you know what today is?"

She answers correctly while the flurry of activity continues around her.

"Do you remember what happened to you?" The paramedic continues to ask questions, but I think he's checking her mental status more than anything. He's already performed a rapid medical assessment on the rest of her body.

"Shot." Her voice is weak, but I thank God it's there at all. Her sweet voice is music to my ears.

He looks up at me again. "Do you have any idea what caliber bullet hit her?"

"Yeah, he had a 9mm." The paramedic nods before signaling the rest of the team to wrap it up.

"We're taking you to the hospital now, dear. You'll feel a lot of hands moving you onto the gurney then we'll load you into the back of the ambulance. I'll be back there with you the whole time." The paramedic asks which hospital she prefers, so I give him the name of the one where she works and assure her that I'll be right behind the ambulance until I'm by her side again.

Only minutes after arriving, the ambulance takes off, running lights and sirens at breakneck speed out of the area. The fire and rescue crews are still on the scene, picking up discarded medical supplies and plastic wrappings. The police canvass the scene, writing up reports of the shooting and gathering information from eyewitnesses. A young rookie cop calls out to me to stop when I jog toward my truck.

"Hold up. We need to talk to you about what happened here." The young buck puffs out his chest and gives me his practiced stern expression.

"Ask all you want—at the fucking hospital, you moron. I'm not standing here one more second with you while she's fighting for her life."

He yells at me again when I turn to leave, but I ignore his commands. I hear a familiar voice tell him to let me go. When I glance over my shoulder as I slide into my truck, I see Spencer taking charge of the scene. He nods at me, knowing there's no stopping me, and he wouldn't try to anyway. I grab an extra shirt from my gym bag in the back seat and quickly pull it over my head before throwing the truck into gear.

Red lights and stop signs are all one big blur on my way to the emergency room. My lead foot lets me catch up with the ambulance before they even pull it into the emergency bay. By the time they're unloading her, I've already parked and run to the double doors to walk in with them. There's no way anyone can make me stay in the waiting room and leave her back here alone. My badge comes in handy when my presence is questioned—it gets me out of speaking at all. They just nod and keep working. As long as I'm not a psycho civilian, I'm allowed to wait here, out of their way.

Watch and wait.

The emergency room doctor orders X-rays and imaging immediately, telling the staff to clear the way for Savannah—"stat." Then he instructs another nurse to page the specialist in female pelvic medicine and reconstructive surgery for an immediate and urgent consult. Two nurses wheel Savannah by me on the way to radiology. Her skin is pale, and her breathing is slow. Tubes are attached to each arm, and an oxygen mask covers her nose and mouth. Bags of IV solution hang above her head as do bags of blood. Wires snake out from the blanket covering her, and my eyes follow them to the heart monitor. I'm not a doctor, but I know a fast heartbeat and a low blood pressure are not good signs in an emergency situation. But as long as that heart monitor records a beating heart, my heart will keep beating too.

The logical part of me knows she's only been away for mere minutes, but it feels like an eternity. I pace back and forth in front of her room in the emergency department, straining my ears to catch any word of her condition. She's lost so much blood. They have to get her into surgery immediately and fix her.

Don't they?

"Nick!" A frantic voice yells my name from behind me. I whirl around to find Karen rushing toward me. "What have they said?"

"I don't know anything yet." I relay the bits and pieces I've picked up while stalking outside the door. The color drains from her face.

"You're sure they said to page the reconstructive surgeon?"

"Yeah. That's not a title I'd know without hearing it first. Why? What does that mean?"

"That's Dr. Jeff Smith. He's a brilliant surgeon, but he's only called in on the very worst cases. The ones other doctors don't want to attempt because of the complexity and bad odds. He will definitely help her, but it means the bullet did extensive damage, Nick."

Karen and I talk for a few more minutes while we wait together. This is where Karen works too, so she has access to every bit of information we could possibly need, but she opts to wait and hear it from the doctor with me. She's a good friend, because if I had her access, I'd be on that computer reading every single word.

"Karen, are you here with Savannah?" A tall man wearing a white lab coat approaches us. He's not much older than me, but one glance at the name embroidered over his chest pocket tells me this is the genius surgeon who holds the love of my life's life in his hands. Dr. Jeff Smith.

"Yes, Dr. Jeff. This is Nick, Savannah's…fiancé. You can tell us both—I'll vouch for him."

"Come with me. She'll need your support."

We follow Dr. Smith through several twists and turns in the hallways until we reach doors with bright red no-entry signs and large white AUTHORIZED ADMITTANCE ONLY lettering across them. Behind those secure doors, several people in surgical scrubs are preparing Savannah as quickly as they can.

We reach her bedside, and I place my hand on her arm. Her eyelashes flutter a few times before she opens her eyes to look up at me. I can see and feel her relief, the reassurance she feels from simply knowing I'm here with her.

"Savannah, I've been called in because of the severity of your pelvic trauma. The impact of the bullet has injured your uterus and is causing a lot of bleeding. The damage to your uterus is severe and irreparable. I am uncertain as to the damage to your ovaries. In order to save your life, I have to perform an emergency hysterectomy to remove the uterus. After this surgery, you will never be able to become pregnant. Do you understand what I've just explained to you?"

His tone of voice is kind, but his message is direct. As a federal agent, I understand the need for bluntness. It leaves no room for misunderstanding or confusion. As a man who only wants to protect the woman he loves, the finality of the doctor's words strikes like a knife to my gut.

I wish that bullet had hit me instead.

I should've shot him instead of waiting for him to comply with my commands. He was unarmed and fleeing at first. My training kicked in—I couldn't use lethal force against an unarmed man. Had I merely pulled the trigger, Savannah wouldn't be in this position now and Butch would be dead. I'd gladly pay any price to go back and change my decision now. The strict rules I've followed have now cost me more than I could've ever imagined.

This is all my fault.

Tears stream out of Savannah's eyes like free-flowing waterfalls. Her bottom lip quivers uncontrollably until she pulls it between her teeth to try to stop it. She closes her eyes, but that does nothing to stem the tide of tears falling. She nods her head and weakly whispers her consent to surgery. "I understand, Dr. Jeff."

"We're taking you into the OR immediately. I'll give you a minute or two with your friends, but that's all we can spare." He turns his gaze to me. "The OR nurse will call the surgical waiting room to give you periodic updates during the procedure. Try to make yourself as comfortable as possible. We all have a long night ahead of us."

He claps me on the shoulder as he leaves, a sign of understanding just how devastating this news and this predicament is for all of us. I lean over the side of the bed, being careful not to jar her too much, but I want to be as close to her as I can get.

"Darlin', I'll be right here waiting for you when you get out of surgery. No matter how long it takes or how long I have to wait to see you again. And I'll be by your side, taking care of you every minute of every day afterward. I'm so sorry I didn't get to you in time. I'm so sorry, baby."

She squeezes my arm—not hard, but it's there. I don't know how she has the strength or energy to move at all, but she doesn't respond verbally.

"I love you, Savannah. I loved you yesterday. I

love you today. And I'll love you tomorrow. Nothing can ever change that. I only love you more every day."

Her tears increase again, but she remains quiet. I know what's running through her mind. Her self-esteem has been battered and beaten for years. This blow is too much for her to take. All at the hands of that fucker Butch. When I'm finished with him, he will regret not turning that gun on me instead of her. He has no idea what he just unlocked deep inside of me. No one does. Not yet anyway.

"We have to go now. You can wait just outside those doors in the surgical waiting room. We'll call the phone in there to give you status updates." The OR nurse unlocks the wheels of the bed and takes Savannah away.

Karen wraps her hand around my arm and tugs me toward the direction we came in. "We'll be here for a while, Nick. Let's go find some coffee and the waiting room. She's in good hands. Trust me."

Karen's emergency room training must be running on all cylinders, but my training just flew out the fucking window. I can't think straight for shit. My brain basically just shuts down, allowing Karen to lead me through the hospital corridors until we're seated in a room full of uncomfortable chairs with bad hospital coffee in hand. I don't even remember getting here.

Some undercover hero I turned out to be.

"Nick?"

"Yeah."

"Did you hear a word I just said?"

"No. Sorry."

"I said, she's going to be fine. She has lost a lot of blood, but they got her here fast. She has the best of the best surgeons. She's strong, and she was conscious when we just saw her. All very good signs."

"You're right. They're absolutely good signs that she'll pull through. But she never should've been in this predicament in the first place. She wouldn't have been hurt if it hadn't been for me."

"That's not true at all. She's tried getting away from Butch for years. He has hurt her in so many ways. This is all on him. Not you, Nick."

"I'll lose her after this. She won't see me anymore once she's released from the hospital."

"Why do you say that?"

I think she knows why, from the expression on her face. But in case I don't know everything about Savannah, she wants to reserve the right to reassure me.

"Because one night when we talked about our future, Savannah told me she wanted to have fertility testing done first. She had doubts about her ability to become pregnant and said she wasn't sure she would marry me if that were the case, because she felt like she would be taking an important part of my future away from me. Well, now we know the answer to that question for sure, don't we?"

"You told her it doesn't matter to you, didn't you?"

"Of course, I did. And I meant it. All I need is her for the rest of my life. Everything else is optional."

"Give her some time, Nick. What happened tonight is already a lot to take in, and now she knows she can't have kids in addition to almost being killed. On top of that, she thinks she's letting you down, because that's just her personality. Let her come to terms with the trauma first, then she'll come to terms with you and your acceptance of her—just the way she is. One step at a time and it'll all be okay. Eventually."

"I'm not so sure. She wouldn't even look at me back there once she knew the severity of her injuries. Under normal circumstances, she would've turned to me for comfort. Before Dr. Jeff gave her the news, I felt how much she needed me. After, she wouldn't look at me at all. She's already pulling away from me."

Hours pass with frequent updates from the OR staff.

She's doing well.

Everything is going as planned.

She's tolerating the surgery well. Nothing unexpected.

The surgery is over. They're just finishing up. The doctor will come to the waiting room to talk to you when he's done in here.

She's being moved to recovery. They'll monitor her back there for about an hour. Dr. Smith is on his way to you now.

My nerves are shot, waiting for Dr. Smith to walk into this waiting room. They've already assured us she did fine in surgery. But the specifics about the damage that 9mm bullet caused are what I'm dreading now.

The surgeon finally comes in and pulls up a chair across from us. The expression he wears is serious—all business—but maybe he has to separate his work from his life like I do. Compartmentalize to survive and stay sane.

"Savannah is in recovery now. The surgery took longer than I planned because the internal damage was extensive. I had held out hope to save her uterus going in, but that was not even remotely possible. To stop the bleeding, I had to remove it and close several nicks in her uterine artery. She'll have to stay in the hospital for a while. We'll need to monitor her closely for bleeding and any signs of infection.

"She'll be moved to ICU for close observation over the next several days, but I've left instructions for them to let you two see her for a minute or two. Don't expect more than that, though. The ICU nurses have a lot on their hands and not a lot of extra time. Also, don't expect her to be able to stay awake. She has a pain pump and we've already given her quite a lot of pain medicine, but I know just seeing her will make you feel better. Any questions?"

"Does she know for certain you had to do a hysterectomy?" I hold my breath and wait for the reply I know is coming.

"She knows. She may not remember all the details when she first wakes up, though."

CHAPTER 19

Savannah

The intense stinging slices through me before I even open my eyes. I'm not sure where I am, why I'm here, or what happened to me at the moment. The searing pain makes it hard to concentrate on clearing my foggy brain. When I try to move, my limbs feel extra heavy, almost like dead weights are attached to me.

The faint beeping of the heart monitor and hiss of the oxygen cannula are unmistakable clues, sounds I'm used to hearing on a daily basis. Fighting against the lead weights on my eyelids, I finally pry them open and glace around. The dim room with curtain partitions between the rows of beds and soft lights overhead is all too familiar. I'm in the recovery room at the hospital.

I've had surgery. Major surgery, if my pain level is any indication. All at once, the events come rushing back to me like scenes playing on a movie projector. Butch. Nick. Linda. The family crisis center. The gun hidden in his motorcycle. The crude remarks. The cruel smirk. The blast from the muzzle. Then complete darkness consumed me as Nick screamed for me to hold on.

Dr. Jeff telling me I'll never have children of my own.

Even though I knew that was a possibility before, now it's a certainty beyond the realm of medical intervention. My thoughts are jumbled in a haze of anesthesia and pain medicine, but my heart understands perfectly. Nick's words of reassurance swirl in my head, but that was when the situation was mostly hypothetical—and potentially fixable.

I'm past that point now. Theory has become reality. Tears leak from the corners of my eyes, and I let them flow, falling unchecked to the pillow beneath my head.

"There she is. You sure gave me a scare, Savannah." One of my nurse friends slides up to my side and grasps my hand. Her voice is low and reassuring, but she can't mask the tint of sadness in it. "You're in recovery now, sweetie. You came through the surgery with flying colors. Just rest now. We'll move you out of here in an hour or so."

The click of my pain pump administering the

next dose means I'll be out again in about fifteen seconds or so. The pain in my body and the pain in my soul will disappear into the black abyss, where even dreams can't reach me. My thoughts revert back to Nick just before I slip into a deep sleep, squeezing my heart with a pain that's every bit as real as any other part of me. I wish he were here with me.

When I wake next, I'm being moved into my bed in the intensive care unit. While I shouldn't be surprised since I'm a gunshot wound survivor, I'm still alarmed by the level of care and attention Dr. Jeff obviously thinks I need. Glancing around the room, I see more nurses I know very well since the ER and ICU share nurses in dire situations. Then I see those whiskey-colored amber eyes locked on me. He's with Karen and one of the nurses appears to be briefing them on my condition, but his attention is homed in on me.

"Excuse me." I read his lips as he steps around the nurse and makes a beeline for me. He's immediately beside me, his long legs making quick work of the distance. He grips the side rails of the bed so hard, I wonder if he'll leave imprints. "Hi, darlin'. How do you feel? Do you need anything?"

I shake my head from side to side, thinking about how sad he seems. The pain radiating from his eyes is palpable. He blames himself for Butch's actions. Opening my hand, I signal for him to take it in his. First, I look down at our entwined fingers, thinking

about how much I love him, before meeting his penetrating gaze again. My throat is still raw from being
intubated, but I manage to speak to him in a whisper.
"This isn't your fault, Nick. None of it. I don't blame
you, so you can't blame yourself either."

A pained smile makes a brief showing before
retreating behind his mask of steel. "Savannah, I wish
he'd shot me. I thought he was gunning for me—I
completely read him wrong, and look what my fuckup
caused. This is my job, it's what I'm trained to do,
and I failed. I failed you. That is all on me."

I shake my head again. "Then this is my fault for
ever getting involved with him in the first place."

"No, babe, you are the victim here. You're the
survivor. But you're not responsible for him."

This time, I nod. "Neither are you, Nick."

He stammers for a few seconds, wanting to argue
with me but knowing he'd only be arguing with his
own point if he does. Then he smiles—really smiles
—at me, and my heart does flips in my chest. The
heart monitor picks up on the effect he has on me,
making his eyes jerk to the screen. When he looks
back down at me, he squeezes my hand and leans
over the rail to kiss my cheek. "They won't let me stay
long because you need your rest. But I wanted you to
know I'm here. I'm not going anywhere. I love you."

"Go home, Nick. You won't be able to see me for
several more hours. There's no need for you to live in
the hospital."

"She's right." Karen speaks up from the foot of my bed. "Listen to the ER nurse, she knows what she's talking about. The fact that she's talking at all tells me she'll be okay."

My only response is a small smile. I don't think I'll ever be okay again. But I don't say that out loud.

"Hey, get that thought out of your head right now," Nick's soothing voice chastises me. "You're alive and soon will be well. That's all that matters to me."

Emotion nearly chokes me, squeezing my throat and threatening to overcome me. Tears well up in my eyes without warning and without mercy.

"You know, don't you, sweetie?" Karen asks.

I nod, my chin and bottom lip quivering too much to risk trying to speak.

"I'm so sorry this happened to you, Savannah. We talked to Dr. Jeff before your surgery and afterward. There was no other way he could save your life. Believe me, Nick and I would both much rather have you just as you are than risk losing you completely.

"All this tragedy is too much to deal with right now, but when you've healed, you'll see things more clearly. Listen to me, babbling on, trying to console you and really sucking at it. I'll be my usual blunt self now, so listen up. Even though it feels like it right now, I promise you this isn't the end of the world. This isn't the end of your life. So, wallow in your grief for now, get it all out while you're in here. When you're discharged, Savannah's new outlook on life starts immediately. Got it?"

I love my best friend.

"Got it. Now, get out. My drugs are kicking in."

"That's my girl. Love you, doll. I'll be back to check on you later today."

Nick leans over, places a lingering kiss on my forehead, and cups my cheek. "I love you, darlin'. Nothing will ever change how I feel about you. Just remember that. I'll be back this evening during visitor hours."

Time passes but means nothing in here. I don't know if it's daylight or dark out, but the pain management drugs are working wonders, so that's all that matters. Well, that, and I've come to a decision during my more lucid moments. It's not a huge revelation or anything, just a facet I hadn't considered until I had so much time on my hands.

I'm letting Nick go.

I believe him when he says my inability to have children won't affect his love for me. He's too good of a man to let that sway his feelings. But he will blame himself for Butch shooting me for the rest of our lives. Every time he looks at me, he'll see what he deems as his failure to protect me. When Karen's belly starts protruding, he'll be consumed with guilt over not being able to give me the same. Guilt, because he thinks he neglected to do his job, even though reading Butch's mind was never in his job description.

I've argued all the points in my mind, wavering between breaking up and breaking down, but the dilemma always ends with the same solution. Now to tell him I don't want to see him anymore, so he doesn't spend another moment of his life waiting for me. This is not a conversation I'm looking forward to having, and I'm sure he'll blame the medications as he refuses to accept my decision. Eventually, he'll understand this is what's best for both of us.

Maybe, eventually, I'll convince myself of that too.

When he shows up for the evening visitation, I know with one glance he's had no rest. He looks worse than I do…or at least than I think I look. Having no mirror in this room is both a curse and a blessing.

He picks up my hand and kisses the back of it before holding it to his cheek and closing his eyes, reveling in our connection. The stubble of his beard prickles my skin, reminding me of the intimate times we've shared. My fingers develop a mind of their own, turning to stroke his skin and lightly scratch his beard. My heart is already breaking inside my chest, just thinking about telling him goodbye.

"Nick." My voice cracks on his name, and his eyes fly open. "Sit down. There's something I need to say."

"No. No fucking way. You're not doing this to me, Savannah. I love you, and you're not pushing me away from you now. I'm not the type of man who tucks tail and runs at the first sign of trouble. This is important to you, and I respect that, but it's only a bump in the road to me. Nothing we can't work out and move past. I'm not running or walking away from you. Ever."

"Nick, I need you to listen. It's hard for me to talk."

"Good. Then shut your mouth and let me just be here with you. I'll do all the talking, and you can just rest your jaws. I've already told you, whether or not you can have a baby doesn't matter to me. You matter to me, and no one else will ever take your place in my heart. Now, if you want me to live the rest of my life alone, without anyone to love because you took my heart with you when you left me, that's up to you."

"You know, my mother tried to guilt-trip me my entire life. Really doesn't work on me now that I'm grown. Please listen to me."

"Go ahead and say it. My answer won't change, but I'll listen to you anyway."

"I need you to leave and never come back, Nick. I love everything about you. You're truly the best man I know. Because of that, you shouldn't have to spend the rest of your life feeling guilty for something that wasn't your fault. Every time you look at me, or see a baby, or anything related to children, that's exactly where your mind will go. Then I'll see that disturbed expression and know it's because of me. We'll never fully be happy together with this between us. I love you too much not to want to see you happy. This is how we're both hardwired, so there's no blame."

He stares hard at me, his brain working overtime to process everything I've said and play it out in his mind. "Darlin', please don't do this. I love you."

He can't deny the truth of the matter. Every ounce of pain, regret, and acknowledgment shows in his features. The despondent look in his eyes. The gloomy expression on his face. The downward turn of his mouth.

"I know you do… I love you too. And it's because of that love that I have no choice *but* to do this. You have to go, Nick, and don't come back. Move on with your life knowing that I want you to be happy and I want the very best for you. More than anything, that's my hope for you." My heart disintegrates inside me when I untangle my hand from his.

He straightens his spine and pulls the mask back over his face. "Savannah Fields, I refuse to let you push me away or cut me out of your life because you have some crazy idea that I could ever be happy without you. You are my happiness. Without you, there's no reason for me to even try. I'm going to go now because you need to rest and recuperate, but I'm leaving you with these words to mull over."

I raise my eyebrows in question, unable to formulate and verbalize the question in my mind to ask what he means.

"There's nothing we can't get through together. You've been my rock since day one, before I even realized it. You saved me when I wasn't able to save myself. Now, let me be your rock. When you feel like everything is at its worst, think about how much I love you. That's one thing you'll never question or doubt."

My words…used against me in the worst way possible—because I believe he means it. I watch him walk away, shoulders hunched and sadness permeating every part of his being. Knowing I caused him more pain than anyone else ever has kills me. Where is that pain medicine when I need it because I'm sure this broken heart will kill me before anything else can.

OVER A WEEK LATER, I'VE BEEN MOVED OUT OF THE ICU and into the step-down unit. While my care isn't as critical, they still keep a very close watch on me. The change in my demeanor has been a sore subject lately. True to his word, Nick has stayed away, but only because that's what I asked him to do. He'd never force himself on me, though I know he still asks about me multiple times a day because Karen's phone pings constantly while she's here.

Karen knows I'm miserable without him, but she's giving me time to figure that out on my own.

The problem is I don't need time to know how much I miss him. That's not the problem. I've never questioned my feelings for him. Only our ability to slay the monster in our closet.

"You look better now that you're able to sit up a little more." Karen washes my hair in the plastic bin made specifically for bedridden patients. A real shower would feel like pure heaven right now.

"I really can't tell you how badly being unable to take care of myself sucks."

"Well, I must admit, you're making a much better patient than I would. You've already been in the hospital ten days without losing your mind."

"It's only been ten days? I was sure it was more like thirty."

She chuckles. "I'm sure it feels like it. But Dr. Jeff said you're healing faster than he thought you would. A couple more weeks in here and you'll probably be ready to go home."

A couple more weeks without Nick. Then a few more. Maybe in a few years, I'll stop counting the days since I last saw him.

Karen called my mom and sister to tell them what happened to me the first night during my surgery. The two of them were here every day during the first week—before I sent them home because there's not much they can do to help while I'm still in the hospital. Every time they knocked on my door, it made me hope it was Nick coming to see me, to convince me I was wrong, and he can be happy with me. Karen hears my gasp with the current knocking, but her only response is to arch an eyebrow at me.

"Come in," I call out.

When Miranda steps into my hospital room, I'm shocked beyond words. She never leaves the crisis center for her own safety. Even after Butch terrorized every woman and child in the place, I was told Miranda still refused to step outside the doors.

"Miranda, I'm surprised to see you. But I'm so glad you're here." I introduce Karen and Miranda, briefly explaining how I know each woman.

"I'm sorry I didn't come to see you sooner. Believe me, it's not because I didn't want to check on you. After everything that happened, I was even more afraid to leave my room than usual. Then I realized, you're the only friend I have. There's no excuse for me to let you down after all you've done for me. I also brought your cell phone. It's been going off several times a day, and it was selfish of me not to bring it to you. Other people care about you, and I'm sure they're looking for answers."

Karen finishes washing my hair, so I tell Miranda to have a seat while she dries and styles it in a messy bun. Miranda hands my phone to me, and I scroll through the messages while Karen performs her magic.

Every single message is from Nick.

I love you.

I miss you.

You're wrong, you know. Every time I look at you, all I see is happiness for the rest of my life.

You're so beautiful—even when you drool in your sleep.

Darlin', you are my life. Don't you see that?

Longer texts tell me about his days at work and his nights sitting out in the hallway, guarding my door. Butch is still at large despite a city-wide manhunt, but Nick assures me he will get his man. He tells me not to worry because he has everything under control. The messages are a daily journal of his life since I've been stuck in this hospital room, keeping me updated on everything he's doing as if we're still speaking. As if everything is completely normal.

Those butterflies take up in my chest again, making my heart flutter like crazy. When I glance up at Karen, I see a knowing smirk on her face.

CHAPTER 20

Nick

Savannah just read all my texts from the last ten days. I know because the read receipt finally showed up on my phone. The three little dots dancing on my text message screen give me hope she's realized this whole breaking up with me bullshit won't work. I'm not going anywhere. If she didn't love me anymore, that would be different. I'd leave her alone to live her life. But she does love me, and we both know it. She's throwing away the best thing either of us has ever known, all for a complete misconception she's convinced herself is reality.

I won't let her toss me aside that easily. I won't let her toss *us* aside that easily. We've proved time and again we're perfect for each other. She'll have to work a little harder at convincing me she doesn't want to be in my life anymore. Karen told me Savannah didn't have her phone with her but encouraged me to keep sending my daily messages anyway, keeping her informed of every mundane detail of my day, reminding her of our deep connection that time apart can't diminish. The impact of reading one after the other all at once would be immense. I hope she's right, because I'm legit dying without talking to her every day.

It's so good to read about your days. The highlight of mine was a shampoo and hairstyle by Karen.

I stare at the message far too long, trying to read between the lines instead of just talking to her while she's in a talkative mood.

Me: *I volunteer as tribute to give you a sponge bath. You don't even have to get out of bed.*

Savannah: *Very kind of you to offer. Can you guarantee hot water and silky-smooth skin? Because you'll have to shave my legs to make good on that promise.*

Me: *Darlin', for you, I'll promise silky-smooth everything.*

Savannah: *You're not in here yet.*

She doesn't have to tell me twice. I'm running down the hospital corridor before I've even finished reading the message. When I burst through the door, Karen is putting away her hairbrushes and shampoo,

Miranda is kicked back in the visitor's chair, and Savannah is in her bed with a beautiful smile on her face.

"Miranda, let's go grab some coffee and give them some privacy." Karen winks at me as she and Miranda leave the room.

"Karen told me you've been here every morning, every lunch break, and every night. Nick, you know that's not healthy. You have to go home and rest." Savannah looks every bit as beautiful as she did the first day I met her.

"You don't have to worry about me. I get enough rest. I come here every day in case you need me. Or in case you decide you want me again."

"Nick." She breathes my name. "I've never not wanted you."

"Then what are you doing, Savannah? We're meant to be together. No matter what, we'll work through any issues together. We're stronger together than we could ever be apart. And being apart is killing me."

"And the other thing? The whole never forgiving yourself for what you can't control?"

"I've given that a lot of thought over the last ten days. Honestly, I can see why you'd think I'd react that way. Everything you've known about me has been duty, honor, and keeping my word. And that's exactly why you should believe me when I say, I could never look at you and feel hurt, disappointed, or as if anything is lacking in my life. Would kids be nice? Sure. But winning the lottery and buying that private island just for the two of us would too. As long as we're together, I don't need anything or anyone else to make me happy. Do I want to give you the world? You bet your fine ass, I do. But I want to give you all my love first and foremost. Without your love, nothing else matters."

Tears fall from her eyes onto her cheeks, but this time, they're tears of joy instead of pain. They're tears of relief instead of burden. They're tears of love instead of goodbye. She holds out her arms, and I rush into them, holding her close to me without jarring her still-recovering body too much. She squeezes me as hard as she can, burying her face in my chest and releasing all the pent-up tension she's held on to alone.

When she calms down, she gingerly moves over in the bed, giving me room to settle in beside her.

"If you're going to sleep at the hospital, the least you can do is sleep with me. You know I sleep better with you by my side."

"That's the best offer I've had in eleven whole days."

"One day longer than we've been apart, huh?"

We both chuckle and settle back into our relationship as if nothing happened. Because it really didn't. She had a moment of doubt and needed to let it play out naturally. When her theory lost steam, she knew there was no other option but for us to be together.

"Thank you for not giving up on me. I was in a really dark and heavily medicated place that day. Karen had a long talk with me today while doing my hair and helped me see the error of my ways."

"Hmm. I guess I owe Karen the best damn baby shower ever thrown, then. We're talking parade-sized balloons, tons of confetti, and a full jazz band. Whatever she wants."

"She wants us to be happy, and she convinced me of how miserable I've been without you and how stupid my decision was. Mostly, she helped me to realize I pushed you away before you had a chance to push me away, and that wasn't fair to either of us since neither of us actually wants that."

"She's a very smart woman. I'm glad you listened to her. This isn't something I'm proud of, per se, but my next option was to kidnap you and keep you chained to my bed until you relented. Although, I still say that plan has merit."

"See, this is part of why I love you. You make me laugh even when it hurts."

After I give her a very thorough bed bath, her dinner arrives and I help feed her, despite her protests she can manage that task on her own. I know she can —but it feels good to be here with her again. And I know I'll have to leave her in a few minutes for a previous engagement.

"I'll be back later tonight. There's something I have to go take care of right now. Is that offer to sleep with you still good?"

"That's a standing offer, Nick. You're welcome in my bed anytime."

With a thorough kiss goodbye, and a thousand-pound weight lifted from my chest, I reluctantly leave her side. There's only one person who could pry me away from her, and I have a bullet with his name on it. Butch slithered out of his hiding place long enough to be spotted, so now I'm holding my own venomous snake roundup.

There are a few lights on inside the dilapidated house in Washington Highlands when I drive by, but I keep going until I'm a couple of blocks away. The sun has already set, and the dark of night is quickly falling, giving me inherent cover when moving between the houses. Some are vacant, long ago abandoned and never claimed by new residents. The working streetlights are spotty at best. Most have been shot out or shattered by rocks. The cold has driven most people inside, huddled around open fires to try to keep warm.

Tonight, the cold doesn't bother me. The ice in my veins has numbed me to the chill in the air.

I held Savannah in my arms as she lay dying in that parking lot. More of her blood soaked into the asphalt than ran in her veins. Time was not on her side, and had we not been so close to a hospital, she would've died in the ambulance on the way. Part of me did die that day when I thought I'd lose her. The pallor of her skin matched the coolness when I held her, begging her not to leave me. In that moment, I realized I can cross that fine line between right and wrong. For her, I will cross every line, break every rule, and annihilate every man who tries to take her from me.

Tonight, one man still poses a direct threat, and he'll pay for his crimes. All of them. Tonight, I'm the judge, jury, and executioner all rolled into one. If his friends get in the way, it'll be their own fault when they're little more than collateral damage. Moving through the shadows toward the back door of the run-down shack, I listen to every sound and watch every shadow. He will not escape my wrath one more day.

The lack of shades or curtains on the back window gives me a perfect line of sight into the house. Five men, two women, and Butch are camped out in the main room. Worn-out mattresses are scattered across the floor, and beer cans litter the walkways. A metal barrel sits in the middle of the room with an open fire still burning inside. A shed at the rear property line catches my eye, no doubt where they hid their motorcycles to avoid being spotted in this neighborhood.

A quick look in the shed reveals all six motorcycles are stuffed inside. The red plastic gasoline can gives me an idea of how to evacuate the house in one fell swoop. Once the gas can is empty and the motorcycles are drenched, I strike a match I pilfered from the shed and toss it into the middle of the room. The fumes catch up in a roaring blaze instantly, so I retreat to the side of the house to enjoy the show. One thing a motorhead loves is his ride, and these guys have no other possessions to their names. When they hit the back steps, they'll be frantic to reach their bikes.

Loud, agitated shouts carry on the night air as the occupants of the house empty into the backyard. At first, they try to bat the flames away to get through the door to their bikes. Then, one of the geniuses decides to grab the water hose instead. While they're busy fighting with the frozen-solid hose and with each other, I steal into the house and kick the barrel over, the fire and hot coals spreading across the floor and bedding. The old wooden house is basically one big pile of kindling, ready to disintegrate into ashes with a single spark. I exit out the front door, leaving it standing wide open to ensure the fire has plenty of fresh oxygen and whipping winds to feed it.

"What the fuck is going on?" one of the men shouts when he looks over his shoulder and finds his hideout nearly fully ablaze.

The fire in the shed heats the motorcycles' gas tanks to the tipping point, causing one after the other to explode. Pieces of metal and rubber and unidentifiable parts land haphazardly in the yard. I smile, pleased with the devastation they feel, but I'm done with the tit for tat games. This ends tonight, and it ends on my terms.

Stepping out of the shadows with my gun drawn, suppressor in place and arm extended, I realize what Shadow and Silas have tried to tell me over the years is true. While CIA officers work under much different rules than the rest of us, sometimes their methods are necessary. Sometimes their course of action is the best way in the long run. When Savannah no longer has to look over her shoulder, waiting for some low-life asshole to take his revenge, every move I've made tonight will be worth it.

The shock of seeing me registers on Butch's face first before morphing into anger. Then he realizes I have no intentions of arresting him. I have no plans of taking him anywhere. This is it for him. The murderous rage written on my face tells him more than words ever could. He opens his mouth to spew his vitriol at me, and I pull the trigger, hitting him square in the chest.

He falls to the ground with raucous screams, grabbing his wound and writhing in pain. I take a step closer and fire again, hitting him in the head and silencing him forever. The other five men decide to rush me at once, thinking they can overtake me before I pick them off one by one. But they're wrong. Dead wrong.

The two women huddle together, crying loudly and begging for their lives.

"Go. If you say a word to anyone, I'll hunt you down, and no one will ever find your bodies."

They run off into the night. Where, I don't know, nor do I care. By the time they sober up from all the drugs I just burned up inside the house, they probably won't even remember where they were.

"I'm impressed." Silas steps out of the shadows, catching me off guard.

"Fuck, man. I could've shot you just now!"

"No, you couldn't. You didn't even know I was standing here watching your entire show. Sloppy, Nick. That kind of shit will get you killed. But if you're looking for a new job once the trial is over, I may know an agency that's hiring someone with your skills and brass cojones."

"I'm definitely interested. Let's talk more—somewhere away from here before we're both caught at the scene of the crime."

Silas lifts his cell to his ear and smiles. "I need a cleanup and containment crew immediately." He gives the address of our current location and a description of the two women I just let flee from the scene. My eyebrows draw down, and I tilt my head to the side, silently questioning his motives. Surely, he didn't just order an agency-sanctioned hit on those two women.

"What? We leave no witnesses, Nick. Ever. Better

get used to change, buddy." He claps me on the shoulder, understanding the conflict I'm fighting inside me. "Those women were running to more bikers a few blocks over. You know better than anyone, the sheep are loyal to their masters. These men are dead, and that house will be nothing but rubble in a matter of minutes. They're already looking for new guys to replace the dead ones because they have no one else. Go back to the hospital, lie down next to Savannah, then tell me if you'd change one single thing about tonight. If not, you know you're ready, and I'll help you out. If your conscience still bothers you because you didn't make the world a safer place exactly by the book, maybe you should stay with the DEA."

His words circle in my thoughts on the drive back to the hospital. Everything has always been black and white for me. There were no shades of gray in between. There were no alternate lines in the sand. It was this or that. Period. Now, there's an entire rainbow of colors separating the line between right and wrong. That fine line just became a great divide, and I'm not sure how to jump across it.

I leave Silas to direct the cleanup crew and head back to where I'm needed most. When I step into the hospital room and find Savannah sleeping soundly with the first happy expression on her face since all this bullshit started, I feel a sense of peace envelop me like never before. That's when I know that Silas was right, and there's no going back for me now. Once the trial is over, I'll tender my resignation to the DEA and join him at the CIA. Though it means more international travel and visiting dangerous places, I won't be recognized in those circles. Changing my appearance will mean more than unkempt hair and a scraggly beard to hide my face.

She stirs when I slide into bed beside her, her eyes flittering open to make sure it's actually me. Her eyes close again automatically, but she's smiling, safe and secure in my embrace. We have a long road ahead of us, months until she's fully recovered and back to her usual self. But those months will be filled with love and laughter and the discovery of a whole new world, one we've never known before.

One I only want to experience and explore with her. With my head back against the pillow and my love at my side, I slip into the most peaceful sleep I've had in the last couple of weeks. The events of the night are not even an afterthought now—because she's safe and because she's mine.

"I'm glad you came back, Nick. I was afraid you'd get busy and wouldn't make it back tonight. You have no idea how much I've missed you."

"Darlin', I think I have a pretty good idea, if it's anywhere close to how much I've missed you. I thought I was going to lose you forever in that parking lot. Holding you while telling you to keep fighting will always be the worst memory I have. But holding you while telling you how much I love you will always be my favorite. Never leave me again, Savannah. I'm a strong man, but losing you is one thing I can't handle."

"You don't have to worry about that, Nick. You'll never get rid of me now. I'm afraid you're stuck with me for life." Her voice is sleepy, and her words are meant partly in jest, but I'm completely serious.

"Savannah?"

"Hmm?"

"Marry me," I whisper against her head.

"Okay," she whispers back.

CHAPTER 21

Savannah—Three Months Later

"Put that box down! Are you crazy?" Nick grabs the box from my hands and gives me an irritated look. It doesn't work, but he gets an A for effort.

"Nick, I'm completely healed now, and this is a box of scarves. It doesn't even weigh as much as my purse does."

"Please go pack up your kitchen items so I can move you out of this condo before you change your mind." He leans over and kisses me for the hundredth time. Maybe I'll keep picking up light boxes until he becomes more distracted.

"I can read your mind. Go pack your shit, right now."

Anyone listening would take that as a threat, but I know my sweetheart of a man, and that simply shows how much he wants me to move in with him. Permanently. I'm as giddy about this move as he is; we've just been waiting for the right time after my stint in the hospital. Now that I'm completely—and finally—healed from all my injuries, I can't wait to start my new life with the man of my dreams.

In our new home—a real house in the suburbs, where there's plenty of bright sunshine, cherry trees in bloom, and spacious yards with beautiful green grass. We chose Arlington, Virginia as our new spot to put down roots. It's just outside the craziness of DC, but it still is every bit as vibrant and upbeat as Adams Morgan.

Nick sold his brownstone almost as soon as he put it on the market. He, Roman, and Silas talked to my superintendent about letting me out of my lease early. With all the security upgrades they made to my place, the building management isn't losing any money by letting me out of my lease early. Plus, the super is really afraid of these three hulking men, especially when they all crowd into his office at once, so he didn't put up much of a fight.

As I'm in the kitchen throwing pots and pans into a moving box, doing as I'm told, my cell phone rings. One glance at the screen and a smile crosses my face. "Hey, Miranda. How are you?"

"Hi, Savannah. I'm fine, thank you. I need to ask

you for a favor, and I feel like a terrible friend for even asking."

"What do you need, hon?"

"I was wondering if you could come by the center to talk with me? I have an idea I want to run by you, but it's not the kind of thing we can talk about over the phone. It's about a way I really think I can help you, after everything you've done for me. But I know this is probably the last place you want to see right now, so I feel terrible even asking. Believe me, I wouldn't if this wasn't important."

She's right; I haven't returned to the shelter since the ambulance carried me away that awful day, and I haven't wanted to even one time. The sights and sounds of that day are never far from my mind. As happy as Nick makes me, the nightmares threaten to return every night. There's one nightmare that will never return, that much I'm sure of. Though I don't know the details of what happened, and I'm probably better off that way, Nick assured me I never have to worry about running into Butch again.

That's all I need to know.

I'm learning techniques to keep the monsters at bay on my own because I can't always rely on Nick to save the day. Or night. Whatever. Finding my own strength and standing on my own two feet are impor-tant to me, even if it takes time to overcome the demons when I close my eyes.

But Miranda's voice is so hopeful, while simultaneously being cautious. She doesn't want to get her hopes up in case I decline her request. But at the same time, whatever it is she wants to discuss is important to her.

"Do you mind if Nick comes with me?"

"No, I don't mind at all. Actually, that would be perfect. Please? I'm sorry to ask—I know it's really very selfish of me, considering I have such a hard time leaving here, so I should understand why you'd have a hard time coming back."

"No, it's fine. I understand why you're concerned about leaving. You don't know where your ex is or where you could run into him. We're packing right now, but we can come later this evening. Is that okay?"

"Perfect. Thank you so much."

We chat for a few more minutes until Nick stands in the kitchen doorway, staring at me like I've grown an extra head, then Miranda and I disconnect. I smile up at him from my spot on the floor, and he simply shakes his head at me. "Do you plan on finishing this room anytime today?"

"It's on my to-do list."

"You're definitely feeling better. Getting all sassy and feisty. I love it."

"Good, because you're only going to get more and more of it."

"I'll take it all, darlin'. Every bit you have to offer."

"Hey, I have some potentially upsetting plans for us this evening."

"Okay. What's up?"

I relay the call with Miranda and her request for us to come talk with her. A dark shadow passes over his face, the memory of that day nearly three months ago still fresh in his mind too. "She wouldn't ask for no reason, Nick. Whatever she has to say, she really wants to talk to us about it. I'm okay with going back there as long as you're with me. Are you okay with it?"

"As long as you're by my side at all times, yes."

"I'll go too. You two may need backup," Silas says as he passes by with another taped box.

"Perfect. We're both safe since Silas has our back. So, we're good to go, right?" I stand and wrap my arms around Nick's waist, push up on my toes, and press a long kiss to his lips.

"You know, this kind of distraction works on me a little too well. How can I say no to you when you ask me like that?" His arms encircle my waist, and his mouth covers mine. The panty-melting kiss he lays on me is hot enough to make me spontaneously combust.

And he thinks I hold the magic power over him. No way that's an accurate assumption.

"We're never going to get Savannah moved out of here if you two keep taking kissing breaks." Silas walks back by again, heading to grab another box.

"Okay, now I feel guilty. Let's get back to work. Our friends are doing all the hard labor." With one last kiss, I start taking my plates down from the cabinets and wrapping them in paper.

Before I know it, we've finished packing and carrying all my boxes down to the moving truck. Well, I watched Nick, Silas, and Roman carry the boxes down, but telling them where to put them in the back of the truck was a full-time job in itself.

Roman offers to drive the truck to our new home so we don't have to make an extra trip back into DC to visit Miranda at the shelter. We found a great deal on a three-bedroom home in a nice neighborhood. It's close enough to drive back into the city for work, but far enough away that we don't miss the craziness of the congested traffic at other times. There's a mother-in-law apartment over the detached garage that would be perfect as an office.

When I was first able to sit up after surgery, Karen brought my laptop to the hospital so I could continue working on my book. Since I've been off on medical leave, I've finished writing my story and found a talented editor to help make me sound halfway decent. I'm excited to see what the future holds when I release this self-help book. If just one woman saves herself and walks away from an abusive relationship after reading my story, it'll have been worth the time and effort.

After two more weeks, I'll finally be headed back to my job as a nurse, too. I've traded the night shift for days, though. Karen also moved to the day shift since it's easier on her both while she's pregnant and after the baby is born. I'm thrilled we'll still work together, and the added bonus is I'll be home with Nick every night.

"So, Undercover Lover, are you glad the trial bull-shit is over?" Silas asks from the back seat.

"Absolutely. Having my entire life splashed across every news outlet on TV and the internet got old really fast. Thank God for Axle, huh? He showed up with all that video footage of Bobby Blalock ordering hits and shit, and all of a sudden, the lawyers were clamoring for deals. Hey, that reminds me, how'd you get my picture scrubbed from everywhere so fast?" Nick glances at Silas in the rearview mirror.

"Ah, you know, the delete key works wonders. You should try it sometime." Silas hedges, refusing to give us a straight answer.

"I will, as soon as you get me in at The Farm."

"You'll hear from them anytime now. Actually, you and Roman both will. I've proposed a three-man team of CIA officers for special operations, working in conjunction with the NSA. Good news is we'll be stateside most of the time. An occasional trip here or there, but no long stints or moving to foreign field offices in our future. They're reviewing your files and background information now, but they'll contact you soon."

"Sounds like a great opportunity. Let's get started."

Nick's enthusiasm is contagious—and magnificent to hear. He's changed so much from the man I first met. He's still the best man I know, but now he's also the happiest. The changes we've made in our lives and in each other's is nothing short of fate. He's my soul mate, regardless of what obstacles have been thrown in front of us.

We walk into the center hand in hand, with Silas covering our backs for good measure. Terrifying memories try to halt my forward motion, but Nick's hand on my lower back reminds me of how far we've come in a short time. There's no going backward now, and no letting old ghosts ruin the good thing we've found.

Miranda meets us just inside the door, throws her arms around my neck, and bounces up and down. She's virtually giddy with excitement and eagerness, though I don't have a clue why yet.

"Miranda, this is Silas Steele. Silas, this is my friend, Miranda Petrovio."

"Hello, Silas." Miranda extends her hand to Silas. When I look up at him, he has an odd expression on his face as he studies Miranda.

"Hi, Miranda. Have we met before? You look very familiar."

"Um, no, I don't think so. But I hear that a lot. I always say I have a very common face. Maybe you just remember me from that awful day. I was here in the middle of everything." She laughs nervously and turns her head away, extending her hand to an empty table in the common room. "Let's have a seat."

"I'll wait over here by the door, just to be on the safe side. Yell if you need me. Nice to meet you, Miranda." Silas walks backward, keeping his eyes trained on us.

Odd.

"It's nice to meet you too, Silas." Miranda takes the seat with her back to Silas, which I notice immediately.

As paranoid as she usually is, she would never sit with her back to the door anytime I volunteered here. In fact, she was adamant about having her back to the wall so she could keep her eyes on the door at all times. My initial thought is she's uncomfortable with Silas's probing stare, and I quickly dismiss my uncertainty as paranoia from coming back here. Besides, Silas can be rather unnerving at times to anyone who doesn't know him. I chalk it up to the CIA officer ingrained in him.

Miranda leans forward, a wide smile covering her face, and grasps my hands in hers. "Thank you so much for coming. Hear me out before you say anything, please, because I know how crazy this is going to sound. But you've been such a good friend to me when I had no one, and if there's something I can do to help you, then I want to do it. You've helped me, talked to me, and trusted me to help you. I've literally had no one else for so long, but you've made me feel like part of your life. There's a way I can help you both with something you want more than anything. I want to offer to do this, because I know you'd never ask it of me."

"What are you talking about? Tell me!" I'm getting excited just listening to her enthusiasm.

"When you were in the hospital, I saw how deeply depressed you were over not being able to have a baby. But I realized it's more than that—it's who you are. You love, you take care of others, you give your whole heart, and it's a beautiful thing. I want to help give that opportunity back to you, Savannah. I'd love to carry your baby for you so you two lovebirds can be parents. You don't deserve what that monster did to you. You shouldn't have to pay for his sins for the rest of your life."

She stops talking, but I can't find my voice or even a coherent thought to attempt to muddle through. I stare at her in disbelief, positive I've misunderstood her intentions. Nick seems to be under the same mute spell because he's sitting beside me, motionless and slack-jawed.

"Let me try to explain further. I'd be a gestational carrier only—not a surrogate mother. Your egg will be fertilized by Nick then implanted into me, so the baby will be one hundred percent yours and Nick's. I would literally only be an incubator for your embryo until the delivery, but this way, you can still have your own baby. Do you understand what I'm suggesting?"

I'm shocked beyond words. How do I respond to an offer like this? How can I say yes, but then again, how can I say no to a baby that would be wholly Nick's and mine?

"Miranda, we—"

"Yes. The answer is yes, we would love that." Nick cuts me off before I can reject such a generous offer. My head jerks toward him, and any question I have in my mind clears when I look at his handsome face. "This is what you want, darlin'. This is why I almost lost you—because you were afraid of what I'd constantly think about not having children of our own. That's not what I think about at all, though, babe. But I know how important this is to you, and she's offering the opportunity of a lifetime. I think we should take it and enjoy every minute of the journey."

"Listen to him, Savannah. He understands. This is the best way I know how to thank you for all your kindness. I want to do this for you. You're the only friend I have left in the world."

With pure joy bubbling up inside my chest, I fly out of my seat and around the table to hug Miranda. Once I wrap my arms around her, I can't force myself to let her go. This amazing gift she's offering gives me more hope than I've had in this area of my life in years, even if nothing goes right in the process. I've never felt whole, thinking I was unable to conceive all those years, even though my logical side chided my emotional side for even entertaining that notion.

"I have one condition," I state when I finally release her. "Nick, do you mind if she moves in to the apartment above the garage while she's pregnant? I want to have her as close as possible during the pregnancy. Just in case she needs help or protection or ice cream."

"That's a great idea, darlin'. We would be right there to help you, Miranda. We'll help take care of you and protect you, but you'd still have your own private space. More so than here. And I'd feel better knowing Savannah would have a friend there when I'm away for work. Plus, your ex would have no idea to look for you in Arlington. I think we'd all feel better with you living close by. What do you say, Miranda?"

"Oh my gosh—I can't believe you'd want me to live there with you. If you're sure I won't be in the way, then yes, I'd love to. After the baby's born, I'll find a job and get my own place, I promise. I won't overstay my welcome."

"We'll worry about that when the time comes." Miranda and I giggle together like two adolescent school girls making plans for a sleepover party.

I'm overwhelmed with hope because of the mere possibility she's offering us. After all these years, after the deep depression and dark hole I found myself in after my hysterectomy, I can see a light at the end of the tunnel. And it feels a lot like a dream coming true.

CHAPTER 22

Nick

I've never known Silas to be so transparent before. The way he watches Miranda is uncharacteristically obvious for him and goes against everything in his training. He observes and handles people for a living, yet he's giving away the home field advantage when it comes to his interest in Miranda and who she is.

When he asked if they'd ever met, I almost choked on the very air I'd inhaled. This is a man who doesn't forget a face and is a master of disguise. He knows damn well if he has met her before. My guess is he'd know the date, time of day, and circumstances surrounding the meeting without a hitch. And it's much more than seeing her face when he was my backup when we faced down Butch and his demon buddy. His tone was certain, and he was testing her honesty.

But then he backed off. And I mean he backed all the way to the door, like a sentinel standing guard. If she were a threat to us, he wouldn't have budged, and he would've called her on it immediately. Still, there's a story to be told there, and my gut tells me we'll be hot on that case soon enough. Makes me wonder if she's why he volunteered to join us for the meeting at the center.

That's one reason why I jumped at the opportunity she so readily offered before Savannah could turn her down. If her offer is bona fide, I'm all for giving Savannah a baby right now. Tomorrow, if I could. If her offer is a ruse, I'm all for exposing her treachery as soon as possible. Either way, Savannah's suggestion of having Miranda move in to the apartment over our garage was perfectly timed and expertly played, even though she doesn't realize it.

Keep friends close and enemies closer mentality.

One thing I know for sure, Savannah is overjoyed with the idea. Miranda had better not be playing on my girl's emotions, only to use her for some bullshit scheme. Her disappointment would be unbearable. My anger would be unmanageable. My plan is to take it one day at a time and watch Miranda like a hawk in the event I need to step in and knock heads around.

On the ride home, Savannah can't stop talking

about Miranda's generosity and how incredible she is to give us such a wonderful gift. Her faith in humanity is beautiful and balances my constant suspicion of everyone in the world. We're complete opposite ends of the spectrum, but the way we complement each other just works for us. In this case, her excitement seeps into me, making me hope for the best despite my wariness.

The Special Agent in me says to prepare for the worst-case scenario, though.

Savannah researches gestational surrogacy and in vitro insemination protocols on her phone and relays the information she finds. The procedures. The time frames. The number of eggs they implant at one time. The odds of having multiple babies if more than one embryo is implanted. The odds of the fertilized eggs not taking. Through all of her chatter, Silas is silent in the back seat, never weighing in one way or another.

"What's on your mind, Silas?" I get straight to the point. I'd rather have all our cards on the table.

"A trip I have to take that just popped up. I'll probably be out on a flight first thing in the morning, but I'll be back before you're even settled into your first training class at The Farm, though."

"Where are you headed?" I raise my eyes up to the rearview mirror, meeting Silas's stoic gaze, while knowing his reply will probably create more questions than answers for me.

"Moscow."

Fuck me running. That is the last place I would've expected him to say. This just became much more complicated than I originally thought.

The sinking feeling in my gut warns me this will not end well.

"You'll let me know if plans change?" Savannah is still busy on her phone, not paying much attention to us, but Silas understands my question perfectly.

"Absolutely. As soon as I know for sure, you'll be the first to know."

Roman is already at the house with the moving truck and has carried in all the boxes, saving us a lot of time. The three of us start moving the furniture into place while Savannah begins unpacking the boxes and identifying where she'll hang the wall decorations. By the time we finish unloading the truck and getting everything in place, it's late and we're all more than ready to crash.

While Savannah is busy in another room, I catch Silas alone. "Just before Savannah was shot, we started walking home one evening from a rooftop bar in Adams Morgan. Two guys were tailing us, a little too obvious to be one of ours. At the time, I thought maybe it had something to do with the case and the trial, but now I'm not so sure. What do you think?"

"What did they look like?"

"Extremely average—from their features to their build. Nothing remarkable about them. Except their very angry expressions when we jumped into a passing cab and sped off in the opposite direction."

Silas nods, his expression giving nothing away, as usual. "I don't think they had anything to do with the case or the trial. But I'll find out more as soon as I can. If they posed a threat to you, you wouldn't still be here three months later. You haven't seen them again since then?"

"No, and I haven't seen a new tail replace them either."

"Good. They were probably reprimanded for being spotted and losing you, so the teams have been pulled back to give you some space. I'll find out more as soon as possible. Keep doing everything you'd normally do until I get back...then we'll talk."

After seeing Roman and Silas off with a promise of an elaborate dinner out somewhere with unlimited alcohol to repay them for all their help, Savannah and I climb into our shared bed in our new house. She lies on her side, and I move close behind her, sliding my arm over her waist and pulling our bodies together. A small moan escapes from her lips, fully content in my arms. I get it—this is the best feeling in the world. Well, it runs a close second or third anyway. There are other feelings I can think of that are much better...in fact, at the moment, I can't seem to think of anything else but how damn good it feels to be buried inside her.

"Mmm, did you bring your gun to bed with you, or are you just happy to see me?"

"Both. I definitely brought my gun to bed with me. Let me show you how I use it."

Sinking into her body, I lose myself in the warmth that envelops me. The noises she makes fill the room, rising on a crescendo until the exquisite tones of her desires prompt me to seek the next and the next. Everything about her is intoxicating. The way my name sounds falling from her lips. How she grips my shoulders and claws my back when the pressure inside builds. The way she shudders and shakes under my touch. Her heavy breaths from all the attention I lavish on her from head to toe. The feel of her muscles contracting and relaxing around me before her body falls limp, exhausted from our endeavors but with an expression of complete satisfaction on her beautiful face.

We lie in the soft glow of the moonlight streaming through the blinds, our bodies still entwined and each breathing heavily. Our house is now a home and holds every ounce of love we possess. What's funny is this was never the life I wanted. When I was a younger man, the adventure I sought was in faraway places and dangerous situations. The thrill of the chase and the excitement of living the escapades most people only read about was my idea of a perfect life. Single. No attachments to tie me down.

That version of life is as far away from what I

want now as east is from west. Without Savannah, without what we have, I'd have no life at all. No reason to go on. As cliché as that sounds, it's the fucking honest truth. Finding her, getting to know her, and falling in love with her changed me from the inside out. I don't have to question if I'm a good man anymore. One look in her eyes is all the proof I need. She sees straight into my soul and what she finds is good enough for her. I never want to be only "good enough," though, so I keep reaching, keep striving to deserve the adoration she so easily gives me.

"You saved me, Savannah." My confession is barely a whisper in the darkness, but it's out there now.

"I think you have that backward, babe. How did I save you?"

"When I moved back to DC, I was a completely lost soul. My compass was broken, and I just wandered aimlessly between my brownstone and the coffee shop. Even though I was a good actor and I was good at keeping people at arm's length, I was nowhere near being happy. You brought all the light, love, and happiness into my life. I didn't even know this level of bliss was real. If I'm living in a fantasy world, don't ever burst my bubble. I like it here."

"I love living in this bubble with you. But it's not a fantasy, this is our life, and it only gets better from here. You've rescued me physically, you've literally saved my life—you've convinced me that heroes do exist. More than that, you've shown me that true love is real, regardless of how messy life gets or how hard it is. I know you'll never desert me, you'll never hurt me, and you'll never break my heart…because you're the best man I've ever known, Nick."

We fall asleep wrapped in each other's arms and secure in our love. Whatever happens next, happens. But we'll get through it together…good or bad.

Over the next few days, Savannah and I work to finish unpacking every box, setting up every room, and hanging every picture. When I say we, I mean me, of course, since I insist on doing all the heavy lifting. She supervises. It works. When we reach the apartment over the garage, she drags me to the furniture store and chooses a few new pieces to make it as homey as possible for Miranda. We venture over to the nursery furniture, and I watch as she fingers every item, from the crib to the rocker-glider chair to the changing table. She keeps saying if it's meant to be, it will be, but she can't hide how much she wants it to be.

"Have you thought about setting a date for our wedding yet? It may be caveman-ish of me, but I really want to see Savannah Fields changed to Savannah Tucker. Soon. How about tomorrow? Is tomorrow too soon?" I intentionally change the subject before her thoughts go too far down the baby-making path.

Her nervous laugh causes a flash of alarm to run

through me. "I actually thought I dreamed you proposed to me. It was a wonderful dream."

"It definitely was not a dream. You already said yes, so you can't take it back now."

"Zero chance of that happening, my love. What about a long weekend trip to Vegas, a drive-thru wedding in a rented car, and a honeymoon where we never leave the hotel room? They have room service. We can be back before you start with the CIA Monday morning."

"Can you be more perfect for me? I'm making the reservations tonight. Nonrefundable tickets." I lean down and kiss her, but I'm not kidding about making travel plans.

"Fine with me. I'll go pack our clothes. Let's leave tomorrow when I get off work—Thursday to Sunday is a perfect short getaway."

AFTER A LONG WEEKEND OF DRIVE-THRU NUPTIALS, champagne and strawberries delivered to our suite, and nonstop lovemaking on every surface in our expansive room, we're flying back to DC as Mr. and Mrs. for the first time in my life, and the only time this will happen. Six months ago, if someone had told me that getting married would've made me the happiest man on the planet, I would've shot them in the head and put them out of their misery. Now, I'd buy them a beer and convince them to join the newlywed cult if they hadn't already.

When we pull into the garage back at our home, we sit in silence inside the truck, holding hands and staring at our wedding bands. The diamond will come, we'll pick it out together, but the forever bands on our ring fingers hold the most meaning to me. "Mrs. Tucker, are you ready to be carried across the threshold and start the rest of our lives together in our own home?"

"Absolutely, Mr. Tucker. I love you...so much."

After getting her out of the truck, I carry her across the threshold and straight up to our bedroom. We have a few hours left before I have to report to The Farm for training. Thanks to my previous experience, I don't have to live there like some of the recruits do. I'll be home most every night and weekends, but some of the spy boot camp sessions will require more of my time than others. With our combined work schedules, we're flexible enough to work around the time apart.

Speaking of flexible, the gorgeous redhead beckoning me with her big emerald-green eyes is very bendy and flexible, and I'm one lucky son of a bitch to have landed her. She straddles my waist, lowering herself on me until she's fully seated, taking all of me. She begins to move, throwing her head back in ecstasy and releasing the sexiest fucking moans I've ever heard. Like a jigsaw puzzle that's been completed at last, being joined as one with the only woman I've ever honestly loved feels as if the missing piece of the puzzle inside me found its mate.

My soul mate.

Before I drift off to sleep, exhausted from the long day and nighttime acrobatics, my phone chimes with a text. I pick it up and glance at the screen, releasing a sigh of relief over the message from Silas.

Okay to move forward with your plans, but there's much more to the story than we thought. I'll fill you in when I get home. See you tomorrow.

CHAPTER 23

Savannah

The past few months have been nonstop running from one place to another for both Nick and me. After our whirlwind weekend in Vegas, Nick started his new job, and the grueling training schedule has kept him super busy. Miranda didn't have many possessions at the shelter, so she and I were able to move everything without help. She was thrilled to have more than a single room at a crowded shelter. The privacy and proximity afforded by her new home brought her to tears—happy tears. Karen has been over several times, looking as if she is ready to pop at any time, but she's as invested in Miranda as I am. I've enjoyed having another friend nearby as much as Miranda has enjoyed getting to know Karen.

Nick comes home most every night, but sometimes it's very late and he's completely exhausted. However, his schedule hasn't stopped him from making time to help ensure the entire in vitro fertilization process flowed smoothly. The first few appointments were for Miranda and me—medication to synchronize our ovulation cycles to prime my body for the extraction. Medication for her so her body can prepare to accept the embryo. Then the trigger shot for me—the last step before they collect my eggs.

Nick and I talked at length about how many embryos we'd want implanted, then sat down together to share our decision with Miranda. Since she'd be the one impacted the most, we wanted to make sure she was on board with us and understood what she faced. I shouldn't have been worried about her reaction, but I couldn't just assume she'd be fine with whatever we decided to do with her body.

Turns out, she was fine with whatever we wanted to do with her body.

We assured her that two implanted embryos were enough for us. If they both take, we'd get two for the price of one, considering we may never have the opportunity for such an amazing gestational surrogate again. If only one embryo implanted, we'd be equally as thrilled and consider ourselves blessed to have a baby at all.

After all the buildup—watching the calendar, going to doctor appointments, getting shots, taking medication, having the egg retrieval performed, and fertilizing the eggs in a laboratory then having them transferred to her uterus—we were finally ready for the big day. It was time for the pregnancy test. I was so nervous and excited, I couldn't eat or sleep all weekend, waiting for the end of the fourteen days to pass. The wait was more than excruciating—it was downright cruel and unusual punishment. The entire process was mentally grueling.

And it all came down to one little test and a positive or negative sign.

While Miranda took the test into the bathroom with her, I slipped into Nick's lap, wrapped my arm around his neck, and laid my head on his shoulder. He smelled so good, the combination of sandalwood and coffee reminding me of the first day we met. Believe it or not, that memory calmed my racing heart. I remembered how I felt, looking up into his eyes when he knocked Butch on his ass. Nick was my hero that day, and he's still my hero today. He was my rock that day, and he's still my rock today. No matter what Miranda's pee showed, we would still have each other, and that was all that mattered.

A few minutes later, Miranda emerged from the bathroom with the stick in her hand. Her eyes were downcast and her feet moved slowly toward me. The doctor warned us several times that the embryos might not attach the first time. That's why they take plenty of eggs and freeze the embryos that are not implanted right away. If she was willing, I reasoned we could always try it again after another cycle of medication and clinic visits.

She handed the positive pregnancy test stick to me and grinned from ear to ear. "Congratulations, Savannah. We're pregnant!"

At first, I was completely speechless. I had prepared to be let down after the first try, knowing many people have to try more than once before an embryo attaches. But I sat there holding my breath and pinching myself, waiting to wake up from a wonderful dream. Nick squeezed me, wrapping both arms around me and burying his face against my neck. He kissed the delicate skin there, moving up to my jawline, across my cheek, and finally capturing my lips. His soft, lingering touch brought me out of my trance. He pulled his head back, looked into my eyes, and smiled warmly at me.

"We're having a baby, darlin'."

With screams and shouts loud enough to alert the entire neighborhood, I jumped up from Nick's lap and danced around in excitement. Then I grabbed Miranda and hugged her, so very thankful for this incredible gift she's given us.

That was six weeks ago. It's now June, the beginning of summer, and we're preparing for an ultrasound to confirm the embryo is developing and thriving. This has been another excruciating wait. Are we having one or two babies? Does it even matter? We're having a baby! Another concern I've pushed to the back of my mind is the frequency of miscarriages after IVF. But Miranda has been great about my overprotectiveness and checking on her multiple times a day, even between patients while I'm at work. She refers to me as her helicopter mom, but I think she secretly likes the attention.

"Miranda Petrovio family." The nurse stands in the doorway, holding it open with her hip when she calls us into the exam room.

Miranda is already in her paper gown and leaning back on the exam table. She looks relieved when we join her, and the full understanding of the enormous task she's agreed to hits me like a runaway train. She's completely alone without Nick and me. No family to help her. No one to turn to for advice or just to lend an ear and a shoulder. And now she's pregnant with a baby that's not hers, all to help someone she barely knew just a few short months ago.

Nick and I take seats beside her, and I reach over to grasp her hand. She squeezes mine in return, and I notice her visibly relax. The doctor steps into the room, and the sonogram technician readies her supplies. When they find what they're looking for, they turn the screen so all of us can see the images with them.

And there it is…

Or, I should say, there they are…

Two distinct embryonic sacs.

We're having twins.

I'm hyperventilating.

I don't think Miranda is breathing at all. Her eyes are bugging out of her head and her mouth is wide open, but I don't see her chest moving. I can't stop mine from heaving.

"Hell yeah!" Nick shouts from beside me, drawing everyone's attention and breaking the spell Miranda and I are both under.

Everyone in the room bursts out in laughter and huge smiles. At least we're breathing normally again. Congratulatory hugs are passed around freely. Miranda doesn't release me when we hug, though. Instead, she slides over a little to give me room to recline beside her. Then she looks at the technician.

"These are her babies. I'm just carrying them for her. Can you please show her again?"

"Of course. Congratulations, mamas. You should both be very proud." The technician slides the wand over Miranda's stomach again until she finds the two raspberry-sized babies. Two separate, tiny heartbeats. Two distinct pieces of Nick and me that I love instantly at first glance.

Yes, I do believe in love at first sight. Because I'm totally and completely in love with our babies right now.

"No wonder I've had so much morning sickness and been so tired lately. These two babies are already zapping my energy." Miranda laughs but keeps her eyes glued to the screen. "Savannah, I'm so happy for you. You're going to be the best mom ever."

We leave the clinic with the next appointment scheduled at the regular obstetrician's office. Miranda is doing well, and the babies seem to be thriving in her womb, so the IVF clinic's job is done. We climb into Nick's truck, and my phone starts to ring.

"Hey Karen, I should've known you'd call right about now." I love my best friend.

"Oh yeah? Is all the magic gone from our relationship? Am I that predictable?"

"Only when you want to know all the details about my baby mama." It's a running joke between us. I've told a few people at work that Miranda is pregnant with my baby and then laugh hysterically when they're unsure of how to reply.

"How is your baby doing?" Karen asks with a smile in her voice.

"My babies—plural—are doing good. Twins, Karen! We're so excited!"

"Oh, love, I'm so happy for you and Nick! That's the best news I've heard all day. Well, maybe the second-best news."

"You have other news? Tell me!"

"My water broke. Spence and I are on the way to the hospital to have this baby today!"

"Oh my God! Nick—you have to turn around and get to the hospital right now!" I realize after I scream at him that my words could be misconstrued.

His horrified expression confirms my suspicion a little too late. "Sorry, Karen's in labor. We're having a baby today. Let's take Miranda home first so she can rest, then we'll go to the hospital."

"Thank you—I was going to say the nausea is a little much. I'd love to see her baby, but I'm afraid the hospital odors would completely do me in right now."

"You got it. Tell Karen we'll be there as soon as we can." Nick keeps a level head while I freak out enough for both of us. Excitement overload.

Hours later, I'm sitting beside my best friend, holding my goddaughter in my arms, and promising her I'll always be here to help take care of her. After we returned from our impromptu wedding in Vegas, Karen chastised me for not asking her to be my matron of honor but relented after I reminded her that she couldn't travel. She forgave me then asked me to be Kate's godmother. Naturally, I said yes. Holding this precious baby and showering her with love, I can't imagine how much stronger my love for my babies will be when I finally hold them in my arms.

"When you have yours, I'll be there with you, Savannah. I can't wait until that day."

"I can't either." My gaze lifts to meet Nick's, and I instantly feel his love flowing into me. "We're going to have a great family."

"You bet your sweet ass, we are." Nick winks then takes Kate from my arms.

If I could actually get pregnant, it would spontaneously occur from seeing Nick Tucker with a tiny baby girl in his arms.

Time flies when you're having fun, a best friend with a newborn, a woman pregnant with your twin babies, and a husband in training day and night at The Farm or wherever else they decide to send him. Another holiday season has passed, and another new year has now begun, bringing promises of everything I've ever wanted. But time really doesn't care if you're ready for the upcoming changes or not. They happen regardless of the best-laid plans or whether it's under the ideal circumstances.

For us, those changes are a baby boy and a baby girl who will be delivered via a scheduled Cesarean section. Thankfully, both Miranda and the babies had an uneventful pregnancy, by medical terms. Every day was a magical event for me. The first time they moved. The first time they had the hiccups. The protruding feet and elbows just under her skin. All the major milestones that I was able to experience with her as if I experienced them myself.

When I step back inside the labor and delivery ward, I feel as if I just left here after Karen's little bundle of joy was born. That was more than half a year ago now, and this time, we're here for our own flesh and blood. A day I didn't think could happen just a short year ago, yet here I am, waiting for my twins. I'm scared and thrilled and scared some more and so damn happy, I can't keep it all inside.

Nick and I scrub in with the doctors to give Miranda all the support we can and watch the delivery of our babies. Nothing in the operating room will bother me—I've seen much worse in the emergency room. But my heart is pounding so hard, I feel light-headed. Two pediatricians are on standby to grab the twins and perform assessments the moment they emerge. They've appeared healthy all along, but the doctors' presence just makes sense under the circumstances.

Nick and I sit on either side of Miranda's head, and I slip my hand under the sterile cover to hold hers. She grips it tightly, scared and nervous about what's to come, but there's no turning back now. She turns her face toward me and whispers.

"I'm so glad you're here with me. I know there's nowhere else you'd be right now, but I'm so grateful for you, Savannah."

"I'm the grateful one, Miranda. You're giving me the greatest gifts I could ever ask for—and they're both fully Nick and me. I've never known anyone as selfless as you are. No one else would've done this for me." I lean over and kiss her forehead. She's become like a younger sister to me, especially in the time since she's been living over our garage.

Once the obstetrician begins, the entire birthing sequence seems to be over in the blink of an eye. Everyone proceeds in orchestrated movements, the entire team knowing their specific job to the point of perfection. Once the pediatricians have given the all clear for the twins, two nurses approach Nick and me, each offering us a swaddled baby. Pictures are snapped and too many tears to count are shed, but every single moment is perfectly perfect.

Once we're moved to a private room, Miranda sleeps while Nick and I enjoy quiet time with our babies, lying on the fold-out couch with Gavin and Kinsley Tucker snuggled between us. For the next eight weeks, I'll take care of Miranda along with the new loves of my life. It's the least I can do to repay her for this incredible life she's given Nick and me. Now I understand what it means to wear your heart on your sleeve, because my heart is now completely laid bare, embodied by these three perfect humans lying here with me.

In the last seven months, while Miranda rested and Nick worked countless hours, I spent my free time working on my book. Refining every word. Pouring my heart and soul into every chapter. Reliving the hell that I endured under that monster's thumb. Sharing the wholly embarrassing details of why I stayed, why I allowed the abuse, and why I didn't tell anyone. Writing that and baring my soul for the world to judge was cathartic for me, even if no one else appreciated my work. That book was for me; it signaled a major turning point in my life that I wouldn't change if I could. Everything that happened, regardless of how painful or humiliating it was at the time, brought me to where I am today. Made me the woman I am right now. Gave me the strength to stand when every cell inside me screamed to crumble into a million pieces.

When I hit publish, I rushed to the bathroom and vomited from sheer nerves.

Then I put the marketing tips I'd learned to use and started promoting my book. All 352 pages contained bits and pieces of me, and I was proud of what I'd accomplished. When I poured that energy into my campaigns, women from all walks of life snatched it up and sent it soaring up the charts. The success I realized from that one book will never outweigh the validation I received from the very women I expected to tear me apart.

Emails from all over poured in, thanking me for being brave enough to share my experiences. Many fled from the abusive relationships they'd been imprisoned in for years because they realized if I could do it, they could too. Two weeks before Gavin and Kinsley were scheduled to be born, I turned in my resignation from the ER department to write full time, working from home where my whole life exists.

My next book will be for women who can't have children of their own, and I'll share my amazing story with them. A story of hope and love and laughter and tears and amazing people along the way. Again, if I can help just one, it's worth all the blood, sweat, and tears I pour into it.

I never actually believed I'd have a happily ever after. I thought those were only meant for dreams and fairy tales, the stuff fictional books were made of. But now that I'm living a life that's better than anything I could've dreamed or hoped for, it's clear what was missing in those early days of bitter disappointment.

Nick Tucker was missing. My soul mate. My forever. There's a fine line between heaven and hell, and I know without a doubt I've crossed that line. From my torturous hell before Nick, and straight into my blissful heaven with him.

I simply couldn't ask for more than what I have right now.

I don't need locks on my heart and locks on my door anymore.

EPILOGUE

Silas—Moscow, Russia

"I'm surprised to see you. I didn't know you were coming." He narrows his eyes and stares at me suspiciously. He's a large man, formidable back in his heyday, but that was many years ago. Today, he'd sooner reach for his gun and blow a hole in my gut than spar with me. Can't say I blame him.

My Russian contact is leery of surprise visits, especially when I haven't been here in quite some time. That's what happens after living in a military-ruled country that still leans strongly to Communism and enjoys torturing citizens for information. Sure, to the rest of the world, they're now a republic. But that's just the face they wear and the front they show.

Walk a mile on the wild side of Moscow then tell me that bullshit party line is real.

The KGB would haul Dmitri away right now if they thought it would gain them an inch. The cold war may have ended years ago, but there's a secret war still raging with no signs of slowing down. And they're playing for keeps, though most of the world has no idea what's going on behind the iron curtain. And that's exactly how they want it.

"If you'd known I was coming, it wouldn't have been a surprise." I purposely keep my hands visible. I mean him no harm. I'm here for answers only he can give.

"What do you want, Silas? I'm in no mood for fun and games. It's been a long day, and I'm ready to get out of here."

I walk farther into his office at the government's fortified complex in the heart of Moscow. There are cameras and voice recorders all over the building; I'm not stupid. But then, they knew I was here the second my plane touched down on the tarmac. My visit here is for unofficial business, but if it turns out to be even remotely what I suspect, the NSA and CIA will duke it out for investigating rights. Good thing I've already assembled a team of three highly skilled and able officers to handle just such an investigation.

Two of them will be starting their training next week with a significant advantage over their classmates because of their previous experience. Now they're learning the spy and asset component, the psychology behind turning a loyalist to a separatist, along with how to blend into a crowd, to become unrecognizable, to become invisible when needed. Very special skills when "sharpshooting assassin" is added to the curriculum vitae.

Glancing over his shoulder, I rest my gaze on the only personal item I've ever known Dmitri to display in his office. It's a picture of his twin daughters—beautiful girls with long black hair, eyes almost as black as coal, straight, thin noses, and perfectly bright complexions.

"I'm here as a friend, Dmitri. How about you and I go find the bottom of a Chernobyl-poisoned bottle of vodka and catch up?" Friends in our business are hard to come by. Dmitri knows this better than anyone, I'm sure of it.

"Your Russian has improved since the last time I saw you. Have you been practicing on someone?"

"No, my Russian has always been impeccable. You were just too drunk to notice when I was here the last time."

Dmitri laughs, the smile reaching his eyes and showing he's warming up to me at last. That's no small feat in the bitter cold of Moscow, even in early spring. "Okay, let's have a drink and regale each other with tales of the good old days."

We walk silently through the corridors until we're well outside the building. There's a time and place for everything, but his office inside the Moscow Kremlin complex is not the place for idle chitchat. And especially not for the questions I have for him. The beauty inside the walled compound—the five palaces, four cathedrals, and the Kremlin Towers with spires reaching to the sky—masks the true inner workings of the secret government operations. To the public eye, most of the government's work is handled at the Moscow White House, a few miles away. But to those of us in the trade, we know the Kremlin is where the clandestine operations begin and end.

We walk along the Moskva River, then cross the bridge to head to Gorky Park. Despite the cool evening temperature and the time it takes to reach our destination by foot, I'd rather walk the entire distance than chance getting into the wrong car. Besides, traffic in Moscow is terrible, and driving would probably take longer than walking. The time out in the cold air gives me time to think and breathe. Being back here isn't exactly easy for me, but with the high stakes involved, I don't have another choice.

The odds of someone from the KGB following us are high, and I'm not keen on being snatched into an unmarked van and whisked away for questioning. On paper, the KGB as it once was doesn't even exist anymore after it was disbanded and split into two units. But as the powerful regime leader declared, "There's no such thing as a former KGB man." That same leader has worked behind the scenes to reestablish his elite police force, full of henchmen, assassins, and ruthless torturers.

Dmitri and I are careful and take our time before deciding where to stop for a drink, leisurely strolling in the old section of the park until we find a pub tucked away on a side street. We choose a booth away from the other patrons, one that allows a view of the front door and anyone who may try to get too close. The music playing in the background is enough to drown out our conversation on any external listening devices their government has in their arsenal.

My toys are slightly more advanced and higher tech. If the tables were reversed and I were spying on them, I'd have their every word in my ear, clear as a bell. Thankfully, they haven't quite caught up with our advanced gadgets yet. However, their medieval torture methods to extract information are top of the line, and I prefer to avoid them at all costs.

Dmitri orders shots and beer for both of us before turning his keen and penetrating gaze on me. "Silas, why are you here?"

"Tell me, Dmitri. How are your daughters, Mira and Kira?"

He strikes a match, lighting his cigar and taking a few drags on it before hardening his eyes and staring me down amidst the smoke swirling between us. The blunt end of his cigar glows in an angry red shade, much like the coloring overtaking his face at the moment.

"I told you I'm in no mood to play games. Speak your mind or get the fuck out of my sight. I'm giving you this one warning because we've been friendly in the past, but don't mistake this pass for weakness. I will gut you like a fucking fish and dump your body in the river, never to be seen again."

The waitress sets our drinks down in front of us, then pauses to take our orders. Dmitri dismisses her with a simple wave of his hand. I wait until she's out of earshot to continue.

"Calm down, Dmitri. I'm here to help you and your daughters. But I need you to level with me about what's really going on. What has happened to them?"

"You're not only asking me to commit treason against my country, you're asking me to put my family's lives in real danger. This I cannot do. Go home. Mind your own business. Forget you know me." He throws his shot back then chases it with the entire pint of beer before slamming the mug on the table.

Before he has an opportunity to slide out of the booth, I stand and toss enough rubles on the table to cover our drinks plus a hefty tip. He cuts his eyes up at me, distrust and murderous contempt shining in his eyes.

"You know, your daughters are very beautiful. I know you've always been very proud of them. Their picture is the only personal memento you have in your office. That's a very telling sign, one I'm sure your superiors also picked up on and used as leverage against you. But I assure you, I'm not the guilty party in this. It seems there's something awry in your own government. A blurred line is far too easy to cross— and that's exactly what they created when they used your children against you after all your years of faithful service."

I begin to walk away then stop and look back over my shoulder. "There are slight differences in your girls, even though they're identical twins. For one, Mira has a much softer expression in her eyes than Kira does. Mira's a considerably gentler soul, isn't she? Not quite as fierce and resilient as Kira."

Before I reach the plane for my return flight home, I predict Dmitri Petrov will desperately want a meeting to resume our conversation.

And I'll be waiting for him.

Outside the pub, I pull my heavy overcoat tightly around me, flipping my collar up and pulling my hat down lower on my head. The wind whips around me, and the setting sun makes the air even colder. Without Dmitri's help, I'll have to go off my own assumptions and start directly with the source. I'd hoped to have a little more intel in my back pocket first, but his lack of answers is telling enough.

"Silas, wait."

That didn't take as long as I thought it would.

I stop and turn sideways, casting a glance at Dmitri over my shoulder. The primary reason I'm here is to help make sure a friend doesn't get caught in the cross fire of whatever covert operation the Russians have underway. The fact that I've known Dmitri almost the entire time I've worked in the CIA is a distant second. Our friendship, loosely labeled, is one of convenience and mutual benefit. The moment I'm no longer of use to him, he'd throw me under the bus. As it turns out, we can both help each other this time.

"Suddenly feeling chatty, Dmitri?"

"Do you really think you can help?" The pleading in his eyes isn't fake, but that's about the only fact I'm certain of right now.

"Do you really think you have any other options? I have an idea of what's going on, and if I'm right, you're the one who's playing games—very dangerous games."

He nods, not so much in agreement with my jab that he's behind the duplicity, but that knowing and doing nothing about it makes him complicit.

"Come to my house tonight. You can stay in our guest bedroom, we'll talk, and I'll drive you back to the airport in the morning."

"When you say airport, you don't really mean Siberian prison camp, do you?"

"Not this time. Next time, maybe."

He calls his driver to come pick us up, and we wait inside the pub, throwing back shots of vodka and snacking on caviar, until he arrives. The black sedan idles alongside the curb, and we walk out together. A moment of hesitation hits me before I slide into Dmitri's car, but I'm banking on his love for his kids to overrule his love of Mother Russia.

Our conversation on the way to his house in the suburbs is benign—nothing the driver or any other prying ears can use against us. When we arrive, his wife Natalya waits for us in the doorway, wringing her hands. The telltale sign of excessive worry gives me comfort—that I'm not walking into a trap.

"Silas, hello, it's been a long time." Natalya greets me with a wary expression despite her warm words.

"Don't worry, Nat. I'm here to help if I can." I kiss both of her cheeks, trying to reassure her of my intentions. She visibly relaxes, dropping her hands to her sides before inviting me in.

"This house is clean. I do my own bug-proofing so Nat and I can have private conversations. We can talk freely here." Dmitri sits at the dining table and begins filling his plate. Nat grabs another plate for me, and I join them for a full meal.

"Dmitri, tell me what's going on. I know you know, so don't bullshit me. And don't leave anything out."

He lowers his fork and levels me with his keen glare. "Will you save both of my girls? No matter what you find?"

"You know I'll do my best, Dmitri. That's the only promise I can give you."

"They were taken to America…by the GRU."

So Russia's largest foreign intelligence agency is hard at work on US soil.

***

**Silas's story continues in *Blurred Line*.
Roman's story is coming soon in *Hard Line*.**

Want more of Nick Tucker? Read ***Her Dom*** and ***Her Dom's Lesson***!

Want more of Nick, Silas, Roman, Reaper, Bull, Rebel, and Shadow? Find them and more the ***Steele Security series***: ***Wicked Games***, ***Wicked Ties***, ***Wicked Nights***, ***Wicked Intentions***, and ***Wicked Shadows!***

～

ABOUT THE AUTHOR

A.D. Justice is the award-winning USA Today best-selling author of the Steele Security Series (Wicked Games, Wicked Ties, Wicked Nights, Wicked Intentions, Wicked Shadows), the Crazy Series (Crazy Maybe, Crazy Baby), the Dominic Powers series (Her Dom, Her Dom's Lesson), the Immortal Obsessions series (Immortal Envy), and a few stand-alone romance novels, such as Saving Grace, Completely Captivated, Just One Summer, Intent, and Mistletoe Not Required.

When she's not writing, she's spending time with her own alpha male character in their North Georgia mountain home. She is also an avid reader of romance novels, a master at procrastination, a chocolate sommelier, a twister of words, and speaks fluent sarcasm. An avid animal lover, A.D. Justice has two horses, two dogs, and three cats.

While the primary focus of her books has been romantic suspense, she has expanded into different sub-genres of romance. Stay tuned to read what she has in store for you!

Connect with her online!
Newsletter
Facebook Reader Group
Website

facebook.com/adjusticeauthor

instagram.com/adjbooks

bookbub.com/authors/a-d-justice

amazon.com/author/adjustice

BOOKS BY A.D. JUSTICE

Steele Security Series

Wicked Games (Book 1)

Wicked Ties (Book 2)

Wicked Nights (Book 3)

Wicked Intentions (Book 4)

Wicked Shadows (Book 5)

The Crazy Series

Crazy Maybe (Book 1)

Crazy Baby (Book 2)

Crazy Love (FREE Short Story)

Dominic Powers Series

Her Dom (Book 1)

Her Dom's Lesson (Book 2)

The Vault

Warning, Part One

Warning, Part Two

Warning, Part Three

Crossing Lines

Fine Line

Blurred Line

Hard Line

Immortal Obsession

Immortal Envy (Book 1)

Stand-alone Romance Novels

Saving Grace

Completely Captivated

Intent

Just One Summer (Novella)

Mistletoe Not Required (Novella)

ACKNOWLEDGMENTS

Writing a book is no small feat. As for me, I put my heart and soul into the story, taking time away from family and friends to finish writing just one more chapter. When I finally reach those two little magical words, a weight is lifted from my shoulders and I'm able to breathe again. Until I start the next book.

My writing journey includes conferring with several people I trust and admire to give feedback and suggestions. There are also people who encourage and support me along the way, taking a chance on a new type of book or a storyline outside the norm. Those who aren't afraid to step outside the box and give "different" a chance. These are my people—my tribe—whether they realize it or not.

Acknowledgments are hard to write because I never want to leave anyone out or make anyone feel their place in my life isn't important. If you've ever read my books, you hold a special place in my heart. There are a few special people I want to recognize for helping make this book special to me.

First and foremost, I thank my Lord and Savior, Jesus Christ, for his unending love, mercy, and forgiveness of a sinner like me. Without Him, I am nothing. Yes, when I say I fall short, I realize I fall way short, but thankfully, there's no such thing as being too far from Him. He knows my heart.

Dr. Jeff in this story is a real person, doctor, and specialty surgeon. He provided the verbatim narrative he would've used for a patient in the situation described in this book. Many thanks to him for taking time to help ensure the scene was as close to reality as possible.

Vanessa, Dr. Jeff's wife, is a very good friend of mine, and she acted as the go-between for our conversation despite her own hectic schedule. As always, she was so gracious and willing to help in any way she could. Thank you for being such a good friend.

Nita Banks, thank you for all the questions you answered and insight you gave. We both know you love me…it's really past time for you to admit it.

Michelle Dare and T.K. Leigh, thank you for all your support—every single day. I'm so thankful for your friendship, your insights, and all your advice. You can never leave me…because I'd find you. Love you ladies with all my heart!

A.M. Hargrove, Liv Morris, Beth Hurley, and Tabitha Charisse, thank you for being my guinea pigs and reading this story before this book was made available to the masses. Your friendship and your feedback mean the world to me!

Lisa Hollett with Silently Correcting Your Grammar, my editor and my friend, thank you once again for working through this book with me, polishing it until it shines, and laughing with me along the way. Your witty banter makes editing (more) fun. Funner? The Funnest? Just kidding!

Wander Aguiar, the photographer for the covers in this series, is always wonderful to work with—although he does make choosing one photo very difficult.

And to my readers, whether you love, like, or hate this book, thank you for taking your time to read it. Thank you for your reviews, even if all you say is you liked it or not. Thank you for your support—you have no idea how much every little bit means to an author.

All my love to you,
Angel